ALL YOU NEED TO KNOW...

Get Annelie's Bookish & Writerly News:

www.anneliewendeberg.com

THE JOURNEY

ANNA KRONBERG BOOK 4

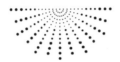

ANNELIE WENDEBERG

Bonus material at the end of this book:
Preview of *Silent Witnesses* - Anna Kronberg Book 5

THE JOURNEY

ANNA KRONBERG BOOK 4

Hear my soul speak.
  Of the very instant that I saw you,
  Did my heart fly at your service.
W. Shakespeare

MAY 1891

*H*unger, exhaustion, and cold stiffened my every move. We had been walking for three days. Our provisions were reduced to two handfuls of salted meat and a sliver of stale bread. A curtain of drizzle surrounded us. The dripping of water from above merged with the *squish-squish* of two pairs of feet: mine and the ones of the man walking a yard ahead of me. The broad rim of his hat hung low, feeding streams of rain down on his shoulders, one of which was still drooping. He had dislocated it while throwing my husband off a cliff.

With my gaze attached to his calves, I placed one foot in front of the other, imagining him pulling me along on an invisible string, forward and ever forward. Without his pull, I wouldn't go anywhere. My knees would simply buckle.

Holmes led the two of us with stoicism. His trousers were rolled up to his knees, bare skin splattered with mud, feet covered in it. He avoided the coast, with all its roads and people. We walked through the heath without cover from view or weather. Then we took off our boots and continued through moorlands. Sickly white feet emerged, toes wrinkled like dead raisins, heels raw from friction and wetness. Water had stood ankle high in our footwear.

When the day drifted toward a darker grey, I saw him growing tired. The slight sway of his hips became stiffer and his gait lacked its usual spring. Within the hour, he steered us to a suitable place to set up the tent and protect our few dry belongings. It had been one frigid night after the other. A series of dark and restless hours, all lacking a warming fire, all without enough food to fill our stomachs.

There was nothing to be done about it.

'Over here,' he called, his hand motioning toward a group of trees. I was hugging myself so hard now, I felt like a compacted piece of bone and skin. He took the rope from his bag and strung it low between two crooked firs, then flung the oilskin off my backpack and over the rope, securing it with rocks on its ends. As I hunched over the rucksack to protect it from rain, I watched Holmes, knowing precisely which move would follow the last, as though my eyes had seen it a hundred times and his hands had done it equally often. As soon as the oilskin was in place, I stepped underneath, pulled out another piece of oilskin and spread it out on the ground.

I extracted our blankets, and anxiously probed for moisture. But my fingers were so numb they felt little but the needling cold. As exhausted as we were, wet blankets would bring pneumonia overnight. Brighton, the closest town large enough for a chemist and a physician, was a brisk six-hour walk from where we were. No one would find us but foxes and ravens.

During our first day on the run, we had established a firm evening routine. One might call it effective. And it was indeed so. But I, for my part, didn't care too much about how quickly we got out of the rain, as long as we did, so I could shut out the world and the struggle.

The peaceful moments between closing my eyes and beginning to dream were all I looked forward to.

In less than three minutes, we'd shed our soggy clothes and let the rain wash the stink and dirt off our skin. We hung our shirts, trousers, skirts, and undergarments out in the rain. They wouldn't dry in our makeshift tent anyway.

We squeezed water out of our hair and dove under the blankets. Holmes opened my rucksack to pull out the one set of dry clothes we had for each of us. We stuck our trembling limbs into them, and clung to one another, sharing our blankets and the little heat that was left in our bodies.

While necessity demanded close proximity, we avoided each other's eyes. And we avoided talking. Attached to Holmes, I felt like a foreign object with my flesh about to wilt off my bones.

He had to spend an hour each evening attached to the woman who had bedded his arch-enemy. How uncomfortable he must feel, I could only guess.

But I tried not to.

Holmes shot his wiry arm out into the cold and retrieved the meat from his bag. He cut off a large slice and gave it to me, then cut off a smaller bit for himself. This was the only trace of chivalry I allowed. The day we had left my cottage, he had insisted on carrying my rucksack. I told him I'd have none of it, and walked away. The topic was closed.

But I sensed his alertness, his readiness to run to the aid

of the damsel in distress should the need arise. His chivalrous reflexes annoyed me greatly.

We chewed in silence. The food dampened the clatter of teeth. Gradually warmth returned. First to my chest, then to my abdomen. As soon as the shivering subsided, we each retreated into the solitude of a blanket. And only then did we dare talk.

'How do you feel?'

I nodded, taking another bite. 'Warm. Good. Thank you. How is your eye?' I had seen him rubbing his right eye frequently.

'Not worth mentioning.' He gazed out into the rain, as though the weather might be worth conversing about. 'We need to replenish our provisions,' he said, and added softly, 'We have two destinations from which to choose, one is a city large enough for a skilled surgeon.'

'It's too late. Choose what place you judge best for your needs.'

'Too late?' Again, that soft voice as though words could break me.

'Five months now. The child is as large as a hand. It cannot be extracted without killing the...mother.'

He lowered his head in acknowledgement. The matter required no further discussion. 'We have to talk about Moran.'

I didn't want to talk about that man. All I wanted was him dead.

'Tell me what you learned about him,' he pressed.

'Nothing that you wouldn't know.'

'Anna!' He made my name sound like a synonym for pigheadedness.

'Damn it, Holmes. I tried to avoid the man whenever possible. All I can provide is what you already know: best heavy-game shot of the British Empire, free of moral baggage, in the possession of a silent air rifle, very angry, and out to avenge his best friend and employer, James Moriarty.'

I stuck my hand out into the rain where the oilskin was dispensing water in a thick stream, filled my cup, and washed the salty meat down my throat.

'You lived in Moriarty's house. I didn't. It follows that you must know more about Moran than I.'

'If he cannot find us, he'll set a trap. It was *you* who said that he once used a small child as tiger bait.' I coughed and rubbed my tired eyes.

'Precisely. Now, what trap would he arrange for us? I cannot use information of his behaviour in India ten years ago and extrapolate it to the near future. How does this man's mind work? You *must* have observed something of importance!'

I pulled up my knees and tucked in my blanket, trying to keep the heat loss at a minimum. 'Just like James Moriarty, Moran doesn't have the slightest degree of decency. He made a fake attempt at raping me so James could stage a rescue. Perhaps they hoped I would be naive enough to sympathise with James after he *saved* me from Moran. But whatever their true intentions, they enjoyed themselves, I'm certain.'

Coughing, I turned my back to Holmes and shut my eyes. Sleep would take me away in mere minutes. 'Moran's brain is exceptionally sharp when he is hunting,' I added quietly.

'Your cough is getting worse,' he said.

'So I've noticed.'

Listening to his breathing, I wiped the memories of Moran and James away, knowing it wouldn't be long before they returned. As soon as the dreams woke me, I'd take the second watch.

~

SOMEONE SCREAMED. My eyes snapped open. Oilskin above my head. The gentle tapping of rain. A hunched figure next to me. I wasn't in bed murdering James.

'You can sleep now,' I croaked and sat up. Tinted with fear, my voice was a stranger to me.

He settled down and rolled up in his blanket. 'Wake me in two hours.'

I didn't want to talk about James, nor did I seek consolation. Our first night, Holmes had accepted my wishes with a nod. I was glad I'd never detected pity or disgust in his face.

He could conceal his emotions well.

The sound of water rolling off leaves and cracking down onto our tent, along with Holmes's calm breathing, were all I could hear. Nature's quietude was a beautiful contrast to London's bustle. It almost felt as though we were silent together, nature and I.

Holmes's feet twitched a little. Only seconds later, his breathing deepened. I waited a few minutes, then struck a match. A dim golden light filled the tent, illuminating his face. It amazed me every time. He looked so different. His sharp features were softened, his expression left unguarded.

I flicked the match into the wet grass, peered outside, and thought of the day I'd kissed him. The memory was far away. Violence and betrayal had bleached it to a dreamlike consistency.

A shy flutter — as though I had swallowed a butterfly and it now brushed its wings along the inside of my uterus. I put my hand there, trying to feel more than just the touch. Where was the love I was supposed to feel for the small being inside? For the first time in my life, I didn't know what to do. I didn't know where to find the energy to keep fighting. Hadn't I found solutions to the most impossible situations? Even the fact that women were prohibited from studying medicine hadn't kept me from entering a university. My abduction by James Moriarty — a master in manipulating the human mind and will — hadn't stopped me from manipulating him in return, and breaking free.

But giving birth to his child, and raising it, seemed a very high mountain to climb.

Too high for me.

I listened to my own heartbeat. How fast was the child's heart beating? Like a sparrow's, perhaps?

Was this non-love based on my hate for its father? Or was I so egoistic and driven that I could not endure the life of a woman?

Being of the *lesser sex* and unable to disguise it any longer, medicine and bacteriology were out of my reach. A single mother was hardly acceptable, but a widow and mother who refused to marry long after her mourning year was over wouldn't stand in much higher esteem.

No medical school would take me as a lecturer. The only alternative for me was to open a practice. But who would choose to be treated by a woman if there were plenty of male practitioners? No one, certainly.

But these were mere difficulties, easy to overcome with enough willpower and energy. Why could I not welcome this child? Was it truly so dreadful to be a mother? Until a few weeks ago, I had no reason to even think about it, for I'd had believed myself barren.

Mothers were other women, and I was something else entirely.

Gradually, realisation crept in and a chill followed suit. I was terrified of never being able to love my child, of not being the mother a newborn needs. All my accomplishments had been won through lies and pretending. I had pretended to be a male medical doctor, affected a wish to develop weapons for germ warfare, and faked love for James.

I would never be able to feign love for my child, the one person who would surely see through my charade.

Holmes began to stir, coughed into his blanket, and cracked one eye open. 'You did not wake me.'

'You said two hours.'

'How long did I sleep?'

I shrugged. How would I know? His watch had produced its last tick yesterday when it fell in a puddle.

'It stopped raining a while ago,' I said. 'Sleep. I'm not tired.' At that, my traitorous stomach gave a roar. Holmes reached for the bag, but I stopped him. 'At my rate of food intake, we'll have nothing left by tomorrow morning.'

When he gazed at me I wished I were far away. 'I'll hunt fowl,' I mumbled.

'We cannot make a fire.'

'Humans must have eaten raw meat before they discovered what fire is good for.' I pulled my crossbow and the bolts from the rucksack. It was an old and worm-eaten thing, made for a child to hunt rabbits and provide for his family. I had found it hanging on the wall of my cottage, and its small size and lightness served me well.

I pushed the oilskin aside. Water dripped from the trees. The ground was muddy.

'I will stay close and watch for any movements. This,' I held up a bolt, 'makes even less noise than Moran's rifle. Go back to sleep now.'

Holmes grunted, pulled his blanket tighter around his form, and shut his eyes as I slipped out of the tent.

2

I wiped my hands on the wet grass. The fresh green turned to a dull red. Holmes opened his eyes as I entered the tent. The light grey of one of his irises was rendered pink.

'Your right eye is even worse today. Let me check.' I bent closer to examine him. Yellow pus encrusted his eyelashes. 'Infected. I'd thought so. Hmm…' I threw a glance outside. The sun was rising. Her golden rays tickled fog from the heath. 'I'll make a fire. Pine might burn well enough. I need to prepare medication before the infection spreads to your other eye.'

'But the smoke—' Holmes began.

'Fog is rising. The smoke will not betray us.'

'Well, then. I will make the fire.' He sat up and rubbed his sticky eyes. 'You haven't slept enough.'

Sleep wasn't my best friend those days. Reluctance slowed my movements as I climbed out of my boots and under the covers.

When Holmes was leaving the tent, I called, 'If you come across chickweed, pick a handful.'

~

A HAND GRIPPED my shoulder and pulled me away from Moran's fist. I found Holmes's knees next to my chest, his face close to mine. Much too close. Coughing, I turned away from him.

'Breakfast,' he announced.

I followed him outside. The odour of fried meat produced a puddle on my tongue. A log served as a bench next to the fire he had made. The resin in the pine branches popped and crackled, spitting wood shrapnel at the animal that hung over the flames. My metal cup had already filled with rainwater. I placed it next to the embers to warm it up. 'Did you find chickweed?'

Holmes pointed to a small pile of green behind me. I took a handful, picked off the dirt, and stuck it in the cup while he cut off the hare's hind legs.

I wondered why he wanted us to be so careful about the fire. If Moran was tracking us — and I doubted it very much — I preferred him close. Arm's reach would have been perfect.

'A rather ropy specimen,' Holmes remarked at his attempt to bite off a piece.

'You look happy enough, though.' My mouth was so stuffed with meat that my words came out mushed.

'I merely stated a fact, not an emotional state.'

The water in my cup began emitting wisps of steam. I wrapped the hem of my skirt around my hand and moved the cup away from the fire.

'What a curious little plant.' He motioned at the chickweed. 'I wasn't aware it could be used to treat infections.'

'Chamomile infusion is used more frequently for that purpose, but it leaves the cornea dry. Chickweed, on the other hand, doesn't. There is only one thing that cures eye infections quicker than this plant.'

'Which is?'

'Breast-milk.'

He burst out laughing — one brief bellow accompanied by a flying piece of hare. We watched it land in the fire and transform to a fleck of coal. 'I can't imagine anyone wanting to pour mother's milk into a patient's eyes.' He wiped his mouth with his sleeve, and took another bite.

'The middle and upper classes live a much more restricted life than us poor sods,' I supplied. 'And breast-milk is not poured. It's squirted.'

Another piece of hare shot into the fire.

We stripped the animal to the bone, and for the first time in four days, our stomachs were full to the brim. I touched the cup with the chickweed infusion. It was lukewarm and ready to use.

'You'd better lie down on the log. I'll wash both your eyes with this.'

Holmes did as asked. I knelt at his side, my skirt soaking rain off the grass.

'Eyes are extremely sensitive to temperature,' I cautioned. 'Tell me how this feels.' I spilled some liquid onto his cheek.

'Good.'

With my one hand to hold his lids apart, I poured the infusion into one eye, then the other, until the cup was empty. I wiped his face with my palms, flicking the green droplets out of his four-day stubble. 'We'll have to repeat this.'

'Thank you,' he said, avoiding my gaze.

~

IT DIDN'T RAIN the entire day and — according to Holmes —

we were making good headway. Good headway to where, precisely, I didn't ask. I could see plans brewing in his head, his half-here, half-there expression, his working jaws. Once in a while, my lack of interest surprised me, but the void of energy and willpower muffled all thoughts. For me, the days consisted of rising in the morning, walking from one place to another, and going to sleep to be woken by terror. The whys and whens and how-fars no longer mattered.

Twice, we spotted a farm and gave it a wide berth. Once, as we walked past a shepherd and his dogs, Holmes spoke in a thick accent I didn't understand. I kept my head low and greeted the man with a nod.

When we set up the tent for the night, Holmes opened his mouth, then shut it again. He said, 'Hum,' narrowed his eyes, and shook his head.

'You often talk to yourself when you are alone,' I observed.

'It usually helps to listen to someone with an intellect.'

'You are a lonely and arrogant man.'

He froze for a moment, then ignored me, and settled down for his first watch.

Surprised at myself, I wondered where that acidic remark had come from. It might have been the truth, but thinking it and slapping it in his face were two very different things. After barely a week, we were already annoying each other.

I wrapped the blanket around my shoulders, and asked, 'What would you do if I weren't here?'

'Don't waste your time with *what ifs*.'

'Would you hunt Moran? Or would you first go back to London to see your friend Watson and your brother?'

He was silent for a long moment, perhaps hoping I would fall asleep.

'Colonel Moran escaped, and I know of two other men who eluded capture.'

'What would you do if I weren't here?' I repeated.

'Find them,' he said.

'I agree. That would be the best thing to do.' Saying it felt like brushing a weight off my shoulders. Being so close to him hurt, and the last thing I wished was to be a deadweight. 'We will part when we reach the next town.'

'We will do no such thing.' He turned his back to me with finality, cutting off all protest.

'You are being sentimental.'

'Go for a walk. Your foul mood is unbearable.'

'No thank you. I'll climb a tree instead. Good night.' And off I went, wondering what was wrong with me. One moment I could lie down and weep, the next I felt the urge to kick his balls.

3

*S*unlight drew the moisture from our clothes and the tiredness from our limbs. Holmes's eye was healed, and his interest in plants that had uses other than poisoning people grew.

With all our provisions eaten, we had to rely on what we found on our journey. During the day, we picked dandelion and chickweed leaves, chewing them while we walked. The dandelion roots were dug up to be cooked at night, together with a rabbit or pheasant either Holmes or I had shot. Now with the rain gone, he was more concerned about watchful eyes than protection from the elements. The spots he picked for our nights were in depressions, often close to a stream. The small fires we made were always well hidden.

With cold and hunger at bay, dark thoughts slammed back into my mind at full force. I longed for solitude. Perhaps when we arrived wherever it was he planned to go, I would…disappear.

But my brain was numb. Planning how best to escape Holmes felt tedious. Unable to invent anything complex, I settled upon simply turning a corner when he wasn't paying attention. I knew this non-strategy was utterly foolish. No need to even attempt it. What I truly needed to escape from, was James and his child.

Three hours before nightfall, when the woods formed a dark and inviting line at the horizon, Holmes informed me that we were now turning south toward Littlehampton.

THE ORANGE SUN hung heavy among the trees when I set out to hunt. Holmes didn't seem to mind the odd distribution of tasks. While he collected wood, cleaned and oiled our revolvers, or explored the surroundings for emergency hide-aways, I would venture out, armed with my crossbow.

I was glad to gain some distance from him and was certain he enjoyed the time of solitude just as much as I did. He appeared highly alert for the slightest change in my mood. Whether it was my physical condition or my reticence that annoyed him the most, I didn't know.

Pheasants were easy prey that time of the year. Mating season had tired the cocks, and they settled on their sleeping branches early after sunset. If I'd had very long arms, I could have picked them off the trees like overripe pears.

Soon I found a sleepy specimen halfway up a beech. I raised my crossbow, aimed and fired, and was back at the tent less than an hour after setting out.

I plucked and gutted the quarry. Holmes poked at the embers, and I sat down opposite him, throwing some of the bird's yellow fat into our skillet to melt. The instant it touched the hot metal, it hissed and bubbled. Heart and liver followed, sizzling and shrinking, blood oozing from the meat to mix with the melted fat, darkening to a deliciously crisp brown and throwing off a scent that made it hard not to reach out and snatch a piece before it was done.

While I busied myself with slicing meat from the bones, Holmes flipped our food in the pan.

'Delicious,' he hummed. Then his sharp eyes met mine. 'You have been evasive long enough. It's time for a longer conversation.'

My chest clenched. I nodded automatically.

'It's now eight days since we left your cottage. I very much doubt that Moran is closing in on us already. But I'm certain he will try everything in his power to catch us. The more information you provide, the more reliable my calculations on his exact plans and whereabouts will be.'

'Naturally,' I answered.

'Excellent. Now, what precisely happened to you and Mycroft after Watson and I departed from Dieppe?'

That trustworthy brain machine of mine hauled in memories as demanded. 'Nothing remarkable occurred on the train to Leipzig or on the ride to my father's home. Once we reached the village, I instructed the driver to drop us off in the woods. That was about half a mile from my father's home. The path led uphill, rather steep, and Mycroft fell behind. I had no patience so I ran ahead.'

Holmes listened, his eyes half-shut, his hand lazily poking a fork at the frying meat.

'The garden looked as though he had not returned. The house was empty, the curtains drawn. Once inside, I noticed the lack of dust. The room smelled clean and fresh. There were two explanations. One, that he had asked someone to clean for him. But he wouldn't have done that. The second and more likely possibility was that he had returned, but left again.'

Holmes held out the skillet and a fork for me. 'Thank you,' I said and impaled a piece of liver. He selected his dinner and leant against a tree, chewing and gazing into the void. I wondered whether he pictured himself inside the house, seeing the things I described.

I took my time eating and collected myself. 'I did not notice the man until he spoke to me.' At that, Holmes focused on my face, eyebrows angled sharply. 'He said my father was in the church. He said he wouldn't be buried in sacred soil, for he had taken his own life.'

I swallowed. 'I was talking to my father's murderer. He had poisoned him and let it appear to be suicide. I asked him how he was planning to kill me. He answered he'd kill me slowly, but not immediately. James had forbidden his men to harm me, he said. I would be allowed to give birth to his child and three years later, they would come to find me. Or...*us*.'

'Intriguing,' Holmes muttered, and stared at the tree tops.

'The moment the man turned to leave, Mycroft entered. They fought, and your brother shot him. But...there is more. The man also said that James had set this trap. His plan was to separate you and me, to weaken us. What he did not consider, though, was that neither of us would be alone. You had Watson, and I had your brother.'

Holmes merely nodded. 'What poison did he use to kill your father?'

My throat closed.

'You didn't examine him?' A sharp shot with both tongue and gaze.

I grew cold and let the drop of temperature reflect in my voice. 'What does it matter what poison was used? My father was dead. No matter how well I examined or studies my father's corpse, he would not come back.'

Holmes cleared his throat. 'I merely wished to know whether the mixture used to murder your father was identical to the one you used to poison Moriarty. That would indicate the scheme was far more complex than I was able to divine.'

I shut my eyes and drew several deep breaths. 'I went into the church to see my father. I touched his skin, examined his eyes, sniffed his face, licked his lips even, but found nothing to indicate what poison was used. However, Belladonna can be excluded. His pupils weren't dilated. And an overdose of arsenic would have caused a blackening of his fingertips or discolourations in the mouth, eyes, or hands. I found none of those symptoms.'

Holmes lowered his head and folded his hands, tapping his index fingers against one another. 'We can conclude Moriarty suspected you might poison him one fine day—'

'He said that he had always suspected the wine,' I interrupted.

'But apparently he did not know what poison you would use. He did not discover the flask you asked me to obtain for you. Let us go back to what your father's murderer said. That Moriarty had forbidden his men to harm you is quite revealing, don't you think?'

Knowing James, the games he had played, the layers of lies concealing one another, I wasn't certain his actions revealed anything at all. I picked another piece of meat from the skillet, and thought about various strands of possibilities.

'When James saw his blackened fingertips,' I began, 'he must have known what poison I had used and that the arsenic would kill him soon. He would have wanted his murderer to suffer and die. What *might* have made matters more complex was that his murderer was also the mother of his unborn child. He had to make a compromise if he wanted it to live. That he would give me three years to raise it is odd, though. Why not have someone take it right after birth and kill me? All that's needed is a wet nurse.'

Holmes scraped his heel over a bump of moss. 'Hum... If I

wished to abduct a small child, what would be the best time to do so? If I had to pay a band of ruffians, I'd make sure the child was old enough to survive a hasty and possibly long trip under harsh conditions.'

'That would explain the three years.'

'And should the child not be what he wanted?'

'Why would...' I trailed off, thoughts racing, picking up pieces and rearranging the picture. 'Assuming he didn't care about his unborn child, which is quite plausible, the ultimatum would only serve to torture me. He would allow me to give birth, to love the child, to live in fear for three years, and then take the child away to punish me with the ultimate pain caused by the loss of my child.'

He pointed a long finger at me. 'Precisely. We need to take precautions that cover both possibilities.' With that, he extracted his tobacco pouch and rolled a cigarette.

I had long lost the appetite for a smoke. 'How ridiculous. I cannot believe he would have expected me to love his child. But... Perhaps he...'

'Yes?' Holmes asked, his fingers pinching the tobacco snug into a piece of paper. He held up a tinder and puffed until a small flame shot from the cigarette's end.

'I believe that James wanted this child. There were signs. He was upset when I tried to abort it. It seemed to hurt him deeply.'

Frowning, Holmes stuck his smoke between his teeth. He surely missed his pipe. His gaze flickered behind a cloud of tobacco smoke, his lips were pressed together, face hardened. Everything else about him seemed to relax and tense in waves, telling of his busy mind.

A long moment later, he pressed the cigarette butt into the grass. 'What you need is a miscarriage.'

I snorted. 'I would have liked one much earlier. But right away would be convenient, too.'

'Quite obviously, that's not what I mean.'

'But that's what *I* mean.'

He shut his eyes and leant his head against the tree trunk.

A miscarriage… I thought of Moran possibly tracking us. What fun that man must be having. If I had a miscarriage and he learned of it, that wouldn't throw him off our scent. And that James had forbidden his men to harm me until his child had turned three, that wouldn't keep Moran from hunting Holmes.

'We need to see his solicitors,' Holmes said. 'As James Moriarty's widow and soon-to-be mother of his child, you have the right to a dower. And we should be able to move all of Moriarty's assets to a trust fund for his heir-at-law, and that would cut off all financial aid and reward to the assassins. That would certainly dampen their motivation.'

'Are you sure you don't want to let Watson know you are alive and well?'

His expression shuttered. He had no wish to discuss this issue yet again. 'I am very sure.'

I frowned at him, but did not dig any deeper. It was his decision, and it could not have been an easy one. 'But what about Mycroft?'

'I sent him a telegram on my way from Meiringen to London. And I plan to contact him in a day or two. We'll need his help.' A dissecting glance later, he said, 'You don't believe it can be done. A feigned miscarriage.'

'No.' I inspected my hands as though they could speak for me. 'It would require hiding my stomach from Moran and simultaneously convince James's solicitors that I am preparing to raise the child. A wire from James's solicitors to his family, followed by another to Moran, would destroy the charade in minutes.'

'There is a risk, indeed. But I believe I can use it to our advantage.'

'How so?'

'Too many strands of possibilities at the moment,' he said, picking at fragments of greenery stuck to his boots. 'The most essential is to make Moran believe your child died before it was born. He will inform the others of that *sad* fact, and once he learns that you received your dower and have moved all of Moriarty's money to a trust fund, Moran must try to convince the solicitors of the child's death. Moran knows that without Moriarty's money, he is nothing. We must arrange it so that no one believes him. We must destroy his reputation. But most importantly, we must track his messages in order to identify his accomplices.'

I nodded, focusing on the main goal. 'It should be fairly easy to obtain a stillborn from any hospital in London. Mycroft could bring one.'

'I'm sure he'll be delighted,' grunted Holmes sardonically.

'Do you occasionally wonder that people think you heartless?' I asked softly.

'It is a waste of time to wonder what others might be thinking. One only has to look at people. One opinion here, another there, and rarely is either based on facts. The heart is a thing that beats, that pumps blood to the brain. Quite obviously, I have one.'

'I know you do.'

'Ah, the romantic! I must disappoint you. I avoid emotions wherever possible. They represent an unacceptable distraction. I am an intellect. The rest are bodily functions.' He leant back, prepared another cigarette, and lit it.

'Nonsense!'

Smoke shot through his nostrils. Grey eyes flashed in amusement.

'I can prove it,' I said.

'A challenge? Very well.' He sat up straight, anticipation in every breath.

I rose and approached him, then knelt in the grass next to him with my face close to his. 'Cocaine.'

His pupils flared wide open, as though he could already taste the drug rushing through his veins.

I drew back and said, 'I have seen a great number of scars from a needle on your forearms, Holmes. Your ability to use your left hand almost as well as your right impresses me. Injecting cocaine solution left-handed is quite a feat.' I grabbed his right wrist, unbuttoned the sleeve and pushed it up. He stiffened. Slowly, I ran my index finger across his pale skin, counting the white dots.

He yanked his arm from my grip.

'From what I observe,' I continued, 'I conclude that your emotional landscape is rather complex. So complex, in fact, that your mind must control it. You are a very controlled man, but I wonder what you were before you gained that control? Perhaps that was when you took cocaine so frequently that you scarred your forearms? These are old punctures. You seem to not need it any longer. Or I should say you *do* need it, but you are able control that need.'

His face was set in stone. Only his black eyes betrayed the turmoil within.

'You can make others believe that you don't experience emotions. It fits your mask so neatly. But I don't believe you. Cocaine is but one example. You took it because you craved it. Craving is a very strong emotion, is it not? Once the chemical hits your bloodstream, you feel intense pleasure, most likely you experience sexual arousal as well. You feel the rush of accomplishment, of being better and of higher intellect than anyone. You have a constant need to be the best, and this emotion controls you.'

Heat rose up his throat, colouring his ears. 'Interesting observation,' he rasped. 'But you ignore the fact that it is only my mind that needs stimulation. In the absence of a case, I must invigorate my mental faculties with cocaine. Otherwise—'

'The other emotion,' I cut him off, 'that seems to control you is your fear of me.' Still, his pupils were wide open. Nothing else moved.

I retreated to my side of the fire and sat down. 'Not to forget curiosity and passion — the two driving forces of every brilliant scientist.'

His jaws were working.

'I will stop talking about emotions, if it distresses you too much,' I said.

'I couldn't care less.' He rose, stomped on the cigarette butt, and walked away.

*W*e stood on a hilltop. The moorland spread before us, wide and soft and green, interrupted only by splotches of treacherous mud. The sea was a good eight to ten miles to the south, but I already imagined smelling it.

'I'll go first,' I said.

'No. You walk behind me.'

'I'm lighter, my baggage is on my back, which gives me a better balance, and I know how to move over swampy terrain. If you walk first, you'll only block my view.' I pushed past him and walked downhill toward a place most people avoided like the plague.

We walked in silence. Holmes' feet made occasional *slop-slop* noises, telling me that he wasn't always placing his feet where I placed mine.

I listened to birds singing spring songs to their mates who were probably sitting on a clutch of eggs, their eyes half-closed, their feathery bellies fluffed out. Would they feel their chicks moving about and scraping their stubbly wings on the insides of the hard shells? My child seemed to be sleeping now. How would it feel to grow so large that I could barely see my own feet? When its head was lodged in my pelvis, its feet kicking my—

My foot caught on a hidden branch. I tipped forward and slipped. There was nothing I could steady myself with, nothing to hold the world in place; instead, it rushed past without so much as a blink. So quick the fall. And yet, the descent, the sliding into the cold, wet bog, felt like an eternity. As though I had time to turn around and wave goodbye. My skirt billowed about my waist, and then it was around my chest, and my throat, darkening quickly as the fabric sucked up water and mud, growing heavy as a rock.

Holmes jumped toward me. He landed on the clump of grass I had been standing on. His eyes were wild, his cheeks on fire. I heard the sharp *tsreee-tsreee* of a bird warning its kin. Holmes shouted, 'Your hand, Anna!' as water flooded my ears.

Where was my hand? My eyes searched for it. There, that small white thing, holding onto a clump of grass. *Why not?* whispered my mind. I looked up at Holmes, felt calmness washing over me, and let go of my only support.

'Don't you dare!'

Black water swallowed my vision. Here was the solution I had longed to find. An explosion of happiness and relief spread through my chest, down to my feet, tickling my toes. I would have cried out in joy had the swamp not sealed my lips.

Pain shot through my head and down my neck as a hand grabbed my hair. Another hand snatched a fistful of my clothes, and I was hoisted up onto a clump of vegetation. I coughed. And I fought. One cannot easily accept life with death so near and so sweet. 'Why?' I cried, and he did, too.

Grass prickled my wet face. Holmes's hands clawed my shoulders. Sobs pressed against my ribcage.

In an attempt to pull myself together and fix whatever needed fixing, I staggered to my feet. He reached out. My gaze followed his hand. Several buttons had popped off my dress where my stomach had grown too large. He picked at the loose threads, rested his knuckles there, then the whole of his palm.

'We need to reach Littlehampton,' he croaked. 'The blankets and all your clothes are wet.' He took the drenched rucksack from my back, grabbed my hand, and walked ahead.

Shock drove silence between us, muffling the ensuing three hours of brisk walking. Eventually, I had to break it. 'I need to sit down for a moment.' My clothes were steaming from my body heat and the warmth of the sun. My tongue stuck to my palate.

I sat in the cool grass, stretching my aching feet and drinking the little water we had left. Holmes dropped the luggage and himself opposite me.

'I spent two years in an asylum,' he said.

I opened my mouth and shut it. One swallow later, I asked, 'What kind of asylum?'

'There is only one kind.' While he spoke, his eyes held mine. As though every twitch I made he placed under a microscope.

'When was that?'

There, his gaze flickered. 'Later. I promise.'

'If you are thinking of sending me to an asylum—'

His shocked expression shut my mouth.

'Thank you,' I whispered, lay down, and watched the wind herding the clouds.

Attempting suicide was one of the many reasons for sending women to lunatic asylums. In fact, women could be committed for anything that indicated they weren't behaving in normal or acceptable ways. Strangely, the two sexes were measured with different gauges. If a woman laughed out loud in a teahouse, her behaviour would be labelled inappropriate, and she might even be thought a prostitute. If a man did the same, he would be unremarked. A woman who struck back when her husband beat her might end up with a fine, or even in gaol, depending on the injuries she inflicted. A man who defended himself against another man would walk free. What bothered me most was that behaviour seen as normal and necessary bore no logic for me at all. I failed to see logic in many things humans did, especially when they acted in concert.

We set off once more, and about an hour later we reached Littlehampton. Strangers that we were — and quite tattered ones at that — we drew everyone's attention. Holmes enquired after an inn with guest rooms. People pointed, and we found it within minutes: the George Inn.

The landlord was a stout man sporting a mighty moustache, whose cheeks were the colour of maple leaves in autumn. He eyed us with suspicion when Holmes announced, 'Good day to you, sir. I am Dr Cyril Baker and this is my wife, Mrs Clara Baker. We've run into a spot of bad luck. We require your assistance. Of course, we will pay handsomely for your services.'

The man opened his mouth, but Holmes kept chatting, emphasising his educated speech a little too much. 'My wife and I were robbed, but we were lucky the ruffians did not search her dress. Or worse! By Jove! I've just now come to think of it!' He clapped a hand to his chest and turned to me. 'Don't listen to me, my dear, don't listen. It's but the confused babble of a husband who has seen his beloved wife in too great a distress.' He turned back to the landlord and gave him a grim nod. 'My dear sir, have you two rooms for us?'

The man cleared his throat. 'I have a room for people who can pay the rent.'

I slipped a hand into the folds of my dress, extracted two moist pounds, and slammed them onto the counter. The moustache broadened considerably, its corners pointing upwards.

'We both need a bath, a good meal, and clean clothing. Would that be possible, sir?' asked Holmes.

And with that, there started a great deal of fussing by both the landlord and his wife.

~

A TOO-LARGE BED in an empty room, and walls that echoed my footfalls and the shallow breath of my lungs. Devoid of birdsong and the rustle of grass in the wind, this place felt empty. Like myself.

The window dulled some of the chatter from the street below, but it did not entirely shut out loud voices spreading news of the strange doctor and his wife. *Have you heard they were mugged and almost beaten to death? That poor woman, in the family way she is, yes, yes! Thugs have torn her dress apart!* And so on. I was glad their vivid imagination had room for pity.

My hair was wet from the bath, my skin still burning. After I'd removed all the layers of grime, I had tried to remove James. But no matter how hard I pressed the coarse brush down on my skin, no matter how much soap I used, all that scrubbing had only cleansed the surface. The resulting pain, at least, was good. For once it was physical, explainable, logical.

As I emerged from the tub, the stink of my clothes hit my nostrils. More than a week of walking, sweating, and never washing properly had created an odour reminiscent of a fox den. Disgusted, I poked my toe at the layer of grit on the tub's bottom.

A narrow door separated my room from Holmes's. Light

peeked through a crack in the thin wood. Earlier that day, he had dispatched a message to his brother. Then we'd had dinner in silence, the unspeakable heavy on our lips. What thoughtlessness to attempt suicide in front of his eyes. What thoughtlessness to have kissed him a year ago. What thoughtlessness...

I sighed, and began moving around, picking up my few belongings and packing them in my rucksack. I would have to wait until he was sleeping.

The candle guttered. I blew it out.

Darkness fell.

~

A KNOCK DISTURBED MY THOUGHTS.

'Yes?'

'May I come in?' His voice was soft and strangely controlled. As though he walked on raw eggs.

'Yes.' I sat up and lit a candle on my nightstand as he shut the door behind him.

'May I sit here?' He pointed to the edge of my bed. I nodded. 'I see that you packed.'

I didn't reply.

'Did you plan this, Anna?'

'What?' I asked to gain some time, or to prevent me from having to answer at all.

'The suicide.' A bare whisper. He was still shocked. But what else was to be expected? Shame crawled up my cheeks, scorching my skin.

'No.'

He sighed. 'How can it be so easy for you? One minute you don't think of it, the next minute you let go, ready to drown yourself. Did I cause this?'

'You didn't.' My heart did it's best to jump up my throat. I

31

wanted him out of this room. Needed him gone. His presence caused a rawness of nerves I could barely endure.

'But I could have prevented it,' he said, more to himself.

I searched for words, but my brain wouldn't provide anything useful.

His eyes darkened and he rose to his feet. 'I allowed you to stay in that man's house for months!' He ran a hand across his face as though to scrape off the anger. His fingers trembled slightly, his shoulders clenched.

Seeing him like this let me surface from my own self-pity. 'Sit, please.'

He did as I asked, and so I continued, 'I'm a grown woman. The path I chose to walk was my own. But I would be lying if I said I knew what I was doing or where it would lead. Every single day in captivity, I made countless decisions. After my father was set free, I chose to stay with James. It was the only logical next step. After all those days, all those decisions amounted to one horrible thing. Should I have foreseen the outcome? Perhaps. But I didn't. Even if I had, I believe I wouldn't have turned around. The price to pay would have been much higher than simply taking the next small step forward. At the end, James and I broke each other. None of this was your doing, Holmes.'

But what would I have done had I known that James would impregnate me with his brood? I could see myself happily accepting the bullet the day he and Moran broke into my cottage and held a gun to my head.

'What made you let go today?' He pressed the words out. Was there still anger in his voice? To him, watching me escape life must be a defeat. Holmes, the do-gooder.

'Opportunity,' I answered. 'A solution to all my problems presented itself, and I took it.' I meant to say something soothing, but all I could think of was how easy it was to let go, how wonderful to sink.

'So all I need to do is wait until the next opportunity presents itself?'

Upon my silence, he fled to his room.

He returned and placed a revolver on my bed. 'Spare me the torture, woman.'

I flung the covers aside and rose to face him. 'You want me to shoot myself while you are watching?'

His hands clenched to fists and he bent closer. 'You wanted me to watch you drown. Where is the difference?'

'You wouldn't have seen me die. You would have only seen me disappear. This,' I pointed to the gun, 'is an ugly death.'

'Yes, it is indeed. Should you choose to insert it into your mouth and point upwards, pieces of your brain, skull bones, scalp, and hair will soil the wallpaper.' He waved his hand toward the wall behind me. 'Perhaps lying on your side instead, and shooting through your temple, would reduce the mess. If you would be so kind?'

'Stop it,' I groaned. My windpipe constricted.

'Ah, I see. You are worried about the aesthetics. A blown-out brain is disgusting. A floater isn't. Most impressive logic.'

'There is no need to shout! Leave me alone.' My knees were about to give way.

'In a moment.' He picked up the revolver and pulled back the hammer. 'Perhaps you need help?'

His hand shook ever so lightly. His knuckles whitened. Candlelight reflected off the weapon's mouth.

'If you stooped but a little, you could take me in your arms.' The words were out before I could control my mouth.

'I'd rather not,' he croaked.

'You'd rather shoot me?'

'You cannot bind yourself to me, Anna.'

'I bound myself to you long ago.' My gaze slid from the weapon up to his face. My hand closed around the muzzle.

33

Two hoarse clicks, and he had uncocked the gun. Then loosened his grip. I placed it next to me on the nightstand. 'Holmes, I know you don't...' I dropped my gaze. 'I'm not stupid enough to believe I'm not... I'm not...defiled.'

Odd, how heavy one's limbs grow when the heart is full of shame. I couldn't tip my head upward, couldn't tear my eyes off his legs. Unmoving, they seemed cemented to a pair of sharply pressed trousers, framed left and right by a half-open dressing gown. Time crawled agonisingly slowly.

'Go away,' I breathed.

His hand approached and took mine in his. His feet took a step closer, his arms wound around me. I had the fleeting impression I would come undone. The taste of blood in my mouth told me I was biting my tongue. I tried to relax my jaw.

'Stop calling me Holmes.'

I couldn't utter a word.

'Say my name, Anna!'

'Sherlock,' I whispered.

My plan of sneaking away that night was forgotten. Exhaustion burned in my eyes. Listening to his slow breathing, the whispering of his hand in my hair, I tried to calm myself. To no avail. I was vibrating.

He exhaled a growl and said, 'You are not defiled. To even think that... What you did to stop Moriarty was a great sacrifice.'

'It all sounds so reasonable, doesn't it. One can look at a collection of facts from many different angles. Mine is simple: I was his whore.' How curious that hearing my own words made them suddenly sound false. In the dark loneliness of my thoughts, I had fancied myself much wiser.

'Well, yes. You could certainly see it that way. But what does it help to do so?'

'Is that ever a reason? Just choose the most helpful interpretation?' I pushed away from him. His one hand slid off my back, the other off my neck. My skin felt cold there.

'I usually choose the one that makes sense,' he said. His expression was relaxed, soft, even. And yet it sounded as though he wished to mock me.

'Are you that distanced? The automaton Sherlock Holmes?'

'Why, in your opinion, was I holding you?'

'Because you feel guilty,' I said.

'How does that fit your automaton theory?'

I had no answer.

'Is that why you tried to kill yourself while I was watching? Because you believe I don't feel, and hence, it doesn't matter?'

He stooped at little, until we were at eye level. I didn't like the belligerence I saw in his posture.

'I simply took an opportunity. As I told you already.'

'That is correct. But for you to do so, you must have established earlier that it wouldn't matter to me, that I wouldn't care.'

'Yes,' I whispered. It was true. It was precisely what I had thought.

'You make surprisingly little sense these days.'

'I know.' *Life* made surprisingly little sense these days. I watched him for a long moment. He wouldn't meet my gaze. 'Why were you in an asylum?'

He sat down on my bed and exhaled one rattling breath. 'My mother fell ill after giving birth to my sister. She starved herself. At times, she clung to her newborn daughter as though she were drowning and her child, the last straw to cling to. It would then take only minutes for the baby to fuss and cry, and Mother would reject her, telling her what a terrible girl she was. It wasn't long before the wet nurse quit her post. The lady's maid helped take care of my sister while my father tried to find a replacement. One morning, Mother left her room, the child in her arms. She sang for her. It was the first time I'd heard Mother sing. I was about to go downstairs, but stopped in wonder and listened. Mother walked past me, smiled at me, and I was convinced she was well again. She lowered her head to smile at the baby. My sister began to stir and woke up with a cry. My mother's face distorted as if in pain, and she flung...'

Silence fell. I followed his gaze across the room.

Eyelids flickered. He cleared his throat. 'She looked at me with a face so empty that, for a moment, I forgot the sounds of my sister dying on the stairs below. Then she whispered, "You tripped me."'

He blinked again, tipped his head, and looked up at me.

'A hysterical child who threatens the good reputation of the family with an obsession of proving his innocence, or rather, *with a poor version of a lie*, had to be removed.'

'How old were you?'

'Five,' he said.

'A small child?' My eyes stung and rage boiled beneath my skin.

'It is very long ago.' He slapped his knees — a whiplash noise that split reality apart, leaving fake lightness behind.

I kept swallowing, trying to force that clump down my throat. One tear rolled down my nose, hit my nightgown, and disappeared into the cotton.

He regarded me with a scrutinising glance. 'Will you be all right?'

I nodded.

He rose and wished me a good night before I could ask, *And you, will you ever be all right again?*

5

woke to rain tapping on my window. Looking at Holmes's closed door, I thought of the previous night, trying to put myself in his position. That of a highly observant and intelligent child with yet a lot to learn about human interaction, and with the need for motherly care and protection, none of which were likely to be offered in an asylum.

It was common for people to be committed to lunatic asylums, should resist adaptation to what was considered normal. But a small child? Whom had his father bribed to have his son taken away?

I wondered what would have happened to me had my father not loved me and not placed my well-being above societal rules. And what would I find if I searched asylums for the non-conforming, the unadapted and unaccepted? Would I encounter groups of people I could identify with? Would that then label me mad, too?

I pushed up from my bed and shed my nightgown. The fabric caught on my stomach ever so lightly.

≈

WE TOOK BREAKFAST, then went for a walk. Sherlock was expecting his brother that day or the next. He had sent Mycroft a cryptic message, instructing him to meet us between nine and eleven o'clock roughly one mile outside Littlehampton, where a stone wall met a large oak.

We spotted him from afar — a large man leaning against the low wall amid bramble and moss, appearing entirely out of place.

'You are early,' was Sherlock's only greeting as he sat down on the wall next to him. Mycroft was as tall as his younger brother, but carried about twice the weight. When he pressed my hand in greeting, his palm felt large but not muscular, his fingertips fine and soft, those of a man who used them to hold a pen or a newspaper and not much else.

I sat in the damp grass across from the two, observing the movements of their bodies while they talked about what had happened since they'd last met. Small gestures were caught and answered in an instant, the lifting of an eyebrow, the stalling of breath, the blink of an eye. I wondered whether they ever missed this simple language when conversing with other people. It felt a bit foreign to see two sharp-minded and emotionally controlled people sharing a deep connection. Then, two sets of grey eyes turned toward me.

'And how are you, Dr Kronberg?' enquired Mycroft Holmes. His gaze dropped to my stomach. Very inappropriate behaviour for an upper class individual. I frowned at him.

'Unfortunately, the name is Moriarty.' I groaned. 'I know nothing about marriage laws, but I hope you can shed light on the issue. Do you see a possibility of making the entirety of James's riches inaccessible to his family and former employees?'

I didn't mention the other problem: my own resources would soon be gone. No one would employ me as a bacteriologist, and I had little chance to gain employment as a female medical doctor. Marrying to avoid starvation was out of the question.

'I'd also prefer to get my old name back, if possible,' I added.

'Hum... Does Moriarty have a son?'

'I only know of a sister. Charlotte is her name. There were a bunch of children at his house on Christmas. They called her aunt, although they clearly weren't James's. Shouldn't the family have read his will by now?'

'I'm quite sure they have.' Mycroft squinted at his manicured fingernails. 'And I doubt he included you in his will.'

'I doubt it, too. But your brother said there must be a dower.'

'There is. Your dower will not only depend on the assets of your late husband, but also on other beneficiaries, descendants, and direct relatives. I'll need a few days to discover the precise amount of money you should inherit.'

An idea struck me. 'I have another question. It's in your area of expertise, I believe, but if you are not allowed to talk about it, I understand, of course.'

One eyebrow went up, and I took that as an invitation to continue. 'James spoke of the German Empire seeking conflict. He spoke of the Transvaal and the Orange Free State, as well. In his opinion, there was a war coming, and that was his motivation to develop bacterial weapons. Do you have knowledge of an impending war?'

He huffed, slightly amused. 'A complex topic. Your question cannot be answered with a simple yes or no.' He pushed his hands deep into his trouser pockets. 'What do you know about the Transvaal?'

I shrugged. 'Close to nothing. Only that it's in South Africa and has large gold mines.'

'And that is where the problem lies. The Witwatersrand area is so lucrative that the Boers alone cannot exploit it. Uitlanders immigrate in great numbers — they are mostly Britons — expecting to get rich. A clash of cultures and beliefs is the natural result. The Transvaal has a tradition of conflict. A second Boer War might indeed be on the horizon.'

'What about a war in Europe?' I pressed.

'Hum... I doubt it very much, but I cannot claim to have sufficient information regarding possible aggression plans of our neighbours. Making a precise assessment of the situation is close to impossible. Britain's espionage and counter-espionage are notoriously underfunded and undermanned. In case of a conflict, we are practically blind and deaf. Your late husband was, in this respect, quite progressive.'

Mycroft Holmes's face had reddened during his narrative. He dabbed a handkerchief at his forehead, then folded his arms across his chest. I stared at his expensive shoes. They stuck out of the vegetation like two abnormally large, shiny black beetles.

What had James known? He must have had more than mere suspicions. How else could he have convinced others? He had men from the government, and even a spy who worked on the continent. He'd gone to Brussels the one day—

'May I speak frankly?' Mycroft interrupted my thoughts. I wasn't certain whom he addressed, so I lifted my eyes and saw him looking at me.

'You would make an excellent spy, Dr Kronberg. You are highly educated and you speak German and English fluently. You are intelligent and have strong nerves. Staying in Moriarty's house, *especially* given the circumstances, and still able to function — that was an extraordinary feat. Should you be seeking an alternative employment, I'd be happy—'

'No I'm not. Thank you very much.'

'Of course, only after your child had reached an appropriate age to be left with a nursemaid—.'

'I'd very much appreciate if you'd stop talking about James's brood. My condition is none of your concern, Mr Holmes.'

He opened his mouth to reply when his brother growled, 'Mycroft!'

I couldn't interpret what Sherlock's face showed. Heaviness came to mind first. He wiped it away the instant Mycroft turned to him.

'We need to find Moran,' Sherlock said to him. 'If he cannot find his prey — me, that is — he will try to use Watson.'

'I made enquiries,' said Mycroft. 'So far, he hasn't been seen in London.'

'Hum,' Sherlock grunted and tapped his fingers against the wall behind him. 'I can feel it in my bones. Moran's greatest urge is to hunt. He must be on our heels.'

'Do you really think he could have tracked us?' I asked.

'Should he be using dogs, it's quite possible to follow our scent.'

I thought back to our trip, the rain we'd walked through, the moorlands — all that would make it difficult for dogs to track us. And yet, every night we had left enough traces behind — bones of the animals we had eaten, the six by five foot area we had slept upon, not to speak of the regular intervals of urinating during the day. 'I believe you are correct,' I said.

He showed a twitch of his lips.

'Why did you drag a pregnant woman across the Downs when you could have taken a train?' Mycroft asked.

'Because I *want* him to follow us by foot.'

Sherlock didn't seem miffed by his brother's blunt choice of words. *With child* would have been appropriate, while *pregnant* was a term used within the medical establishment, but never, under any circumstances, was it to be uttered in society. The word alone implied that a woman had had sexual intercourse, which was almost as good as saying she was a whore. But neither of the Holmes brothers appeared to have the patience for such foolishness.

I was glad of it.

Mycroft scratched his chin and turned to me. 'I will return to London and learn all about your financial situation. If you are lucky, your former husband did not anticipate your attack on his life, and hence would have had no reason to arrange for revenge in his will.' He turned to his brother and continued, 'I will see to Watson's safety. Do you wish me to tell him you are alive?'

'No.'

'Very well, then. If you'd give me the names of Moran's accomplices, brother?'

'A German engineer with the name Heinrich von Herder. He is an excellent weapons maker, and he might be in Hamburg at this moment. He had, as far as I have been able to ascertain, nothing to do with Moriarty's crimes, but you may wish to keep an eye on him. Another is a comparatively harmless footman by the name of Thomas Parker. A garroter by trade who frequents every public house in Whitechapel, and who should presently be with Moran. The third is an elusive creature. An as yet unknown physician at the Dundee School of Medicine.'

'You haven't found him yet?' I asked. That man had been involved in medical experiments on paupers. And he hadn't been identified him for more than a year.

'Unfortunately not,' answered Sherlock.

'Is he still in Dundee?' Mycroft asked.

'I don't know.'

'Anything else?'

Sherlock shook his head.

We parted then and there. Mycroft's fleshy hands pressed mine for a moment. What a contrast to his wiry brother.

After his broad back disappeared, Sherlock turned to me. 'For more than a year you've loved a man who offers you nothing in return. Yet you seem to believe you will not be able to love your own child. This appears—'

'Illogical?' Behind my eyes, something stung. 'Tell me why I did not love my husband.'

'Because you chose neither him nor the child.' The question burned in his face.

I spoke for him. 'Precisely. You asked why I love... someone who will not love me in return. Is that the point of loving? To expect something in return? I don't think so.'

On our way back into Littlehampton, I cut a glance at him and said, 'Last night, you wanted to make me believe that your past doesn't bother you anymore. But I believe the one thing that bothers you most, besides the stupidity and ignorance that surrounds you, is that you might end up in an asylum once more. You have a need for self-control that borders on the...extreme.'

Without showing the slightest reaction, he marched on. We'd walked almost the entire length of the stone wall when he finally stopped. He pinched a cigarette between his lips, struck a match on a rock, and said, 'Is it only moving objects that constantly beg for your attention?'

'What?'

'I'm being cryptic. My apologies. I observed that most of the time, your eyes seem to dart every which way. For example, when crossing a street, normal people look at their feet to avoid stepping into puddles for example, or they look at other people to avoid collisions. You, on the other hand, seem to be highly sensitive to many things at once, especially *moving* objects, no matter their size. Carts, people, dogs, flies.'

'Sound... sound, too,' I muttered, my gaze dropping to my shoes. How could he leaf through my pages like this? His analytic mind tickling out secrets I didn't share, and that no one had ever observed.

'I thought so,' he said.

ames smiled at me. He slid his hand down my neck, curling his fingers around my throat. His smile changed to a fanged grin. He bent down to kiss me. My tongue slid over his incisors. I felt his hackles rise. He sank his teeth...

'Anna!' A voice cut through the dream. Fingers dug into my shoulder.

A hiss erupted from my throat. I discovered Sherlock by my bed, bending over me. The light from his room illuminated one side of his face. His brow was crinkled.

'Thank you.' I coughed. 'I'm good now. Go back to sleep.'

Slowly, he rose and walked away. 'Good night,' he said before shutting his door.

'Good night,' I answered after he was already gone.

Why was it that I felt so... so hollow and transparent? As though I weren't there. Every night, James invaded my dreams and forced himself on me before he killed me or I killed him. And every morning, I woke up and still felt him between my legs and smelled his death on my skin. It bore no logic. He was dead and I was alive. But I never felt so. I felt as though he were more alive than I.

And yet, I preferred these dreams to the ones about my dead father.

～

THE MORNING SUN shone through my window and through my eyelids, prodding me awake. I blinked and heard a knock. 'Yes?'

'We must leave soon,' Sherlock called through the closed door.

After breakfast, we bought provisions and supplies and boarded the train to Brighton. I had a new dress that could be adjusted at the waist to accommodate my growing stomach. Buying it was almost as painful as putting it on. It felt as though my fate were to be sealed again and again.

When the train followed a sharp eastward bend, my nose dipped against the window. I wiped the print off the glass and watched the dark blue sea come into view over a green countryside littered with small farms, villages, cattle, and sheep.

'I wonder how you observe, or rather, what your eyes see and how your mind analyses,' Sherlock mused. 'Is there anything in particular that you tend to focus on? How loud does a sound have to be? How fast does an object, an animal, or a person have to move to attract your attention?'

He leant forward, elbows resting on his knees, eyes lit up with curiosity. It wouldn't have surprised me the least if he'd pulled out his magnifying glass to attempt a brain examination through my ears or nostrils.

'As we walked to the station,' I began, suppressing a smile, 'we passed an elderly couple. The man was talking about their too-old horse while she told him that the pain in both her hips had got worse. Three children, a few yards to the left, had an argument about a single piece of candied pineapple, the artificial kind that is so very yellow and sticky sweet. The cobbler on the other side of the street moved a crate out of his shop; it caught on a stone that stuck out of the pavement a little. It must have come loose only recently. The man swore into his beard while a woman in the room above him was about to tip cabbage leftovers out a window. The sash needed oiling; it squealed as she opened it. She must do this every day, always at the same time, for a flock of sparrows was already waiting for the food to hit the street. They fought over it while a buzzard called high above the town and a goldfinch snuck past us quietly, flying low. A pair of swallows switched places on their nest that was stuck to the house behind us, and you chatted nonsense about our new home in London. All that happened in merely a minute. Do you want me to go into detail?'

'An example, if you please.'

I shut my eyes, recalling the scene. 'Naturally, my view is somewhat sharpened for injuries and disease. And birds, because I like them. Anyway... The man had a slight limp, but I cannot tell what the cause might have been. It was an old injury or illness. The shape of his shoe had adapted to his way of walking. The slight inward tilt of his foot had worn the heel flat on that side.' I opened my eyes again. Sherlock was listening attentively. 'The aching of the wife's hips was not chronic. She walked carefully, but otherwise placed her feet almost normally. Her legs weren't bent outward. I assume her hipbones were not arthritic. Whatever she was doing to reach this state, I would recommend that she stop it at once to save her from increasing pain.'

'Intriguing. Hum...' He leant back, stretched his long legs, pushed his hands into his trouser pockets and said, 'You never take morphia to shut them out?'

'Shut out what? People?'

'Yes.'

'No! But it is indeed tiresome. Sometimes I feel like screaming to muffle the noises that constantly scream at me. I feel the urge to scream at all these people who are constantly buzzing, chatting, and behaving utterly nonsensically. Keeping my hands busy keeps me sane. Healing people keeps me sane.'

Silently, we watched the countryside fly by.

As the train slowed to a stop in Brighton, he said, 'There are moments when I despise everyone. That is why I'm not in the habit of carrying a revolver.'

He rose and slung the bag over his shoulder. I watched his back, wondering whether that was the reason he avoided humans: we were emotional, uncontrolled, loud, and dumb. We would tend to drive a man like him to madness.

We climbed onto the train to London. As soon as we reached our compartment, he extracted from his bag the telescope he had purchased in Littlehampton.

'That's why you led us along these hills! To watch Moran, should he be tracking us.'

'Precisely,' he said, and leant against the window.

'We should take turns.' I was curious to see if Moran was indeed coming.

'Hum,' he grunted, and then said nothing more as he searched the countryside.

We passed Hodshrove and his body tensed like a spring, his telescope pointing west to a hill about half a mile or a mile away. 'I cannot be absolutely certain. But two men and three dogs are walking precisely where we walked, and they look suspiciously familiar.'

'Let me see,' I said, and he gave me the instrument. The view was a little blurry, and the movements of the train didn't make it easy to focus, either. The locomotive hooted and I saw both men turning toward us. His movements, the way he shaded his eyes, how he slapped at his companion, looked all too familiar.

'It's him,' I said. 'I even know the dogs. They are James's Mastiffs. They know my scent.'

'Excellent!'

'What's your plan?'

His eyes were glittering with excitement, his voice crisp. 'He is faster than I expected him to be. We will reach Lewes shortly. I'll dispatch a telegram to my brother. Tomorrow, we'll return to Littlehampton. These two,' he jerked his head at the window, 'should need another three days.'

'The miscarriage plan.'

'Precisely. It should provoke Moran to contact his men. Their identities will be revealed!' He rubbed his hands and clicked his tongue. 'I hope to learn the name of the doctor in Dundee. But first, we need to make sure you are sufficiently suffering.'

'I will need blood, a pale face, and a coat to warm my weakened body. And of course, to hide my stomach, once the child is officially buried and we are leaving Littlehampton. A new dress would be practical, too, since I'll be spoiling this one.'

'Excellent While I go to the post office, you get a dress and a coat. We'll find an inn later.'

'And bandages, a sharp knife—'

'I have a knife,' he interrupted.

'I know. But I'm not using that dirty thing.'

'You want to cut yourself? We can get blood from a butcher. Ah... no. It will congeal, of course. Good. We'll use my blood.'

'No,' I said. 'We use mine. I'll open a vein at my ankle. It'll be easy to stop the bleeding. A little blood loss will make me convincingly pale and queasy. Besides, you need to be the one running about nervously, fetching ointments and medicine for your ailing wife. If you pass out every other minute—'

'Don't be ridiculous! But yes, we'll do as you say.' He grinned and appeared ten years younger. I wondered how he'd looked as a boy. The images of a five-year-old in an asylum made me nauseous.

'Are you afraid?' he asked.

'No. I was just wondering how you looked when you were a boy.'

'I was a beanpole.' He laughed, then leant back and inspected the window.

The train rolled into Lewes and we parted at once. I dashed to the chemist, to a second-hand clothes store, and then met with Sherlock at Lewes's only inn half an hour later.

'I'm starving,' I announced as we stepped inside.

With trotters, potatoes, cabbage, and ale on the table, we discussed our plans.

'I instructed Mycroft to meet with us the day after tomorrow. He will bring a stillborn of appropriate size and freshness.'

I nodded and poked at my trotter. The naked and gooey sheep foot suddenly looked rather uninviting. On the other hand, if it were hairy, it would have been even less edible. I began to suck the soft meat off the bone.

'I'll bleed myself ten minutes before we arrive in Littlehampton, then decorate my dress with a sufficient amount of blood, as well as your hands. You are my husband, and a doctor, after all, so there should be blood on you, too. I'll walk into town, moaning and heavily supported by you.'

'Precisely,' he said, and plopped his jug with ale on the table. 'How did you manage to poison Moriarty?'

His gaze slid to my hands that now froze around fork and

knife. I wanted to retch. 'I spread a mixture of essence of belladonna and arsenic solution on my lower lip, my breasts, and my vulva, knowing that James would lick it off eagerly.'

'Exceptional!'

The admiring tone was the last thing I had expected. Only a second later, he seemed to arrive at a similar conclusion, that his reaction had been, perhaps, rather inappropriate. The light in his eyes guttered.

'Can you really admire that?' I said quietly, so as not to snarl at him. 'A murder? How can you not be disgusted by how I betrayed a man and destroyed his life?'

'The method is admirable, but more so the strength, calculation, and nerve to accomplish it. Morals are not helpful here. They will twist you either way. Was Moriarty an evil man who deserved to die? Or was he merely a man who had made mistakes that could be forgiven? Simplification of the utterly complex for the sake of self-accusation to uphold morality, is not only stupid and inviting self-pity, it is outright dangerous.'

He was correct, of course. I began to wonder whether the logical mind could help the heart to heal.

'There is no use in regretting the past,' he said.

'But that! How can I not regret that?' I cried. 'This is his child. It will be born in a few months.'

I thought about the risk of dying during childbirth. The thought tasted like an option, not a threat.

'You think of the child as his. But aren't there parts of you there, too? Isn't it half you?'

'Which part of me? The part that manipulates or the part that believes humanity is a mob of idiotic creatures?'

'My father used to tell me that I'm just like his father, a man he despised. He told me I was a perfect copy of his father's character and stature. He knew I adored my grandfather, a grumpy and irritating man whose snide remarks always hit truth in the heart.' A deep laugh rocked his ribcage.

'And you mean to tell me what precisely?'

'That your child could be like you, or like Moriarty, or like your father, or even your mother. But most likely, your child will be a person of his or her own.'

I huffed at him. The chances that a second Anton would suddenly appear were minimal. A series of images flitted through my mind — a row of ancestors, a chaotic mix of Moriartys and Kronbergs.

'I cannot tell you what the right thing to do might be. But should you choose to raise him, you can give him what he needs to be an intelligent and loving man,' he said. 'Or woman.'

He bent forward, pressed my hand for a long moment before releasing it again. How empty it felt now. I curled it around the other to fill the void.

'So, in essence, you propose to me that the child might or might not show James's characteristics, and that I should raise him or her to ascertain later whether the world will or will not be bothered by another criminal mastermind.' I slammed the cutlery on the table. My appetite had disappeared.

'You are terrified,' he observed.

'And *you* believe that locking you up in an asylum one day might be justified,' I retorted.

He signalled yes, and so did I.

Then he changed the topic. 'The man who talked about the too-old horse served in the Boer War. He took a shot in his right lower leg. The injury tilted his foot inward a fraction. The horse was too old to pull the plough, but the couple couldn't afford a new one, so the wife began to work as a help in the post office. The constant sitting made her hips ache. Her wrists had marks from the edge of the counter and her fingers were smudged with ink. She even had ink on her right temple. She must have rubbed it repeatedly. Perhaps a headache?'

'An oncoming cold?' I offered half-heartedly.

'Her eyes didn't look like it. Her voice didn't indicate that, either. But then it could be early.'

'I'm not convinced of that gunshot wound. He might have been injured while working in the fields.'

'He wore a small medal. It was tucked just above his waistcoat pocket; only its top was visible — a black suspension piece with simple ornaments characteristic of service medals from the Boer War. The ribbon was missing.'

'But was he injured at war or in his field?' I insisted.

The corners of his mouth twitched. 'To be absolutely certain, we would have to return to Littlehampton at once and undress the man.'

'It's not too late. The next train should leave in an hour or two.'

He whacked the table top. 'Very well. Shall we wager?'

I grew cautious. He was convinced he was correct. I closed my eyes and imagined possible injuries a farmer could suffer. The horse kicks him hard — fractures, perhaps with bone breaking through skin, could result in a tilted foot if the fracture were not set properly. How had he walked? No shuffling, no limping, and the hip had seemed straight enough, so a considerable shortening of one leg due to a wrong setting of the bones wasn't likely. A fall, perhaps? Or a carriage driving over his legs? All I could come up with resulted in fractures. The tilted foot. Slight inward angle. No limp. No torsion of the hip. On the inside of my eyelids, I saw a bullet pass through various parts of the limb, severing muscles, nerves, tendons.

'There is no way of knowing whether he was shot or cut in the leg. The cut could have been done with a scythe. Or,' I interrupted myself, theatrically poking my index finger into the air, 'his wife's lover attacked him in the middle of the night, tried to cut his throat but ended up slicing the calf muscle instead.' I laughed. 'Or he chopped wood and drove the axe into his leg. Either way, scarring of the calf muscle resulted in a shortening of the same, and ultimately, in a slight inward bend of the foot.'

Sherlock looked at me as though I had lost my mind.

'But then it is rather complicated to cut oneself with a scythe or axe at that angle.' I rose and made a sweeping gesture, trying to hack at the flesh on the back of my leg. The clientele regarded me with puzzled looks.

'The man was lucky he didn't lose his leg,' I noted and sat down. 'Battlefields are awash with germs.'

A satisfied smile flared up, accompanied by a nod.

'But I rather opt for a mild case of polio,' I added.

'Excuse me?'

'As the cause for the man's slightly tilted foot.'

All I got as a response was a click of his tongue and a mischievous grin.

~

ON THE FOLLOWING DAY, we boarded the first train to Little-hampton. A few minutes before our arrival, I took off my left shoe, pulled the stocking down, and unclasped the knife. He held out a cup for me.

A sharp pain, then a tinkling of thick liquid hitting the metal cup's bottom. The cup began to fill and soon, my tongue felt dry and my ears sang quietly.

I fastened gauze over the small wound, pulled up my stocking, laced my shoe, and stuck my fingers in the cup. My blood was warm and was already congealing. The amount and its metallic odour felt alarming. I poured the liquid on my dress and rubbed it over its front and hem, while Sherlock smeared it on his hands and cuffs. We looked as though we had stuck a piglet.

'Ready?' he asked.

I nodded. He slung the rucksack over his back, the bag onto his shoulder, then stepped forward to offer me his free arm. Moaning, I slumped against him.

And that is how we exited the train, called a carriage, and arrived at the George Inn only a day after we had left it.

The landlord carried our luggage up the stairs, constantly calling for his wife and most likely thinking us idiotic for taking yet another trip through the moorlands and then returning, once again, all bashed up. Obviously, Londoners hadn't much brain in their funny heads.

When the landlady finally arrived, she left with a long list of things that needed to be arranged. Towels, hot water, cold water, disinfectants, and surgical instruments for the poor doctor who had left all his tools and supplies at his practice. Who could have known that a short trip to the countryside would have such a detrimental effect on his wife? While buzzing around in the most nervous fashion, Sherlock let everyone in Littlehampton know that his wife was on the brink of a miscarriage and that she should not, under any circumstances, be disturbed.

It seemed all Littlehampton walked on tiptoe. People didn't even dare talk when passing outside our window. Only the sparrows and finches and swallows dared peep.

'Well done,' I whispered as he returned.

'Likewise. And now, my dear wife, you haven't done any moaning for at least ten minutes.'

'Make me,' I quipped. Did I see him blush? I believe I did. Hiding my face, I doubled over and groaned loudly.

The sun began to set. I watched its descent while producing ailing noises every few minutes. He had bled himself to stain our white towels red, then sent them down to the landlady. Littlehampton's practitioner had asked whether we needed his help, but of course we didn't.

'Very good,' Sherlock whispered after he had shuffled the doctor out of our room. 'Should Moran ask questions, he will learn that a doctor's his wife had a miscarriage. He'll conclude that you treated yourself, considering your medical knowledge.' He lowered himself on a chair with a huff of accomplishment. 'After all, a miscarriage is nothing but a birth.'

Yes. And a stillborn is considered nothing but waste, I thought. Should Mycroft make the mistake of offering money for a stillborn, people would throw them at him.

Around seven o'clock, Sherlock went down to fetch supper for us, saying that I was sleeping at last, but should I wake in the middle of the night, I might need sustenance.

He lit the candle on the nightstand and we ate in silence. 'I'd like to wash,' I said when supper was finished. He retreated to his room.

I undressed and removed the bandage from my ankle. The cut was small and pale. I cleansed myself at the wash-bowl, disinfected the wound, wrapped a cotton strip around it, and dressed in nightgown and robe. Then I knocked on his door.

'Yes?' he called and I entered. He had already washed and changed as well.

'I need to disinfect your cut.'

He spotted the iodine in my one hand, the handkerchief in the other, and inclined his head.

He placed his foot up on the bed. I sat next to him and unwrapped the bandages.

'You washed it already. Good.' I dabbed disinfectant on the small wound, and wrapped the cotton strip around it again. 'We can take the bandages off tomorrow as long as our shoes don't rub on the cuts.'

He remained silent, staring at my hand holding his foot. I cleared my throat, rose, and wished him a good night.

Back in my room, I hoped not to cry out in my dreams. I wanted him there when he wished to be — not when he believed I needed consolation.

7

I produced more noise the following morning while Sherlock met with his brother. As soon as he returned, I began screaming in earnest.

'We will need more blood for this.' I glanced at the two packages he placed on the bed. Without comment, he sat and opened a vein on his other ankle. When the cup was half-full, I stopped him.

I spread the blood on my nightgown and on the sheets, then asked him to hand me the first package. Reluctantly, my fingers peeled off the layers of wax paper. Inside lay a tiny girl, wrinkled and grey. A newly hatched moth. The odour of decay didn't come off her yet. She must have died only a few hours before.

I had helped mothers give birth. Mothers from the lowest classes who were suffering from malnutrition and hadn't had the strength to carry a child to term. I had seen many still-borns in my life. And yet, this dead girl hit me in the chest at full force. I pressed my hand over my mouth, growled, and put myself back together.

'You should go down and spread the news,' I said to Sherlock.

A brief nod, then he took his hat and left.

I placed the foetus on the sheet among the red smudges, poured blood on her, unwrapped the other package, took out the placenta and umbilical cord, laid them out, and tossed the paper under the bed. I smeared the last of the blood on my nightgown, then curled up in the mess, warming the small body with my own, and gently bending and massaging her limbs to break the *rigor mortis*.

A timid knock announced our first and only witness. Sherlock stepped in, along with Littlehampton's practitioner. The latter saw that I was alive and comparatively well, and the child was not. He touched her lukewarm skin, nodded at the missing heartbeat, and seemed convinced that she'd died an hour before.

Then he left, for his help wasn't needed. Too normal a sight, even here, far from London's grime, disease, and poverty.

'The landlady will soon bring us water,' he said. 'We can clean up. She informed me that there is no open grave at the moment. I told her that under these circumstances, we will bury our daughter down at the beach.'

'Build a small grave for her with a mound of stones and a small cross, so Moran can easily find it. He will dig her up to make sure there is indeed a dead child.'

'Will you be all right?'

I brushed his concern away. 'Of course.'

We sat on the bed, I staring at my hands and he staring at his knees and chewing on an imaginary pipe until a knock interrupted the grim scene. The landlady opened the door a small crack, and placed an ewer with warm water, and an armful of fresh towels and sheets on the floor.

Silently, she shut the door.

'I will go alone,' Sherlock said after he had washed his hands and put a fresh shirt on. 'Everyone will expect you to remain in bed for a few hours at the least.'

Mute, I watched him carrying away the girl, the placenta, and his blood wrapped in a towel.

With one eye I peeked through the gap in the curtains. His slender figure crossed the street. People stepped out of his way, eyed the package under his arm, quickly drew their fingers across their chests — up-down, left-right — and hastily turned away. Bad luck.

I longed to get away from there, but the show needed to be played out to its end.

I used the rest of the water to wash all the blood off my skin. The red in the bowl reminded me of my days in the slums. So often had I placed my hands on someone's wound. To stitch them up, sometimes to saw off a limb.

I had been tougher back then.

~

LIGHT RAIN TAPPED against the window. The morning sun peeked through cracks in the cloud cover, rays prickling through the drops on the windowpane and refracting into a hundred small rainbows.

Our belongings were already packed. For authenticity's sake, Sherlock carried both the rucksack and the large bag while I was to lean on him. We stumbled down the stairs, through the small parlour, out into the drizzle, and across cobblestones that were steaming with rain and horse manure.

The station emerged from the mist, a red brick building, its roof streaked with white gull droppings. The birds cried and circled as we waited for the train. Soon came hooting and wisps of steam as the locomotive huffed into the station.

The stationmaster saw us step onto the train. None of the Littlehamptoners saw us exit on the other side. Even if we should have been seen by passengers, they were all taken away to New Shoreham, Brighton, or London.

Sprinkling camphor in our wake to spoil the tracking fun for Moran's dogs, we walked to the river Arun. The chain ferry took us across. The ferryman thought we were early tourists. He had never seen us before, and the rumours of a doctor and his ailing wife certainly wouldn't apply to a couple walking about laughing, pointing and chatting, as we were doing.

Once we reached the other side of the river, we went down to the dunes to set up our tent.

'How long, in your opinion?' I asked.

'It depends on the dogs. How quick they tire, how often they lose our scent, and how quickly they find it again. It could be any time from this very moment to up to two days from now.'

He pulled out his telescope and scanned the area where the river spilled into the sea. 'Look. There.'

I took the instrument from his hand and searched where he had indicated. On the other side was a small pile of rocks where the dunes rolled softly down to the beach.

One of us would be keeping an eye on the grave.

8

*W*e watched boats going in and out of the river's mouth, listened as fishermen praised their catch, to oystermen haggling for a better price, and to the gulls screaming at the sea. Wind combed the grass. The tent's oilskin flapped lazily.

While Sherlock kept his telescoped eye firmly on the other side of the river, I gazed up at the sky, one hand on my stomach, feeling the growing weight of the child and wondering what the next day might bring. 'In two or three weeks, this will be too large to hide.'

'Hiding it won't be necessary for much longer. We will go to London as soon as Moran discovers the grave. I need to know whom he contacts. After that, we'll pay Moriarty's solicitors a visit.'

'Moran will be delighted to learn that the child is dead. No need to be patient for three years. He can take revenge immediately.'

'Precisely.' He lowered the telescope, rubbed his eyes, and turned to me. 'If all goes as planned, Moran will take the train to London, believing we are already there. I have only one problem.'

'What problem?' I sat up.

'Evidence against Moran and Parker is weak. If I try to get them convicted, they should have a good chance to win at trial. I need an alternative.'

I leant back and watched the clouds crawl across the light blue sky. 'I have no problem shooting Moran in his ugly head.'

'You are developing an unhealthy habit.'

'I doubt it.'

I grew tired of doing nothing, so I asked him to let me take the watch for an hour or two. He placed the telescope in my hand, and retreated into the tent.

During the day, we would stay hidden. At that time of year, only the first handfuls of tourists were trickling into Littlehampton, too few to conceal our presence, but enough to possibly discover us or disturb the grave.

~

NIGHT HAD FALLEN two hours before. Moran hadn't come. I walked along the dunes, chewing on two thick slices of bread with a piece of ham in between. The grass was soft under my bare feet. Blades tickled my ankles.

A gentle slope led me down to the deserted beach, littered with small rocks and stones polished by millennia of water licking land. The rush of the sea was like a welcome song. I should have lived close by it; it might have healed my soul. Like pulsing blood, a heartbeat, the whisper of caresses — at times gentle, other times as rough as passion — the music would have filled my void.

I lifted the hem of my dress and sat down on a rock close to the water's edge. The sea washed my feet. Sand sneaked in between my toes. I shut my eyes, letting my ears take over my mind. Push and pull. Push and pull. The sea was reminiscent of Sherlock. An almost-embrace, then immediate retreat. A glance, gentle and caring, then a back turned toward me the remainder of the day.

I pushed away from the rock, shed my clothes, and walked into the water. Moonlight glittering on its dark and unsteady surface.

Coldness stung my belly and my uterus hardened to protect the child. Seaweed curled around my wrists as though to pull me asunder. Foam danced across gentle waves, up and down, lapping at my belly. I gulped a lungful of air and dove. With the sound of the sea in my ears and the blackness embracing me, I grew calmer.

I walked back to our hiding place, and spotted a slender silhouette next to the tent. He had his hands in his trouser pockets and stared in my direction. I remembered the first time I'd set eyes on him. He had walked through tall grass, just as tall as it was now. The wind had bent it, just as it did now. And I'd had the fleeting impression that his body was about to be bent by the wind, too.

I walked up to him, my hair dripping saltwater onto my shoulders and soaking my dress. 'I'll take the first watch.'

He lowered his head in agreement. 'Moran is unable to cross the river at night. On this side, you are safe.'

I wasn't shivering because of Moran, but I didn't tell Sherlock. 'He'll not be able to send a wire at night, either. This isn't London.'

Even if Moran arrived this very moment, found the grave, and questioned the few Littlehamptoners who were still awake to learn we had left for London, he couldn't do much. He would have to wait for the post office to open at eight in the morning and for the first train at nine twenty.

Wind gushed through my wet hair. I began to grow cold.

Sherlock slid into the tent, retrieved a blanket, and laid it about my shoulders. My gaze was trapped by his and I didn't know where to put my hands. My heart galloped. I could feel it in my throat and ears, in my legs and stomach.

'I'm not tired yet. Let us sit here for a while,' he said, motioning to the grass at our feet. 'I've been meaning to ask you this for some time now: how could you afford to study medicine? Your father was a carpenter. His earnings would have barely been enough to feed and clothe you.'

I smiled. He would always prefer distraction to an awkward silence caused by a doe-eyed woman. 'A handsome man helped the damsel in distress.' I began, 'Carpenters in Germany and Switzerland, and I don't know what other countries, have a strange tradition. As apprentices, they take to the roads to find a master, but they do not remain with him for any extended period of time. Half a year at the most, I believe. Then they take to the road again. There are some rules they have to adhere to, but most of them are secrets of the trade. All I know is that they are allowed only a certain amount of money while they travel, a maximum time with each master, and a minimum time of apprenticeship. They even have a secret language. They live the life of nomads for three years or longer. During his apprenticeship, my father met Matthias, a Swiss carpenter's apprentice. They took to each other like a fly to shit.'

Upon his low chuckle, I added, 'Not my words. It was their own joke, but they never told me who was the fly and who the shit. As it happened, Matthias was not only charming and intelligent, he was quite handsome, too. Tall, fair hair, blue eyes, broad shoulders. Almost every woman craned her neck when he walked past. At least that's what my father kept saying. He and Matthias were offered work by a wealthy man in Bavaria. He had a beautiful daughter who, upon seeing Matthias's shapely figure every summer day, did not even dream of rejecting his advances. Naturally, her father had several screaming attacks. He wanted her married to a well-bred gentleman. She, however, had her own mind, and the two became husband and wife after only three months of courtship. Her father threatened to disown her, but in the end, he didn't. And before he thought to change his will, he died.'

Sherlock's breath stalled for a moment.

'Are you suspecting a murder, Mr Holmes?' I teased him.

'Always. Pray continue, although it is clear now who your benefactors were.'

'The two friends parted but kept writing, and once in a while, they visited one another. Matthias was the one who stood by my father's side after my mother's death. He paid a wet nurse, otherwise, I would have perished. When I was older, I spent several summers in their home. He and his wife never had children, so they took to me, and I believe, they both loved me dearly. Before I turned ten, I told everyone with a pair of ears that I would be a physician. This wish made me rather unhappy, because fulfilment would never come. As a girl, I would never be admitted to university, nor could I ever afford the tuition. One fine day, however, Matthias asked me whether I'd like to dress up. I laughed at him, believing he thought to put me in a pretty dress, which I'd never liked. They were just plain uncomfortable! No one can climb trees in those things! But he brought me a shirt, a waistcoat, and a pair of trousers in my size. You *cannot* imagine how delighted I was!'

'On the contrary, I can very well imagine,' he said in calm amusement.

'Well, it turned out I looked quite boyish and if I were to cut my hair, I would certainly have made people believe I was a boy. He taught me how to walk like a man, how to burp like a man, how to laugh and talk like a man. I found it utterly amusing until one day I found myself enrolled at university. I was so terrified, I must have trembled all the first semester without interruption.'

'Did they ever ask you to return the money you owed?'

'They did. But they didn't want me to pay it back to them. I was to return the favour to people in need,' I answered.

'Is that why you chose to live in the slums?'

'Hmm...yes and no.' I pressed my palms against my aching back. 'It's a bit more complicated. I guess I would have ended up there, anyway. I needed a safe place to be me. Besides, I wasn't the only medical doctor who provided free treatment to the poor.'

He waved his hand dismissively. 'In all my years in London, I have heard of only three physicians who would offer their services for free. You are one of them.'

'Well, yes. But there were a lot of nurses who did that. Besides, a slum was a good place to hide my short hair and my big mouth. Nothing outrageous about that, among all those criminals, prostitutes, and beggars,' I supplied.

His gaze dropped to my lips. 'Your mouth is not big. I measured it a year ago.'

9

*P*ale morning light brushed across Sherlock's profile as he poked his head through a gap in the oilskin. 'We will separate,' he said. 'Moran must not see either of us and I'm faster without the luggage. I'll follow on his heels while you'll send a telegram to my brother. Then you follow. But you must not be seen in Little-hampton.'

'He's here?' I was suddenly wide awake.

He shook his head. 'But we should pack and be ready.'

We rolled up our blankets and collapsed the tent, while hunching low enough as not to poke our heads above the grass. He folded the oilskin and stuffed it in his bag. 'Can you carry all this?'

'Of course I can.'

Then we waited, he flat on his stomach, telescope in his hand, and I perched on my heels, surveying the surroundings as I cut slices of bread and ham.

We ate and washed our breakfast down with cold, bitter tea from the previous night. The wind pushed grass blades in our faces, held the gulls high above us, and carried their cries on salty air. The sun was hiding behind a thin sheet of clouds.

'Are there any good memories from your time in the asylum?' I asked.

'Hum...' he answered, not taking his eyes from the grave. A boyish smile lit up his features. 'Ha!' he said, and I was all ears, expecting a wild story to be revealed.

'Two ladies taught me a vast diversity of German profanities.' He turned, eyes shining. 'Miss Glücklich and Miss Meier.'

I almost spat out my breakfast. 'Glücklich? You found a Miss Glücklich in an asylum? Do you know that *glücklich* is the German word for lucky or happy?'

'Of course. I speak German fluently.'

It took me a while to digest this information. 'You never told me.'

'On what occasion precisely should I have done so? There was none. Besides, your English is excellent. No need to help you with translations.'

A dry remark and completely logical when one possessed all needed information already. 'Why were they there?'

'They were Sapphists.'

'Oh,' I said, feeling a pang. 'What you people from the higher classes have to endure is...madness. I have no other word for it. Locking up two women because they love each other. Locking away a boy who — even *if* he had made a horrible mistake — was only a small child, and hence innocent. All these useless rules go against logic, compassion, and instinct.'

Feeling quite hot from anger, I fluffed my hair to let the wind cool my scalp and my thoughts. 'If I had abided by those rules, I'd never have become a physician. I would now be sitting at home, with eight children, of whom four would already be dead from undernourishment or disease. And I would have a husband who believes that beating his wife with a stick no thicker than his thumb is appropriate — because the law allows it!'

I threw a handful of sand in the wind. It was blown straight back into my face. 'Dammit to hell and back! I have sand between my teeth.'

A low chuckle rolled up his throat.

I poked my finger in his ribs and said, 'I was kissed by a woman once.'

'As was I.' He turned back to observing the surroundings for any signs of Moran and Parker while I inspected the grass for insects.

'We drank all of the tea,' I said somewhat involuntarily, feeling rather dry in my mouth. 'The water is gone, too.'

We didn't speak for the ensuing two hours. Only the wind whispered in my ears, the gulls screamed, and the sea rushed up against the shore, again and again.

'I've changed my mind,' he finally said. 'You'll leave now. A trap can take you from the ferry to Bognor. Take the train to London from there.'

'No.'

'I will not discuss it!'

'Good. Because I won't, either. There is no reason for me to leave, other than you wishing to tuck me away safely.'

Annoyed, he pinched the bridge of his nose

I smiled and said, 'I know you care. But don't make me smaller now. You know what I'm capable of.'

His set chin didn't relax. 'It is only logical for you to go to London immediately. You are too slow to help me track Moran, and the next instance your presence is needed will be at the solicitors' office to receive your dower.'

'It would only be logical if I would expect you to do everything and think everything for me. And you know I don't expect that. I need to see with my own eyes how

Moran reacts to the child's death. I want to see how hungry he is. I will collect my own data and analyse them with my own brain. You may do as you see fit.'

With that, I turned my attention to the grass and the sand, as though they needed inspection.

~

AROUND NOON, Sherlock knocked the sand off his trousers, grabbed our two bottles and a water pouch, and dashed off to the ferryman.

With the telescope held up against one eye, I watched the pile of rocks and the dunes farther up.

A hat appeared, then another. Shoulders emerged from the tall grass. One of the men turned enough for me to see part of his moustache. My skin prickled. Moran! I turned my head to see where Sherlock was. I thought of warning him, then decided against it. I was sure he'd be keeping an eye out for the two, and would approach our hiding spot with utmost care.

The sun kept behind the clouds. No strong reflections would be cast off the telescope to betray my location. I lifted the instrument to my eye and watched their progress.

Three dogs sniffed eagerly, urging the two men ahead. Moran's companion appeared younger, perhaps in his thirties. His clothing was cheap. His demeanour showed how low in rank he stood. In a flash, he obeyed every flick of Moran's hand, kicked aside the makeshift cross, squatted next to the pile of rocks, and began moving them aside.

He paused, then began scooping away sand, then stopped again. Moran bent down, pointed, and his footman, Parker, picked up the package.

Did I see reluctance in his motions? The girl must have begun to stink. Both men stood still for a moment, gazing down at the bloody towel and its contents. Moran waved a dismissive hand. Parker dropped the girl back in the hole and tossed a few rocks on her.

As they stood with arms crossed over their chests, contemplating and discussing, I heard Sherlock approach. Sand whispered under his shoes.

'Did they swallow the bait?'

'It appears so,' I said quietly and handed him the telescope. While he was observing the two, I told him what I had seen.

'The next train leaves at three twenty,' he noted.

'That will be the last train today.'

A few moments later, he rose. His knees crackled. 'They are gone. Come.'

We hurried to the ferry, and he said, 'Enquire for a trap to Worthing. As soon as you arrive there, send a telegram to Mycroft Holmes, Diogenes Club, Pall Mall. The message "Now" will suffice. He'll know what to do—'

We ducked when we spotted Moran and Parker on the other side of the river.

'I'll keep a very close eye on these two. He'll dispatch telegrams from the post office. You and I will meet at Victoria Station tomorrow morning. Should I be unable to arrive in time, leave the luggage with a porter, then go hide at your Irish friend's home at once.'

'Garret? Are you serious?'

'Is that a problem?'

'We parted rather...unfriendly.'

'We have to agree on one location quickly now. It cannot be a public place, for we might have to change our disguises. I have a few hiding holes, but you wouldn't be able to find them, even if I gave you the addresses.'

'Good. Garret, then. If he doesn't welcome me, he'll certainly take a message for you.'

'Excellent.' He bent down and extracted a revolver, ammunition, and a few bills from the bag. 'The second revolver and some twenty more bullets are in the side pocket...' His face fell. 'Why did I never show you how to properly use a revolver?'

I laughed. The one time he had seen me using a gun was when I'd thrown one at him. 'Cock, point, fire. You can introduce me to the fine art of marksmanship later.'

Littlehampton's church bell banged twice. The ferryman was pulling his vessel toward us. Moran's and Parker's backs disappeared toward the small town. Next to me, Sherlock was vibrating with impatience.

Without farewell, we parted as soon as the ferry docked.

10

From error to error, one discovers the entire truth.
Dr S. Freud

⁓

I woke up early the following morning, aching to leave. And two hours later, a train took me from Worthing toward London.

Once at Victoria Station, Sherlock was nowhere to be seen. With my bonnet pulled down low to conceal my face, I stepped out of the last wagon, left the luggage with a porter, and told him it would be picked up tomorrow. Then I pressed through the bustling crowd and out of the station.

Wary of familiar faces among the masses of people, and their refuse, luggage, chatter, and hotchpotch while adapting to London's overwhelming variety of odours and noises, demanded all my attention. Without thinking, I nearly stepped into the first cab I hailed. I let the hansom drive away without me, walked around a corner, and took another one to Bow Street.

The hansom rattled over cobblestones. Wind slapped my face. I inspected my dress and my shoes, picked at a few threads on my sleeves, and decided I looked worn enough to be safe in St Giles for a few hours. How many people would recognise me? Would Garret roll his eyes and shut the door in my face? Barry would be twelve years old now. More or less. He was only guessing his age. Children came in large numbers, most of them unwanted and unplanned. One had sexual intercourse, one got pregnant, one gave birth. Then the circle started anew. Two thirds of all the slum children died before reaching the age of three. There was no reason to note birthdays.

The cab came to a halt. I paid the driver and stepped onto the pavement. Everything looked the same as when I'd left. The streets were covered with the same amount of dirt. Mule droppings here and there, limp cabbage leaves with caterpillar holes, undefined mush, and rivulets of waste water and chamber-pot contents.

How long would it take to pull sewers through the slums, I wondered. Would the slums still be home to the poorest when the government decided to gift the people with a way to rid themselves of their own refuse? Probably not. Streets would be torn open, houses gutted, grime and beggars shoved aside.

London would look different.

I found Garret's house and was surprised that even the door looked as it had long ago. The brown paint was rubbed off in several places. Naked wood peeked through. It had been a year. Or a little longer, even. But not enough time for a door, a house, or a district to change all that much. But enough time for Garret to grow into an altogether different person. I wondered how much he had changed. He and Barry probably hated me for leaving without even saying goodbye.

I pushed at the door and, as expected, the broken lock

clicked open. I walked up the stairs, and familiar creaking accompanied each step. When I knocked at Garret's room, a child began to wail.

'What is it?' a woman barked through the closed door.

'Could I speak to Garret O'Hare, please?'

'Don't know that fella.'

My heart sank. For a moment, I'd thought he was a father. Now it seemed that he would be hard to find.

I went downstairs and knocked at the door to the landlady's quarters. Or whatever she was. I doubted she owned the house. Only kept it in a somewhat orderly state of decomposition.

'What?' she demanded, flinging the door wide open. 'Haven't seen *you* in a while.' Her arms went akimbo, her eyebrows slid to a V-shape.

'Hello, Mrs Cunningham. Have you seen Garret?'

'Where have you been?'

'Germany.'

'Ah. On the continent. Fancy that. Well, your friend is in Newgate. For two months now, I believe.'

My knees wobbled. 'Newgate? Do you know why?'

She laughed. 'What do you think?'

'He was caught burgling a house.'

Her lips crinkled. She produced a nod.

My hand clapped over my mouth. 'That's the third time. He'll be hung.'

'Pretty much. Don't take it to heart, dear. He's a thief. Getting hung is what thieves usually do.'

I coughed. 'Yes. Thank you. Have a good day.'

Several gulps of air later, I found myself on the street again. Barry was my only thought. I desperately hoped the boy was alive and well. Comparatively well, at least.

Three blocks farther south I walked up the rotten stairs to the room he had been living in the previous year. The stink of urine, rotten potatoes, fetid cabbage, and excrement waved *hello*. And although I knew that stink all too well, it brought up the little breakfast I had eaten. With my hands on my knees, my stomach cramping and nostrils burning, I retched up my stomach contents. There was no need to worry about cleanliness. The rats would soon take care of the half digested porridge.

'Barry?' I shouted, wiped my mouth, and entered a dark room. Something on the floor moved. A cry of surprise fled up my throat as a set of teeth came flying toward me, barking and growling.

'Shit!' a young voice called. 'Come here, you bastard.' The dog stopped, turned around, and left me standing in the doorway.

'His name is Shit?' I huffed, trying to get my bearings.

'What do you want, mum?'

'I'm looking for Barry.'

'What for? Who are you?' Hostility seeped through every crack in his voice.

'A friend. We used to roam St Giles together.' What an unladylike choice of words.

'I'll let him know you are looking for him.' His tone was mocking and I had the impression he was lowering his voice to make himself sound older than he was.

Slowly, my eyes grew accustomed to the dark. Dim light oozed through cracks in the barricaded windows. The dog must be lying somewhere amid the rubbish littering the floor.

'Nonsense!' I shot at the silhouette hunching in a far corner. 'You didn't even ask for my name. I doubt you know the boy very well. You probably ate him.'

A throaty laugh rocked the walls. Almost a man's laugh. Then the voice changed again and I finally recognised it. 'You have some nerve showing up here.'

'I couldn't come earlier. I need your help, Barry.' I stepped closer, trying not to fall over the refuse. 'Garret is in Newgate. They'll hang him.'

He didn't move. 'And what do *you* want to do about it? Break in and toss him over the wall?'

His arms wrapped around his knees as he compacted himself against the wall. There didn't seem to be much flesh on his bones. I knelt down and dimly saw his face. How could he look so much older than the last time I'd seen him? The boy was only twelve! 'Let's go to the pieman.'

'I'm not six anymore.'

'No, you are almost a man. But I'm hungry and I need to talk to you.' I held out my hand. The familiar grin with its four missing front teeth blinked up at me. 'Thank you, my friend.'

'That will cost you,' he said.

'Yes, I thought so.'

We walked along the street and he steered me to an inn. 'No pieman?' I asked.

'I changed my mind. I want a real meal.'

The landlord greeted us with an 'Oy!' and then brought the food and drink we ordered.

While Barry inhaled mutton and bread, I talked. 'I've never been in Newgate. Obviously. But I see two possibilities. The first involves a lot of money. The second involves your skills. If Garret has had his trial already, there isn't much time until he's executed.'

Using Barry's skills was a most unrealistic plan. Newgate was a stronghold. But it gave the boy the impression that his help was badly needed. He wouldn't come with me if he got the feeling I was on a charity mission.

He chucked a potato under the table, wiped his hands on his shirtfront, and bent closer to me. 'Is that why you carry more than fifty pounds, a revolver, and ammunition?'

'You've got quicker. I'm impressed.'

As we'd walked down the stairs of his decrepit house on our way to the street, he had stumbled against me. I had felt his swift hands search the folds of my skirt and I wondered whether he had extracted money.

'Yes. I'm a great pickpocket. I work alone. I don't need anyone. And I don't have to feed anyone. I'm free.' His shoulders broadened and his eyes flared.

'What about your mother?'

'Got the French gout. Died two weeks ago.'

'I am sorry,' I said, and reached out to touch his hand.

Appalled by the gesture, he pulled it back. 'So. You have a bun in the oven. Congratulations.'

'Unfortunately.' I avoided his gaze.

'Yeah. That's what my mom said when she had me.'

'It's the child of the man who abducted me.'

'I am the child of a man who paid my mom to let him fuck her, right after hundreds of others fucked her, and right before a hundred more fucked her. She didn't even know what lucky prick produced me. Never even knew who made her sick.'

He spat. 'Have you got an idea how it *ate* the flesh off her face? Have you got *any* idea how my mom died?' He pushed away from the table.

The clientele threw annoyed glances in our direction.

'I know how syphilis kills.' I was about to say that even if I had been there to help his mother, there was little I could have done. Yet another disease without a cure. But what would it help to say it? It wouldn't make his heart lighter, only mine. But had I been there, I could at least have taken care of him. 'I'm sorry I left you alone.'

'You idiotic do-gooder nurse,' he mumbled, and sat back down. 'I didn't need you. And I still don't.'

'I have never been a nurse, Barry. I worked as a medical doctor and masqueraded as a man for twelve years.'

His fork clattered on his plate. He snapped his gaping mouth shut. 'By the hairy balls of Jesus!'

The dog emerged from under the table, wagging his tail, lolling his tongue. 'Down!' said Barry and used his foot to push the fur ball back into hiding.

'Why did you name him Shit?'

'He's brown, dirty, and he stinks. So, when are we burgling Newgate?'

I smiled down at my hands. 'We will begin our preparations as soon as you have eaten.'

He took that as an invitation to hurry. He gulped down all the ale, grabbed the last two potatoes and stuffed them into his cheeks which basically made him look like an overgrown hamster, then jumped to his feet, grinning.

I steered us onto the Strand and into a tailor's. The man took Barry's measurements with reluctance and with both his pinkies strutting out to ward off contamination. He seemed to have fewer problems running his ruler over my limbs. I gave him sixty minutes to fit the clothing we had chosen. Next was a bath house and a barber.

Without the multiple layers of dirt, Barry looked like a newborn piglet. Scrubbed clean and pink, he smelled of soap and fresh laundry. The new haircut, with Macassar oil, his new suit, waistcoat, and top hat, made him look like a tiny gentleman shrunk from too hot washing.

'That's how you ran around all these years?' he asked once we entered a cab. He had been grinning ever since I slid into my trousers, buttoned my waistcoat, placed the topper on my head, and stuffed fabric above my stomach to make it appear more like a potbelly. The tailor had seemed less amused, but my explanation that we were performers took the edge off his alarmed expression.

'Yes.' I grinned and had to hold myself back to not lift his hat and ruffle his hair. It seemed those days of mischief and do-gooding were too long ago.

The hansom stopped. We alighted, and walked up to the club.

'I speak. You don't,' I said and rang the bell. A man with a solemn face, sharply pressed suit and trousers, and a perfectly starched shirt and collar opened the door. 'May I speak to Mr Mycroft Holmes? He's expecting us, although I'm not quite certain under which name.'

The butler didn't even twitch an eyebrow. We were beckoned in. He offered to take my package, but I declined. We placed our hindquarters on offered seats in the parlour, both of us slightly nervous from all that stiffness surrounding us. The silence was so heavy that my neck began to ache.

I hoped Barry would be able to control himself, but his hands were already roaming, about to pick at a few lilies from a crystal vase.

'Barry,' I growled and he stopped, then sat on his hands to prevent them from trailing off in all directions. The butler returned and waved at us to follow him. We went up the stairs, along a corridor, and into a room far in the back. Mycroft sat at a desk, cigar smoke enveloping his large figure.

'Mr Holmes.' I stepped forward and held out my hand. He turned it and breathed on my knuckles.

Barry choked. 'How did you know she's a woman?' he blurted.

'Hands, feet, and chin too delicate, as is her entire physique, and when she walks, the sway of her hips betrays the child she's with,' he commented in an offended *rat-tat-tat*. 'Fairly obvious, even if we didn't know each other.'

'Is Sherlock safe?' I asked. 'He wasn't at Victoria Station

and the alternative meeting place was... What happened to him?'

'Of course he is safe. At present, he's at your late husband's solicitors. We have been waiting for you.' Mycroft threw a gaze of mistrust at Barry, obviously unwilling to share any more information.

'My apologies,' I said and turned to my friend. 'This is Barry Williams, a dear friend of mine.'

'Are all your friends pickpockets?'

'Of course not. Most of my friends are prostitutes or burglars.'

'How... how did you know?' Barry stuttered. His mouth got stuck at the "ow" and wouldn't close.

'You scanned every single valuable item in this room. Your hands and eyes are quick, as are your feet. Pickpocketing is your second nature.'

'What's my first nature?'

'Eating refuse, judging from the odour emanating from your mouth. Snap it shut!'

'Mr Holmes,' I interrupted, 'if you could tell me where I can meet your brother, I'd be most grateful.'

'Certainly. I'll even accompany you there.' Expelling a huff of smoke, he rose to his feet and extinguished his cigar in a crystal ashtray. 'I assume this is a respectable dress?' He pointed at my package.

'Yes.' I removed my hat. 'Barry, I'll need your help buttoning it. If you would wait just outside the door until I call you?'

Barry made round eyes, then retreated together with Mr Holmes.

The dress hid my stomach to some degree, owing to a number of useless frills and buffs. I pinned up my hair and called for Barry, who let his swift fingers trail up my spine, sending all those small buttons into their holes. He picked at the veil until it fell into place and then we stepped out of the room.

Mycroft led us to the waiting brougham. 'I recommend that the young gentleman remain in the carriage once we reach the solicitors' office.'

I looked at Barry, who nodded obediently. 'Mr Holmes, I have a problem and hope money can solve it. I need to buy the freedom of one of Newgate's prisoners. If I'm not mistaken, he is waiting for the gallows.'

'I'm surprised you haven't considered burgling it,' he said, his voice slightly acidic.

I cleared my throat. 'In fact, I have,' I lied. 'That's why I brought my friend. I'm far from being an accomplished cracksman.'

I hadn't picked a single lock, aside from the ones Garret had used in his attempts to teach me lock-picking. He had called it *entertainment*.

'You will need a considerable sum,' Mycroft said.

'I do hope to inherit it very soon. If necessary, I'll buy the whole damn prison.'

'How amusing,' he said, and cocked his eyebrows.

We arrived and were received by a servant, who led us into a large office with windows spanning from floor to ceiling and furniture that indicated an income significantly higher than the average solicitor. Two gleaming mahogany desks formed the centre of the office and bookshelves adorned the walls, together with a picture of a grumpy-looking Queen Victoria. Seeing Sherlock's face hidden behind a humongous moustache lifted a weight off my shoulders I hadn't known existed.

Two men rose from their seats, approached me with outstretched hands, and introduced themselves as Messrs Palmer and Miller.

'Our most heartfelt consolations,' the older said, while the younger muttered, 'Indeed, indeed.'

Sherlock clapped his hands — a canon shot that split apart the solicitors' pretence. 'Let us begin, gentlemen. My client is in danger and the longer she remains in London, the greater the chance her pursuers find her.'

'Certainly, Mr Wright—'

'And let us not forget the terms of our agreement,' Sherlock cut across.

'Absolutely not, my dear sir! We are deeply saddened by the death of our esteemed client and are, of course, bound by honour to carry out his widow's wishes. Had we known that she was still with us...'

'Yes. You mentioned that already.' Sherlock rushed to my side as though I were about to faint and offered me a seat. I did my best to sort the elaborate mourning dress into the chair, together with myself, without appearing to be the non-lady that I was.

How recent was the information of my supposed death? Was it Moran's fabrication or that of James's family?

'We took the liberty of letting your solicitor, Mr Wright, inspect all of your late husband's papers. If you wish, we can show and explain everything to you—'

'The short version, please,' I said.

'Very well.' He picked through the pile of papers that lay in neat stacks on his desk, then cleared his throat. 'It is most unusual for a man of his standing. And considering his meticulousness, I cannot fathom why... My sincere apologies, Mrs Moriarty, but there appears to be no will. Without it, all of your husband's possessions are to be transferred to his closest male relative, or, in the lack thereof, to his closest female relative. In plain English, his sister Charlotte already inherited everything. However, by law, you are entitled to a dower equivalent to one third of your husband's estates.'

'If there truly is no will, as you stated, Charlotte Moriarty cannot inherit a farthing. I am with child.'

The man coughed in his hand. 'We received intelligence of a miscarriage.'

'Whose?' I asked, feigning surprise and puzzlement.

'Well, obviously the miscarriage of the heir-at-law.' A dignified index finger rose to brush imaginary lint off an impeccable lapel. The man's lips compressed. His eyes searched for evidence hidden by the frills of my mourning dress.

'You also received intelligence of my death, did you not? Do you believe I'm dead, Mr Palmer?'

Blood rose to his face.

'Do you wish to consult a physician, or would you like to conduct the examination yourself?' I asked.

'Well…' He trailed off, swivelled his head, and said, 'I need proof. Considering the amount of money that will change hands, I fear I must insist.'

'Upon my honour!' huffed Mycroft Holmes.

Ignoring the affront, I rose and moved veil and frills aside, presenting the small bulge. 'Would that be sufficient?'

'I need to ascertain its authenticity.'

'I thought so.'

'Outrageous!' barked Mycroft and pushed between Mr Palmer and me.

I grabbed the man's hand and placed it on my stomach. The blood vessel in his throat bulged and his upper lip began to perspire. 'You are obviously terrified of making a mistake, Mr Palmer. I wonder what troubles my late husband's family is giving you.' With that, I released him.

He stumbled backward and wiped his palm on his trousers. I felt an urge to kick his groin.

'Upon clarification of this delicate subject, I suggest we proceed,' Sherlock cut in.

The crackling air in the room cooled at once.

'Your late husband is, or I should say *was*, in the possession of a variety of estates and trust funds, plus a rather large amount of money in various bank accounts,' Mr Palmer began. 'As suggested earlier by your solicitor, Mr Wright, all the money will be withdrawn, trust funds liquidated, and all estates sold. The money that has already been transferred to Mrs Charlotte Moriarty's accounts will be removed, if necessary through a court order, which won't be complicated to obtain. May I assume this meets with your approval?'

I signalled yes and flicked my gaze to Sherlock, who now began to speak. 'We will provide testimony by a certified physician. Should the court prove as sceptical as you about the obvious state of my client.'

A stiff nod answered his offer.

'As for the estates to be sold,' the solicitor continued, 'we are unable, as yet, to give you a precise amount. It depends on the motivations of the buyers, of course. However, before we reach this issue, I have a question regarding the servants. In your house at Kensington Gardens, the servants are still under employ. Do you wish to keep them?'

'No. Pay all of them two months' salary, with the exception of Jonathan Garrow, the coachman, and Cecile Gooding, the lady's maid. Both shall receive five years' salary. Then sell the house. It reminds me too much of my husband.' I pushed a handkerchief under my veil and blew my nose heartily.

The man in front of me cleared his throat, polished his monocle, and inserted it in his left eye socket. 'Very well,' he said, directing his gaze at the younger man, who instantly began hacking away on a typewriter.

'Now,' he continued. 'Estimating the current value of the estates, and adding the trust funds to the much larger value represented by your husband's savings, less inheritance taxes, we arrive at the following amount.' He stared at a piece of paper in front of him. I could see a lot of numbers, slanted and upside-down.

His mouth formed the words with great reluctance. 'Two million four hundred thousand pounds sterling.' His fingertips trembled. 'More or less. Of that, your dower should amount to approximately three hundred thousand pounds, considering that half of Mr Moriarty's assets are in estates. The rest will be moved to a trust fund with you as the sole trustee and will be transferred to the heir-at-law when he or she attains majority.'

Silence fell. I thought of Barry, who couldn't even dream of such numbers, who would probably think to cram the equivalents of eel pies and baked potatoes into his head. And Garret, whose freedom I could simply buy. I could buy the entire Newgate prison and even the ugly street it was built on. I could even pull sewers through St Giles—

'Excellent,' said Sherlock. 'If you please, arrange for the dower to be transferred to the bank account we agreed upon.'

Everyone looked at me. I nodded.

There were papers to be signed, received, and kept. Before we left, I bent close to Sherlock to ask a question. He squeezed my wrist and whispered, 'Later.'

The moment the brougham's door snapped shut, I slammed my head against the wall and cried, 'That idiotic stomach examination! Why is it that all these educated men cannot face the natural consequence of sexual intercourse? I feel as though I'm the only one who...' I looked at Barry, who was severely red-cheeked. When my gaze drifted to Sherlock, I felt heat rising to my face. Mycroft's bored look tried not to reveal a thing. I swallowed the mad urge to laugh out loud.

'You were late,' Sherlock said to me. Upon seeing my clueless expression, he added, 'You didn't meet Wiggins?

Mycroft, we need to find the boy. Driver!' He tapped his stick to the carriage's roof. 'To the Berkeley Hotel. Make haste!' A flick of the whip and the horses clopped along the streets.

I'd seen Wiggins, as well as a few other of Sherlock's street arabs, only from afar. With Moran so close, it was indeed a bad sign that the boy had gone missing.

Sherlock turned to Barry with a look of expectation. The boy woke from his rigour and opened his mouth to speak, then snapped it shut again.

'He is my friend and I trust him,' I said.

Barry finally found his voice. 'Did that bloody devil leave you a lot of money?'

'Two million and a bit.'

He made a croaking noise. 'Can you buy Buckingham Palace?'

I burst out laughing. 'I don't want to live in *that* small shoe box. And I can buy something much better.' I turned to Sherlock. 'Garret is in Newgate.'

'Why?'

'He burgled a house.'

'Did anyone come to harm?'

'I don't know,' I said truthfully. 'I know him as a gentle and caring man. He can hurt people when he defends others. He was caught in the act of burgling a house, but what happened precisely, I cannot say. It's the third time he's been arrested.'

Sherlock's eyes narrowed for a moment.

I curled both hands to fists. 'Yes, he's a criminal. He's far from innocent. But I will not let him die in Newgate. If you'd rather not help, I'll do it alone.'

His gaze drifted to his brother, and it was as if a set of tiny cogwheels were put in motion. 'The Lord Mayor. You know his weak spots.'

'How much is your friend's life worth?' Mycroft turned to

me and interpreted my cold stare correctly. 'Good. Unlimited. His full name, please.'

'Garret O'Hare,' I answered. 'I would like to accompany you.'

'Not to the mayor's office, but you are most welcome in Newgate.'

'Thank you.'

We arrived at the Berkeley. Sherlock rose and opened the door.

'Wait a moment,' I said.

He jumped onto the street and turned to me. 'I'll tell you everything upon your return. You'll find me under the name of Eric Wright. I'll book a room for your two friends as Thomas and Daniel Atkinson. You are Thomas, the son.' He pointed at Barry, and then at me. 'Your room is booked under the name of Olivia Saunders. I'll also arrange for a physician's testimony.'

I turned to Barry, who still sat frozen on his seat. 'Would you wait for me at the hotel? I might need your help once I'm back.'

He blinked and squeaked, 'Sure!' Then he peeled his buttocks off the expensive leather.

'Thank you, my friend. Eat something and stay put.'

The boy climbed out, the mutt on his heels.

Mycroft and I left at once.

11

'*M*ay I ask how you plan to convince the mayor to release a convicted habitual burglar?'

'I'll tell him that your friend has information about a German weapons maker who is now in London and is suspected of planning an assassination. The target will, of course, be secret, meaning open to the wildest interpretation.'

'And you need money to convince him?' I asked.

'Yes. Either that or I'd have to…threaten him. I prefer the former.'

'What are the chances he'll release Garret?'

'Since your resources are now unlimited, I should think the chances are close to one hundred per cent,' he said.

'Thank you. I cannot… let him…die,' I stammered. 'I'm deeply indebted to you—'

He stopped me with a held-up hand, and bent closer to my face. 'One day I'll ask you for a favour and you will not decline.' His voice was quiet, yet full of conviction. More effective than a shout. I squinted at him, remembering his earlier request to work as a spy.

The two horses came to a halt and he alighted at once.

Waiting for Mycroft Holmes to return with Garret's release papers tortured the thin sliver of patience I possessed. When he finally opened the carriage door, sweat glistened on his temples. 'Quick, driver! To Newgate,' he called.

'What is it?' Fear crept in through my pores.

'They've decided to hang him early. Apparently, your friend is sick enough to make the judges fear he might die before they have a chance to wrap a noose around his neck.'

I yanked the veil over my face and stared out the window. My eyes began to water.

'Old Bailey,' the driver he announced a few moments later, and opened the door for us.

Mycroft said, 'I'll introduce you as the sister of the convict, who wishes to see her brother one last time before he is taken into custody to the Special Branch. The police are of course hoping you will help to tickle dark secrets from him.'

I nodded once.

The unhappy building with its small, grated windows glared down on us. We went in through the governor's house, entered a small office where Mycroft presented the papers, and muttered a few words. An officer was called to conduct us.

We walked through a lodge, one of its walls decorated with heavy sets of irons — perhaps to scare the new arrivals. We passed a mighty oaken door held by cast iron bands, complete with studded nails and an armed guard, followed by a series of corridors, gates, gratings, and more guards yet. The maze of terror opened to a yard with a thick iron gate at one end. The turnkey on duty admitted us, and after a sharp left turn, we reached the condemned ward. Mycroft's heels clacked steadily on the stone floor, as though this place didn't touch him in the least. I held on to his steadiness, hoping Garret was still alive at the far end of the dark passage.

We entered a room with cells on either side, each one guarded by a turnkey. I counted twenty-four convicts, all waiting for the gallows. We continued. Yet another yard, framed by tall walls, a narrow and obscure staircase, then a dark passage ending in a massive iron door. The turnkey bowed and admitted us, and another opened yet another door for us. Hinges screeched, locks clicked.

Pushing past Mycroft, I stepped into the stone dungeon and laid my eyes on a man I hardly recognised. His orange mane was matted, his clothes and bare feet blackened with dirt. His breathing was elaborate. I rushed up to him and tossed back the veil, so he would see my face. I took his hand in mine and pressed it hard. 'Garret.'

He blinked at me as though I was an illusion. 'Anna?'

I bent close to his face, and whispered, 'Don't speak, don't ask questions. We'll get you out of here.'

His eyes were round in shock and disbelief. He pushed himself up, and staggered a little. I was relieved to see him stand without sinking back to his palette. I offered him my arm. He gladly took it. His once-muscular frame had become bony. He felt like half the man I'd once known.

I pushed forward, out of that dreadful cell. I would have run, had Mycroft not slowed our escape to a casual walk, warning me with a flick of his finger and a sharp sideways glance. My heart was hammering so hard, it hurt.

When we finally stepped out of Newgate and into the brougham, Mycroft snapped, 'If I had known that you could barely control yourself, I would have strapped you to that bench and not allowed you to enter the premises!'

'What was the problem?'

'You burst into his cell and very nearly kissed him!'

'And what… Of course. The guards will talk. My apologies. It taints your reputation.'

He harrumphed and straightened his lapels.

I turned to Garret. 'How do you feel?'

'Alive,' he croaked, and stared at me and Mycroft, blinked, and let his head drop in his hands. 'When I saw you, I thought I was dead. A whole damn year I was convinced *you* were dead, Anna.'

He sat up, and groaned. 'For Christ's sake!' The raggedness of his breath was alarming.

'I will answer all your questions, but first I need to examine you and find out what ails you and what cure I can give you.'

'There is no cure. I have consumption.'

'How would you know?'

'The turnkey said so. His wife had it. Half of London has it. It's hard to miss.'

He was exaggerating. Perhaps a fifth of London suffered from various forms of tuberculosis. But yes, when the frigid autumn fogs rolled in, it felt as though those deep rattling coughs came from all directions.

'We will part here,' Mycroft said when we had reached the Berkeley.

'Thank you so much, Mr Holmes.' I pressed his hand, and alighted.

'You owe me two thousand pounds. You should receive your inheritance in about a week. My brother will bring me your cheque. And you, Mr O'Hare,' he called after Garret, who exited the carriage, 'will not be admitted to the hotel in such a state.' He shrugged off his coat and handed it to him to hide the grimy, disintegrating clothes. 'I will want it back,' he said, muffling Garret's flood of gratitude.

I pulled the veil over my face, wrapped one arm around Garret's waist, and together we entered the hotel. Money bought silence and smooth service. A bath for Garret, new clothing, food — all were delivered to his room.

I excused myself to knocked on Sherlock's door. When no answer came, I returned to Garret and Barry. Both fell silent when I entered. 'Is it true what Barry said? You are rich now?' Garret's face was that of a stranger. Anger made his voice metallic.

Was that how money changed the world? By sowing mistrust?

'I have been rich before, when I had you and very few problems. I was happy and earned enough to sustain myself. Now it appears I'll lose your friendship over the shine of my newly won riches. To answer your question: Yes, I have an obscene amount of money now.'

'Good,' said Garret, picking at the immaculate fabric of his dressing gown. 'Then I don't need to feel bad about wasting some of it. This place,' he motioned at his room, 'is… is…'

'For wealthy, arrogant pricks?' I suggested.

The corners of his mouth twitched. 'Why did you leave?'

I slumped on the armchair closest to me, all strain peeling off me. Tension had kept me upright. Now gone, it left me exhausted to the bone. I hugged my knees and smiled at the only family I had left.

I got two lopsided smiles in return.

I sucked in a deep breath, and began. 'I left because I had to hide. I never told you about my past, or about that one part of my life as a…' I shook my head. 'Perhaps it's better to explain from the beginning. I've wanted to be a medical doctor since I was a child. It was heartbreaking to know that, as a woman, I'd never be admitted to university. I didn't understand the logic behind shunning women from higher education. Don't all men have mothers they adore? Do they all think them stupid and shallow, not wanting a life that is fulfilling? Or do they believe a fulfilling life for a woman is childbearing and serving the husband?'

I had got a little too loud. Barry was scooting about on his armchair. Even the freshly bathed mutt folded its ears.

It was time to rein myself in. 'I saw only one solution. I had to cut off my hair and masquerade as a man. It worked well enough.'

Garret sat still like a rock, his eyes large as cartwheels.

'I'm still amazed that no one suspected me for more than twelve years,' I muttered. 'Well, not until I met Sherlock... Holmes. It took him only two minutes to realise what I was. That was on a day Scotland Yard called me in to provide an expert opinion on a corpse found floating in one of London's waterworks. The man had died of cholera.'

'What?' shot out of Garret.

I shrugged. 'It was no threat. One infectious corpse in such a huge volume of water poses no risk. But he was one in a series of victims that had been tortured and murdered by a group of physicians. They were experimenting on workhouse inmates and infecting them with tetanus and cholera, with the ultimate goal of creating...' I cleared my throat. 'To create weapons of war.'

Barry blinked, Garret did not move an inch.

'I worked for them while feeding information to Sherlock. Eventually, we took them down. Most of them, that is. Their leader and a few of his men remained at large. The police were looking for me, for they believed I was part of that gang. The head of the gang was trying to find me, too. So I went into hiding. And then a few months later, he found me. He also had my father, and so forced me to work for him. I lived in his house for months. And I developed weapons...made of...disease.'

I swallowed my shame. 'I broke that man and then I killed him. But before he died, I...shared his bed. I carry his child.'

Garret jumped to his feet, then sank back down. His face was greenish, his breathing shallow. 'Why did *you* have to do all of that? I mean, why would you put yourself in danger like that? And in such...' He waved at my stomach, shook his head. 'Was that Holmes fella not man enough?'

'What does that have to do with anything, Garret? Infectious disease is my expertise!'

'Ah, well, that explains it!' He threw up his hands.

'Did you pretend to be weaker than you were so they'd move your execution forward?'

He narrowed his eyes to slits.

'Why would you do that?'

He crossed his arms over his chest. 'All that waiting? It was unbearable.'

I could understand that well enough. 'Would you let me examine you?'

'Sure.' He began to pick at his lapel, apparently not overly interested in my offer.

'Would you give us some privacy?' I asked Barry.

AFTER THE BOY HAD LEFT, I walked up to the man who had been my lover for years. I placed my hand on his cheek and, for a moment, his forget-me-not eyes fluttered shut. 'Can you forgive me?' I whispered.

'For what? That you lied to me for years? That you never loved me in return?'

My hand dropped to my side. Before I could answer, he continued, 'You told me from the first day that you couldn't share everything with me, not certain...information. I could have figured it out myself. I could have followed you. And I did once. You went into the cobbler's at Bow Street. And I stood there, waiting for you to come out again, wondering what you were doing in there. But it felt like I was betraying your trust, so I left. I thought that one day you'd tell me. And I guess you just did. Maybe I shouldn't complain.'

'Are you shocked?'

'That you worked as a doctor? No. But I'm shocked to see you like this. Like...only half alive. I'm shocked to see you with child, knowing that you don't want it, and that...' He picked up my hand again. 'Did he force himself on you?'

'He didn't. Climbing into his bed seemed to be my only way out.'

He dropped his head and squeezed my knuckles. 'Come, Anna. Do your thing.' A rasp of a whisper.

I cleared my throat as he rose to his feet. For want of a stethoscope, I pressed my ear to his ribcage. 'Deep breath, Garret.'

There were the all-too-typical rattling noises, up in the bronchi and farther down in the lungs. The left side seemed to be affected. The right side sounded clear. 'Do you cough blood?'

'Sometimes.'

'How often?'

'For the last three or four weeks, every morning. And every night. At the end of each spell of coughing, a lot of... stuff comes up my throat. Some of it is bright red.'

He placed a kiss on my forehead. 'Don't worry about me. You just extended my life.'

'People live with consumption for years, Garret.' I knew that the disease must have progressed dramatically in Newgate, and that he might not have years left. 'Besides, I can't be absolutely certain that you have it. Dammit! You are strong. I want you out of London. Where you can breathe fresh air. Living by the sea in a warm, clean house. Eating good food. You'll be better in days.'

'Come with me, Anna.' He pressed his face in my hair.

'I can't.'

'Why?'

'I cannot settle down now. Three men are still hunting me. They want to take the child once it's born, and then kill me. Sherlock and I will arrest them.'

'*You* will arrest them? You are with child. Do you want to risk the babe's life? If that Holmes is such a sharp one, he can arrest them without you.'

'I guess he could. But with me, it's easier. The rats gather quicker when one offers them bait.'

'That is…' he fought for words, 'idiotic!'

'No. It's logical. I'm safer playing the bait.'

'Nonsense! Come with me, please. I'll keep you safe. I'll care for you and your child. It can be ours.'

'I love another man,' I whispered. 'I love you both.'

'Ah,' he breathed and pushed himself away to sit on the armchair.

I sat on the armrest, my hand on his. 'How come you let yourself be caught?'

He laughed out loud. I had asked this same question just before I spent my first night with him. I had been ill, running a dangerously high fever, and he had taken care of me, working on lowering my temperature for hours. Since that night, I'd trusted him.

'I burgled the house of a woman. She was a police inspector's widow, as I learned later. He must have taught her things. She came at me from behind. I heard her only when it was too late. She crashed a crystal vase on my head. That woman was tall and strong enough to slam me on the head and knock me out cold!' He buried a chuckle in his sleeve, then sobered up. 'I woke up in a cell.'

He examined my small hand in his large one and said, 'I'm not a gent. I cannot live in a nice house. I'd feel awful if I had servants. All the more awful as they'd try to make me feel comfortable.'

'You grew up in the countryside. Don't you want to keep sheep again?'

A smile flitted across his face. I could almost see him — the little boy Garret holding newborn lambs to their mother's teats.

'I guess that would be nice,' he said.

'We'll find a small farm. Barry needs a home. He has hardened almost beyond repair.'

Garret nodded, his face scrunched up in concentration. 'I need a...a little time. Two hours ago, I thought I was dead. Now I find out you are a rich widow, and that I'm free, and you want me to leave, and probably I'll never see you again. And you love somebody else. My head hurts.' He patted my hand, then took it and placed it in my lap. I was being dismissed.

Before I closed the door, he called, 'Send Barry in, if you see him.'

12

I stood at the window of my room. Below me bustled the multitude of everyday lives. I watched the comings and goings, gentlemen tipping their hats at ladies, porters weighed down by monstrosities of suitcases, children dashing along, and there! — a girl picking a man's pocket. She got away and he entered the hotel, unknowing.

I closed my eyes and leant against the glass pane. On either side of mine was a row of rooms, each providing a home for a day or two, each containing a puzzling story and an aching heart. Barry, who had lost his entire family to poverty and disease. Garret, who had lost his roots and his only love. If I could hold him now, just once, as though we were lovers one last time, I would. But that would cause him more pain than not being held.

That half-love I had given him was just as cruel as half a non-love. And yet, he was ever forgiving. A gentle giant of a man who had shown me that lovemaking has nothing to do with violence, that there is only giving and forgiving. He had been a steady factor in my life while I had revolved about him, always buzzing, always changing shape from male to female and back again. And he had known nothing about it. Until today.

I pushed away and left my room to knock at Sherlock's. His footfall made my heart leap. He opened and I saw caution in his face. 'What's happened?' I asked.

He stepped back and let me in. 'I don't know where Wiggins is. He was supposed to find you in St Giles and bring you to Mycroft at once.'

'And Moran?'

'Three of my street arabs are tailing him. Two are searching for Wiggins. I'm still waiting for messages. What are your plans for the money?'

'Isn't it safe now?'

'Of course it is. But its purpose cannot be to sit in a bank.'

'No, but it's much more than I thought—'.

'On the contrary. It's what I expected it to be. Moriarty came from a rich and old family. He has organised all the major crime in London, if not in the whole of England and parts of Europe. I calculated his riches to be on the order of two to three million. I'm surprised you didn't.'

'I never spent a single thought on it. As for plans for what to do with it — I'll need some thinking time, but I would appreciate suggestions. Regarding his will — I believe he made one, which he hastily destroyed after I poisoned him.'

'Yes, that is probable.'

We hadn't moved. We still stood in the centre of the room, four feet apart. Where did this distance come from all of a sudden? 'Tell me what happened. Who did Moran contact? What kept you from meeting me at the station?'

He took a step back, nodded, then began pacing the room. 'Moran went to the post office. I found it notable that he made Parker wait outside so he could keep the destinations of the telegrams secret. After the two had left, I convinced the woman at the counter that the telegrams and the identities of the recipients were a matter of the safety of the British Empire, and that she was not allowed to tell anyone of them, nor keep the contents in writing anywhere.

'She assured me the law forbade her to release any such information and that I must be mistaken, because the man had sent only a single telegram, and not several. I demanded that she at once burn the slip he had handed her and any copies of it. She was sufficiently shocked. She handed over the slip, swearing by her mother's grave that no copies existed and begging me to burn it on the spot.'

A grin flickered across his face. 'Of course, I couldn't decline. I'll take the night train to Edinburgh to arrest Dr Joseph Walsh of the Dundee Medical School. He and Moran are the last of the men who had a direct connection to Moriarty and our case. Parker as Moran's footman wouldn't know more than absolutely necessary. A great number of criminals had dealings with Moriarty's men, but they are of little importance to our case.'

I sank into the armchair. The ruse had been a success. Moran had given away the identity of a long-sought man. Memories of nearly two years of chasing James and his men washed over me, memories of the bodies of dead paupers being thrown into Broadmoor's enormous furnace, of my murdered father, of disease, torture, and death. I sucked in as much breath as my lungs would take, and let it out with a sigh.

'You said you don't have enough evidence against Moran. I could serve as a witness if the Yard were not looking for me.'

'They are not. I made sure the Yard understand the role you played as Dr Anton Kronberg and that all notes in which you appear must be destroyed to protect you. Lestrade profits a great deal from my services. He did as I asked.'

'Oh. Thank you.' I looked up at him, but he kept his back to me.

'It would still be your word against Moran's. That you masqueraded as a man for years would be made public. Depending on the mood of the judge, you might be deported. Under the circumstances, you don't make for a good witness.'

'What can we do, then?'

'I haven't decided yet,' he answered. 'Moran will have learned that all of Moriarty's funds are to be transferred to you. I'm quite certain the family had concurred with Moriarty's plan for your assassination and the kidnapping of the child. So they'll have promised Moran compensation for his services. Now, with the money gone, we can expect their full wrath. On the one hand, they were told the heir-at-law is dead, and on the other, they've heard of your visit to the solicitors and that the pregnancy is intact.

'Moran is now threatened by unemployment, and the family by an unusually low budget, so they must either find proof of the miscarriage or they will attempt to kidnap the child as soon as it's born, and murder you, whether it be death during childbirth or accident thereafter. Then they would have custody of the child, who would also inherit your dower.'

'And their world is perfect,' I murmured.

'Precisely. And now, what happens next depends on Moran's nerve. Will he be furious because we keep fooling him? Will he have enough control of his temper to construct a plan to catch us?'

'He has enough control,' I said. 'Moran is a hunter. We both know that. He is an excellent planner and he keeps a cool head. He'll try to find a way to get to you first, I believe, because you are an irresistible challenge. I am an easier prey, for I'm only a woman and soon I'll be so large I'll barely be able to waddle away from him.'

'Which brings us back to Watson. Moran will try to kidnap Watson and use him as bait to force my surrender. At least, that's what I would do. I need your assistance. Keep an eye on Watson, please. Carry the revolver with you at all times. I need to act quickly to arrest Dr Walsh, and I'm quite certain that Moran's first step will be to fabricate *proof* for the heir-at-law's death. Therefore, he has to talk to the Moriarty family and to their solicitors. His time will be consumed accomplishing these during the next three days while I'm gone. I wish I could send Wiggins to your aid, but the boy is nowhere to be found.' His lips compressed as he pointed to a note on the table.

'Addresses?' I asked.

'Yes.' He walked to his armchair, retrieved his stuffed pipe, and lit it.

'Don't worry about Watson. I'll keep him safe.'

'Thank you,' he said, shrouded in blueish smoke.

'You took the same train as Moran and Parker,' I began. 'When you arrived at Victoria Station, or shortly thereafter, something happened. Something that kept you from contacting me. What was it?'

'I decided that it was more efficient to let my street arabs take care of you while I did everything in my power to arrange your dower and make preparations for the arrest of Walsh.' He didn't even look at me. 'How is your Irish friend?'

'I believe he has tuberculosis.' My brain began to rattle. I observed him puff his pipe, the tightness of his lips, his half-closed eyes, his body slightly facing away from me. The once open book was now shut. With a pang, I realised that he had withdrawn his help as far as necessity allowed. He wanted to send me back into Garret's arms.

'I understand.' I made to leave his room. The rustling of my dress was too loud in my ears. I wished I could disappear like a mouse — unnoticed.

'I believe Mr O'Hare is the better choice.'

'Propose to him.' Furious, I shut the door behind me.

~

I PACED MY ROOM, trying to walk away from emotions that tangled my thoughts and slowed my mind. I made plans for purchasing a small farm for Garret and Barry, or rather, arranging for Garret to buy it so as not to involve my name. That way, they'd be safe should Moran think of using my friends as bait to get to me. I doubted Moran even knew about the two.

While I waited for James's money to become accessible to me, I would try to find a suitable property.

13

*H*alf an hour after Sherlock left, knuckles hit wood. 'Mrs Saunders? My sincerest apologies, but Mr Wright asked us to let you know when a young man of the name Wiggins called. He is in the hall and looks rather...upsetting.'

'Hold him there!' I called, jammed my feet into my shoes, and tried to smooth the most dramatic crinkles from my dress.

The boy was standing at the front desk, one elbow resting on the wooden table, legs crossed at the ankles, one hand in his trouser pocket. 'Wiggins!' I hissed, and the boy straightened up in a snap.

'Ma'am, I have... Where's Mr Hol—'

'Quiet now!' I shot at him, took the boy's arm and led him to a group of armchairs in a far corner of the entrance hall. 'There, sit, and tell me everything.'

'Where's Mr Holmes?' the boy repeated.

'On a train. He asked me to interview you.'

Wiggins swallowed and began, 'The boys caught up to me at Bow Street, sayin' the man they was tailing was coming with another one. I said, no, this is not gonna work, and I said we mustn't let them get here and find the lady. Er... you.'

He almost poked his finger in my chest. Then, noticing the affront, his ears began to glow. He adjusted his cap. 'Anyways. The boys and I pretended to mug them. Or mugged them, really. Got bad, I tell ya. Everybody was beatin' up everybody.'

He pulled up both sleeves, showing blood-encrusted elbows, then lifted his cap and revealed a large bump. 'But we got his watch afore the rozzers came runnin' around the corner.' A satisfied grin slashed across his face.

I knew that watch. Moran fancied gold. 'What happened then?'

'Boys and I split up. They kept following them two. I went to the address Mr Holmes give me, 'n waited. But you didn't come.' He squinted at me as though I were the culprit.

'What did you do then?'

'Went to the baked potato man,' the boy squeaked.

I tried not to slap my forehead and groan. 'Where are the boys now? Weren't they supposed to report to Mr Holmes?'

'Er... they didn't dare show up. Wasn't no use anyway. Wouldn't get paid by him, now would they?'

'Because they lost Moran and Parker?' I asked. The boy nodded. I wondered why he had bothered coming. Ah! He must have seen Sherlock leave and hoped I would pay him. 'Where did the boys lose them?'

'Just past Guilford Road, South Lambeth,' he answered.

'They knew they were being followed?'

Wiggins dropped his head, nodding.

'Moran is a tough nut to crack. He knows when he's being chased.' I retrieved coins from my purse, sorted through them, and handed him six sovereigns. 'You boys did excellent.'

With an expression of incredulity, he crammed the

money into his trouser pocket, lifted his cap, and pushed it back on his head. Then he dashed off, coins tinkling.

I watched him disappear. He was a quick one. Once I'd seen his injuries, I decided not to ask him for help with Moran.

I wasn't certain that Sherlock's analysis was entirely correct. With the millions of pounds gone, every single one of James's family members would try to protect what remained. Like vultures, they would claw at the last bit of carcass after the lions had taken the largest part. Would Moran rush back to Littlehampton to try to retrieve witnesses and evidence of the heir-at-law's death? Would he act in such a haste as to not ascertain first that I was still pregnant and that the miscarriage had been a ruse? The more likely alternative was that the Moriartys would ask Moran to assassinate the child and me as soon as possible so all money would go back to them at once. Or they might try to kidnap me, and simply wait for the child to be born.

I thought of Garret then, his illness, and Barry, who was about to cut all his ties to humanity. I needed their help for my next task. And this would also me to keep an eye on them a little longer.

A porter interrupted my thoughts. He was carrying a bag and a rucksack — the two worn pieces of luggage I had left at Victoria Station.

$\approx$

'WHERE IS GARRET?' I asked when I stepped into the room.

'Lavatory,' Barry answered.

'How did he sleep?'

'Coughed a lot.' He pointed to the handkerchief next to the bed, an expensive-looking embroidered thing now adorned with ugly brown splotches.

'Did you two talk about leaving London?' I asked.

The boy picked at his unusually clean fingernails, then said, 'I don't know. Garret doesn't like the idea. It's like... you know... a woman is to be paying for him? And everything's hers, the house, the money, everything? It's like chopping his balls off. He'd be no real man anymore.'

Garret entered, hair ruffled, face ashen despite apparent anger. 'What?' he shot at Barry.

'Oy! I was only saying that when she.. when she...' He pointed at me, then his arm wilted.

'Sit down, Garret! And you, Barry — shut your mouth.' I kicked at the bed frame and dug my hands into my hips. 'Here is my offer, take it or leave it. You,' I pointed at Garret, 'are so sick that you can barely walk. You saved my life. You are my best friend, and... such a pig-headed man. Why won't you allow me to help you?

'And you,' I turned to Barry, 'have all the right to make me feel guilty. But I doubt that makes *you* feel any better.'

'But!'

'Shut your trap, Barry! I was married to England's most powerful criminal. His dearest wish was to develop the most gruesome weapons mankind could create. He amassed money through criminal deeds. *That's* the money I inherited. It is time to put it to good use. Shove your pride,' I punched the air for better effect, 'up your intestinal tracts!' Then I sat down on the floor, glowering up at the two.

Garret doubled over, laughing. As his laughs transformed into coughs, I rose and clutched his ribcage. 'Garret,' I whispered in his ear. 'I beg you!'

'So when do we go?' he asked, trying to catch his breath.

'Today. But I have to ask you both for your help before we leave London. I have to keep an eye on someone.'

Garret grunted in the affirmative.

'Barry?' I turned to the boy. He slapped at an imaginary fly and nodded.

'Excellent. Pack your belongings.'

Roughly three hours later, we settled into a room opposite Watson's practice. It was only a single room and we crammed ourselves in it, pretending to be husband, wife, and son who were travelling up north and staying in London for a few days.

Garret observed the other side of the street while Barry and I tried to nap. As soon as night fell, our work would begin.

～

THE BOY and I walked along the street, dressed in dark walking clothes. I hunched. Grey hair stuck out from beneath my bonnet, one of my arms leaning on Barry, the other on a stick. At a snail's pace, we shuffled past Moran's house — one of several handsome villas that lined the street, each with a pretty front yard. Windows on both floors were lit, indicating that not only the servants were at home, but also their master. I could hear the dogs in the back, their playful growls and the scraping of paws on gravel. We searched for a good hiding spot, but found nothing suitable in the immediate vicinity.

I began coughing and bent down. Barry patted my back very lightly so as not to blur my view. I stared through the telescope that was partially concealed by my overcoat. The electric light at the entrance to Moran's house revealed every feature of his front door. 'God bless the Queen's nether garments!' I muttered. 'We can leave now.'

Barry and I stopped at a corner. I took his coat, rolled it up, and stuck it under my arm. He picked up the broom we had left leaning on a tree. I rubbed dirt on his face, throat, and hands, and then we parted. He'd act as the street sweeper and watch for any comings and goings while the real sweeper snored in his bed, ten shillings richer.

I rushed back to Garret, knocked, and entered the room. He sat at the window, guarding Watson's practice.

'Did he not go home yet?' I wondered aloud.

'No. He mostly sits at his desk. Very few patients during the day, and none at all now. What is the man waiting for?'

I approached the window and saw Watson's silhouette, his face in his hands, hunched over a table or desk. I had to fight the urge to run over, ring his bell, and tell him that his best friend was alive and well.

I turned away, placed the telescope in Garret's hand, retrieved pen and paper, and began to draw. The picture of the lock was burned in my mind, but my hands only clumsily copied it.

'Garret?' I called, and he looked over my shoulder.

'Hum. Looks very much like a Davenport rim lock. Are you sure these markings went that way up and not down?'

'Yes. Absolutely sure.'

'It's a two-lever lock. Harder to pick than the ones I've shown you.' His energies seemed to return at the prospect of lock picking. 'You need the right tools. And you need to practice. We'll visit a friend of mine. He can help.'

'Do you know that when you are full of mischief, your hair sticks out every which way? Much like the whiskers of a cat.' I grinned up at him, thinking of times long ago when we'd made love, and how much he resembled a lion then. He must have seen it in my eyes, for his head drooped and his Adam's apple bobbed up and down to move embarrassment out of the way. He cleared his throat, bringing on a coughing attack.

'Go call a cab,' he grumbled.

I nodded and left. Knowing that Moran was yet in his

home, I decided Watson should be safe without us for a little while.

We didn't speak on the ride to Fetter Lane. Once there, Garret asked me to wait in the carriage. Understandably, his friend didn't accept strangers in his lock-pick shop.

Ten minutes later, he returned to show me three different locks. I chose one that looked identical to the one in Moran's entrance door, and we dashed back to our quarters. Watson was still in his practice.

'So, now. I'll hold it and you pick it,' Garret said, pinching the heavy brass and cast iron lock between his knees and hands. 'Try each single one of them.' He nodded toward the lock picks. 'You'll get a feeling for the innards of the thing.'

I wiped the grease off the tools.

'Now, you see on the keyhole that you can stick in the key either end up or end down. Try up first. If nothing moves, try end down. Use only just a little pressure.'

I stuck the first lock pick in and began to wiggle and probe.

'Do you feel the tension in the bolt?' he asked.

I grunted. My medical instinct told me to open the stupid thing, and gut it.

'Not like a brute, Anna! Try another lock pick.'

I tried another three until I could feel something mov when I pressed the metal tool against it. 'The bolt is moving. Perhaps,' I squeezed through my teeth.

'Good. Hold it there. Take the small hook and see if you can lift the first lever.'

I did as told, but it took several attempts, with me dropping the lock pick to the floor each time and swearing through clenched teeth. When I finally heard the first click, I decided not to throw the bloody thing out of the window.

'Good! Now turn it to unlock, then lock it again. Do it several times,' he said. I looked up at him; his brow was as sweaty as mine. We practiced another hour, interrupting to spy on Watson every few minutes. When he finally left his practice, I sneaked out and followed.

He took the direct route home. His wife, and not the housekeeper, opened the door when he fumbled for his keys. She must have been worried. Her arm closed around his shoulders. Then the brightly lit hallway engulfed them both and the door shut.

I kept walking, careful to keep an eye on my surroundings and on anyone with too much interest in the Watson's residence. All seemed quiet, yet I wished I had more men at my disposal. Leaving Watson's home unguarded went against my grain. But Barry would let us know at once should Moran or Parker venture out at night. It was all I could do for now.

On the way back, I bought baked potatoes, bread, butter, cheese, and pies. Garret's appetite was atypically mouse-like, and I hoped the odour of good food would change that. Besides, I was hungry almost constantly now.

Barry returned at around three o'clock in the morning. He told me that everyone in Moran's house was fast asleep, then he devoured what we had left on the table, dropped on the mattress next to Garret, and began to snore like a tiny steam engine.

I slipped from the room to take Barry's watch.

14

'*J*'m coming with you,' Garret said yet again.

'No.' I turned away from him and began to lace my boots. For two days and nights now, Garret had kept his eyes on Watson while Barry and I kept watch over Moran. Moran's footman, Parker, had left the previous day. Barry followed him to Victoria Station and saw him take the train to Eastbourne, most likely with Littlehampton as his final destination. I expected the man to return no sooner than the following day, delivering hearsay and flimsy evidence to his superior. He'd certainly be punished for something that Moran wouldn't have been able to do any better.

Garret's socked feet appeared in my field of view.

'The dogs know me, but they don't know you. They'll bark,' I said.

His left toe began to wiggle up and down, tapping a rhythm of impatience on the floor.

I pressed my teeth together. 'You can barely walk a hundred feet without coughing blood.'

He snorted and walked back to the window.

'Don't worry about me, Garret.' I rose and pushed the lock picks into my pocket, put on a light overcoat, and placed a hat on my head. When I loaded the revolver, Garret grumbled, 'Good luck.'

'Thank you.' I sneaked out the door before he could argue with me again.

Barry was fast asleep and oblivious to it all.

~

PICKING the lock of the gate was quick and easy. Just one lever, well-oiled and quiet. I heard the huffs of the dogs and began to talk quietly before they saw me. They sprinted around the house, tongues lolling, tails wagging, and buried their noses in the folds of my skirt. I patted their sides and ordered them to be quiet.

The walkway was laid out in gravel, so I avoided it and instead placed my feet on grass. A thick apple tree provided cover. I took my hat and shoes off, pressed against the tree's coarse bark, and watched the one lit window. I thought of it as Moran's study, for this was where he would spend his late evening hours before retiring to a room on the other side of the house.

It must have been close to midnight.

Low buzzing pulled my attention to the branch above me. It was too dark to see what was causing the noise, and straining my eyes didn't help in the least. I shut them, and turned my head this way and that, analysing what I heard. It sounded too low to be caused by bees... Could it be hornets?

Carefully, I scaled the tree, keeping my eyes close to where I was placing my hands and shifting my gaze to the branch the noise came from. There, a darker patch among the almost-black of the bark. The insects were using a hole in the tree for their nest. That complicated matters.

I chewed my cheeks. My eyes scanned the few lit places on Moran's property, and I spotted a small flower-pot. A plan began to form. Then, the brightly lit window fell into darkness.

About an hour later, I slid off the tree, approached the house, and tipped the flower-pot's contents out onto the grass. Then I ran back to the apple tree. The dogs believed I wanted to play with them. I stopped, stiffened, and growled quietly. They plopped on their hindquarters, folded their ears, and tried to look like puppies.

I ignored them, hiked up my skirts, yanked off a stocking, then opened my pocket knife and sliced off one leg of my drawers. With that, I covered the top of the pot, wrapping my stocking around its rim to hold the fabric cover in place.

I climbed up the tree again, pressed the pot's bottom hole against the opening of the hornets' nest and tapped a twig against the branch. The tapping grew to light whacks until the hornets began to stir angrily. Their buzzing gained in volume and depth.

'Bloody damn it,' I muttered as I remembered two more holes I needed to plug. Balancing awkwardly with my legs hugging the tree, I cut two pieces off the stocking, took a deep breath, and inched the pot away from the nest. I jammed one piece of fabric into the bottom hole of the flower pot and the other into the nest's entrance.

A few hornets had escaped. I felt them crawling over my shirt, attempting to drive their stingers through the fabric and into my skin. I clamped my mouth shut, and tried to resist the urge to slap at them. One crawled up my throat and cheek, then got caught in my hair. Burning pain told me I had been stung twice; I nearly fell off the tree. Luckily, I made it down without dropping the pot.

Not entirely certain what to do, I placed the pot in the grass. If I should try to slap off the hornets while running a loop in the yard, the dogs would run with me and most likely get stung. The resulting ruckus would wake the whole neighbourhood. I had no choice but to let the remaining hornets crawl over my garments, and try not to agitate them.

I picked up the pot and approached the house. It appeared like a dead organism, dark and still, but somehow waiting for a disaster — a shot, an explosion, something that would expel me as soon as I entered.

I stepped up to the front door and inserted a lock pick. This lock felt identical to the one I had used to practice my crackswoman skills. After barely a minute, I opened the door, stepped in, and shut it behind me. Exhilaration washed over me. I let the feeling of triumph pass, and took a steadying breath.

Silence lowered itself heavily. The cricket song was gone, the quiet noises of playing dogs were gone, no faraway clopping of hooves, no rattling of wheels on cobble stones. If it weren't for the fierce hum in the pot I carried, I might have suspected I'd suddenly fallen deaf.

I pricked my ears and crept up the stairs, carefully staying close to the wall where the steps were less likely to creak when stepped upon. Then I paused and listened, holding my breath and wishing the hornets would shut up for a moment.

The house was quiet.

I went up the corridor, placing first my toes then my heels on the carpet, careful not to disturb any noisy floorboards.

Nothing creaked. I reached the study door, tested the doorknob. It didn't move. My hand extracted the lock picks from my dress, fingers pressing against the tools so as to muffle clinking of metal against metal. I slid the first lock pick in place, pressed, turned, wiggled. Nothing. The second, the third, the fourth, and finally, with the fifth, the lever moved. *A one-lever lock*, my mind registered, as the lock clicked open. I turned the knob and opened the door slowly. A shy squeal made me freeze. Not daring to move, I listened.

One minute crawled past. I squeezed through the gap, pulled up a chair, stepped on it, and placed the pot on top of the door, leaning it lightly against the frame. One hornet crawled over my sleeve. I pulled the fabric out a little, moved close to the wood, and let the insect crawl onto the door.

I stepped off the chair. My eyes took in the room. A half-moon peeked through the clouds and send its light through a single tall window, painting a trapezium of rippled silver on the carpet.

Three steps from the heavy brocade curtains was a desk. One step further to a strongbox mounted in the wall. I pulled at the desk drawers. All were locked. The lock picks removed that obstacle. I lit a candle and leafed through Moran's letters in the top drawer. The strongbox behind me was most enticing, but I'd never be able to open it. I pushed it from my mind and focused on what I held in my hands: his book-keeping journals.

I opened the most recent one. Monthly payments of one hundred pounds sterling — an amount most people would never hold in their hands — labelled *JM*.

James Moriarty.

But from March onward, those payments were missing. Moran was living on his savings. Receipts of various purchases thickened the book. Some looked like tickets. A few were printed or written in a language other than English. I had no time to spend on scrutiny, so I clamped them under my left arm.

In the second drawer lay a photograph inscribed, in golden letters, *Colonel Sebastian Moran, September 1880, Transvaal*. A notation was dated three months before the Boer War. Moran sat in a chair that resembled a throne — one foot perched on a lion's head, his right hand holding a rifle that was propped on his thigh. An idea hit me, spreading a smile across my face. I slipped the picture under my arm, too.

The third and last drawer contained more letters. I took them all, removed every drawer and ran my fingers over all their hidden surfaces: outside of there backs and bottom. Nothing.

The clock on the mantelpiece told me I had spent fifteen minutes in Moran's study. I went over to the door and listened to the silent house. Then I made for the safe. I had no high hopes of cracking the thing, but wanted to at least make an attempt. Three dials secured its door. I pressed my ear right next to the locking mechanism and began to turn the largest dial. *Click-click-click.* I turned it several times until I was certain that it produced a more hollow click in one position. I left it in that position and worked on the next two dials. My ears picked up another sound. That of a low scratch. I jumped the three steps to the curtains, and just before I reached them, the silence was shattered. A crash, then furious buzzing and a hollering Moran. Two shots that found no living target. Slaps against garments. Screams.

I stood protected behind the curtains, waiting for Moran to run. And so he did, crying for help.

Hornets that weren't clinging to Moran now filled the study. I held on to the curtain and tugged with all my might. It fell off, together with the rod. Moran was still screaming, but now an echo was added to the noise he made — he must have been in the bathroom trying to hose the angry insects off his body. The man certainly knew how to keep his wits.

I opened the window and looked down. A ledge ran around the house just above the ground floor windows. It was narrow, but served my toes with enough support. I jammed the curtain rod tight against the window frame, flung my legs out, held on to the fabric, and climbed down. A soft *plop*, and my feet hit the flowerbed. The dogs were already awaiting me. Together we ran to the tree. I retrieved my hat and shoes, and made for the gate. I rubbed the dogs' ears, threw a last glance at the house that was now quiet, stepped into the street, and began to run.

Was it only my imagination, or did I hear footfalls behind me?

'Left,' a familiar voice huffed.

I obeyed, then stopped to press my fists into my burning sides and my back against a damp wall. 'How was Dundee?'

Sherlock ignored my question, pointed to the shoes in my hand, and asked, 'What did you do in Moran's house?'

'A courtesy visit that involved lock picks.'

'Why was he screaming?'

'I filled a flower-pot with hornets, sealed it with my drawers and a stocking, then placed it on a half-open door so it would crash on top of him, should Moran try to enter the study while I was in it. And that's precisely what happened.'

'An undergarment-hornet bomb?' He slapped his thigh and barked a laugh. Then he bent forward. Despite the dark, I could tell he'd narrowed his eyes to scrutinise whatever needed scrutinising. 'What did you find?'

'A few letters, journals, receipts of trips to the continent, and a photograph.' I unfolded my voluptuous bonnet that was serving as the receptacle for my loot. 'Hold this for a moment.'

I put my shoes back on, then straightened up.

'How often were you stung?'

'Once,' I lied. A few more hornets had stung me after Moran crashed the pot.

Nimble fingers probed my forehead.

'Your night vision is excellent,' I observed.

'Hornets, you say? But the swelling is minor.'

'I was stung a lot during my childhood. A neighbour kept

about ten beehives. My body has got used to bee venom and reacts with bumps the size of a mosquito sting. Hornets can make them a bit bigger, it appears.'

An awkward silence fell. He removed his hand from my face. The chirping of a lone cricket and the clacking of a set of hooves echoed from afar.

'Tell me about Dundee, Sherlock.'

'Dr Walsh stepped right into my trap, with the police waiting just outside the medical school.' His voice sounded bored, almost disappointed.

'Why the slight limp, then?' I'd heard it as he ran behind me: one foot was set down with hesitation.

'A mere trifle.' He waved his hand. 'It wasn't even Walsh. The man had surprisingly little fight in him. It was the unfortunate combination of a desperate pickpocket, a clumsy porter, an old lady standing in the way, and a flying, and very heavy, suitcase.'

'I'm glad you survived the ordeal.' I smiled up at him. 'We should probably go back and see if Moran survived the hornets, don't you think?'

'I was already wondering when you would bring up the issue.' He took my hand and marched off.

The house was brightly lit. A hansom waited at the gate. A horse had its nose hanging low over the pavement. Foam dripped from the bit. The doctor had responded quickly.

The door to the house opened, and light spilled onto the lawn. We pushed farther into the shadows. A servant walked up to the cabbie and informed him that he could leave. The doctor would remain at his patient's side.

'We can leave now, too,' Sherlock said, and we turned away. 'His injuries are serious enough to keep the physician in attendance. How many hornets were in your flower-pot?'

'I didn't stop to count them,' I answered, sorting through my limited knowledge of insect bites and stings. 'Almost all that were in the nest; surely more than a hundred. Hornet venom is very painful, much more than that of bees and wasps. If he received enough stings to worry his physician so much that the man is staying overnight, the situation appears serious. Some people suffer a heart attack when stung so many times. But I have the impression that Moran is healthy as a horse. Perhaps he'll see tomorrow, or he might not. I could speculate, but that would be a waste of time.'

We walked along the quiet streets, in and out of the dim light of hissing lamps.

'How is Watson?' he asked.

I didn't want to give him my interpretation of how things stood. After all, my brain ticked differently than his. So all I shared was a summary of my observations. 'Crumbling.'

For a moment — a very short moment, lasting barely half a pace — he paused.

Soon, we reached Watson's practice. Although it was well past midnight, the window was still lit. 'Would you ask him whether he has finished his story on our last case?' He turned toward me, his face hidden in the shadows.

'Now?'

'Yes, please. He needs to know about the danger he is in, and I need to remain officially and believably dead for a little while longer. He can keep secrets, but he's not too good a liar. His report would be too cheerful should he write it knowing I'm alive.'

I nodded, approached Watson's practice, and knocked on his door. When he opened up, a cry of surprise erupted from his mouth. A hopeful peek over my shoulder, and then his face collapsed, and his shoulders followed. I squeezed them, and pushed us on inside.

'My apologies,' he said, straightening his cravat. Then he took my hand in his and said, 'Thank God you are alive!'

I smiled at him and asked, 'Dr Watson, did you finish

your report on your last case with Holmes?' What a most unusual question under the given circumstances and at that time of the night.

He cleared his throat and turned away from me. 'Do you wish to read it?' A painful croak.

'Is it finished?'

'Yes, for days now.'

'Splendid!' I clapped my hands together. Watson turned around, his face ashen. 'My apologies, Dr Watson. I may seem heartless. But you will understand in a minute. May I ask you to sit down?'

'I'd rather remain standing. Say what you must, Dr Kronberg. But then I must ask you to leave. I'm quite... busy.'

'My dear Dr Watson.' I stepped up to him. 'Sit, please.'

All that happened was a broadening of the man's chest and a strengthening of his resolution.

'Very well, then. If you would excuse me for a moment?' I opened the door, stepped outside, and waved.

A slender shadow broke away from the blackness lining the houses on the other side of the street.

As Holmes's face showed in the doorframe, Watson fell where he stood. We rushed to his side to see to his well-being and recovery. A drop of brandy between the moustached lips and life quivered back to his pale cheeks. Bleary eyes cracked open and darted from my face to Sherlock's.

'Holmes! Is it really you?'

'I'll leave you two alone now,' I said. 'I'm sharing a room with Barry and Garret just across the street. Number fifty-five.'

Sherlock dipped his chin. 'I will call tomorrow morning.'

15

*S*herlock chewed his toast, his face hidden behind a most hilarious moustache, his energy sparkling through the dining hall, unnoticed by all the other hotel guests. They muttered quietly, clinking silverware against china, eyes still bleary from the previous night's entertainments.

His invitation for breakfast had arrived early that morning, while Garret was still sleeping and Barry off prowling the neighbourhood with his dog. My stomach yowled as I sat down. A plate of fresh toast appeared from nowhere, a gloved hand attached, followed by a neatly folded white napkin. A sharply pressed black jacket, a pair of black trousers, and two polished shoes disappeared along with the waiter.

Sherlock poured me tea while I tried to sate my ravenous hunger.

'How is Watson?' I asked.

'The good chap recovered quickly. I dare say he suffered a nervous twitch in his right arm.'

'He punched you?' My toast was forgotten for a moment.

He lifted his chin for me to inspect.

I squinted and detected the faintest bruise. 'He must have been quite dazed, judging from the little damage he caused. Though this was a straight punch.' I pointed to the tip of his chin, or rather, moved my fist in that direction. 'I can imagine a swing would have gained more speed, and would have resulted in a stronger impact and a blow to the side of your face.' I paused for a moment, puzzled. 'You allowed it?'

'He deserved revenge. More toast?'

My plate was empty already, so he offered what was on his side of the table. I reached out and stole his eggs and ham. 'Thank you. Why do you want people to believe you are dead?'

'Call it a holiday.' He leant back, brushing bread-crumbs off his lapel. 'There are several things I'd like to do without anyone suspecting my being behind the actions. Only Moran has seen me survive. The few other men he's told about it will only believe him as long as he's seen as trustworthy. I should think they'll doubt his judgment soon enough. Watson has completed the final draft of his latest story. I read it. He'll publish it as soon as possible. It'll have a heart breaking effect on the public. The news will spread like fire.' The corners of his mouth twitched, eyes twinkled. 'So, before I continue, tell me why you've packed.'

I wondered how he knew, but decided to show nothing of my surprise and curiosity. I leant back and observed him. The shine of expectation darkened. He seemed to ready himself for verbal combat.

I yawned. 'I plan to buy a small farm in Dymchurch and take my friends to a safe place. I saw an advertisement in the papers and sent Barry to inspect it. He says it's pretty. I wired the owners to let them know that Garret will arrive with the money today at noon.'

Barry hadn't believed his luck when I'd asked him if he'd

like to take a look at a potential future home three hours from London. At the ripe age of twelve, he had never seen a train from the inside, or even left London, although he had fed himself and his mother from the age of four.

'You've received your dower?' asked Sherlock.

'Yes. Surprisingly enough, the law protects me and the child from greedy relatives-in-law.'

I'd visited my bank daily, for I was in a hurry. The previous morning, the manager himself had received me. The man was beaming as though with an expectation that a considerable fraction of the newly arrived three hundred thousand pounds would magically rub off on him.

'I'll be back late tonight or tomorrow before noon,' I continued. 'In the meantime, could you please retrieve your notes? I need to know details of your investigation of James and his *friends*. Oh! Wiggins appeared. The boy is a little beaten up. Nothing serious, and I'm sure you could ask him to watch Moran's house. The man won't be moving about yet. Parker should return from Little-hampton today. He'll experience Moran's fury at full force, I suppose.'

Sherlock signalled agreement. 'I'll send my street arabs to Watson's practice, and to his residence as well as to Moran's. My notes are deposited at Mycroft's. What precisely do you wish to know?'

'Anything that could give me a clue as to why James was convinced a war might be upon us. And information on the man he thought would be *talented to find useful friends on the continent*. What is his name again?' I massaged my forehead, digging through memories. 'Erving Hooks! I'd like to know what he knows. And that man from the foreign office. Whitman was his name, I believe.'

'Both men are in Newgate. I will question them while you are gone.'

'Excellent! Another thing: What brothels did Moran frequent?'

'Five establishments in Whitechapel. He was a well-regarded customer with a taste for deflowering.' His upper lip curled in distaste.

'That suits us. Whitechapel is perfect. With it being traumatised by the Ripper's activities, and with Moran's liking for young girls and children, his temper...' I trailed off, wondering whether we could arrest Moran for buying the services of underage girls. Probably not. An intact maidenhead brought twenty to fifty pounds to a madam's purse. Surely no one would point fingers at a gentleman who paid such generous amounts, when all a girl was worth for the second, third, and hundredth mounting were a few shillings.

Sherlock's intense gaze interrupted my thinking. 'Having you as an enemy must be rather unhealthy. And it surprises me that I never saw Moriarty visit prostitutes.'

'He had his mistresses delivered.' I thought of the woman with the red mane, her empty expression, the silver brush gliding through her copper hair. 'They came from the lower working class. He provided them with a room, food, clothing, and opium, and bedded them every night.'

He paled. I hadn't told him about that. I hadn't believed it relevant.

'Was that why you asked me about the torso case?'

'Yes. James played with my fears, telling me his manservant had cut a woman into pieces and dumped her under a railway arch. You said the Pinchin Street torso was from a redhead, that she was clean and smelled faintly of patchouli, and that she had a dog's bite mark on her hip. It fit all too well. James used patchouli-scented soap to mark me. His dogs were trained to attack anyone who smelled of it. But these are only pieces, weak evidence and not proof. That torso could have come from anywhere. However, I'm certain that if anyone was doing such things for James, it was Moran.'

'Was a woman still in his house when he began bedding you?' he asked.

'No.'

He lowered his head in acknowledgement. I could see it brush across his calm facade, *every night*.

'We will catch the nine o'clock train,' I said. 'I must leave in a few minutes. Where can I find you once I return?'

'I'll be here.'

GARRET, Barry, and I took the train to Folkestone, then a trap to Dymchurch. The farm was just as Barry had described it: a small stone house with a moss-covered roof, surrounded by rock-littered fields. The basic structure of the building appeared more than solid. The bargain was made, Garret put his signature on the contract, and the former landlord clamped the money purse under his armpit, a shine of triumph on his face. He wished us good luck and bade his farewell.

Once we were alone, I planted the sage and the mint I had bought in London, and instructed Garret how to use it to alleviate his symptoms. Then I examined him one last time. 'Don't let the farm work tire you too much. You need to breathe. Your lungs are not even half as good as they were a year ago.'

'I'm not made of glass, Anna.'

'Yes, you are. For a little while, at least.'

'Are you in a hurry to leave?'

'I must go back to London.' I nodded to myself as though bobbing my head up and down could hammer in the impression that there was nothing left to say.

'Tell me,' he said softly.

I sighed. 'It feels as though my life will end in autumn.' My feet took a step away from him.

'When the babe is born?'

'Yes.' I heard him inhale, about to speak. My index finger poked the air in warning. 'Don't you even *think* of telling me to simply accept my fate.'

'I wasn't going to say that!' His hands went up as though I had threatened to shoot him. 'I wanted to say that whenever you need help, I'll be here.'

My shoulders sagged. 'I'm sorry.'

'You know...the weeks in gaol gave me time to think. A man's last days on Earth and all that. I can let you go now only because you don't want to be with me. But you are always welcome. I'll never ask where you've been. Or who with.'

It was indeed alluring. The thought of hiding here, growing old with a kind man, not having too many worries.

I smiled at myself and took his hand, gazed down at it, stroked its back. 'I won't return.'

I wouldn't make him wait for me. He was my best friend and his offer was safety, and perhaps the only home I might have, should I keep the child.

Impossible. Me, a mother?

'I killed a man,' he said all of a sudden. 'Many years ago.'

My mouth fell open to ask *whom* and *why* and *when*, but we were interrupted by Barry rumbling through the door. He slid to a halt. 'What's wrong with you two?'

'Thank you, Garret,' I said. 'Barry, I'll be leaving now. Would you ask one of the neighbours to drive me to Folkestone?'

'Sure.' He was out of the door in an instant, probably relieved to have escaped an awkward situation.

Garret picked up my bag.

'Why did you kill a man?'

'I… He was a murderer. Please, do not ask me now. I shouldn't have told you. I just… I thought you should know that I'm not as nice as you think I am. And you are giving me all this.' He waved his free arm, a gesture encircling the house, the fields, and the orchard.

I snatched his hand before it dropped to his side. 'I see no reason why I shouldn't give this to you. You are my best friend. I owe you much more, but all I can offer is money. This isn't much, if you think about it.'

He shook his head as though to shake off my words. 'I'll walk you to your cart.'

'No.' I stepped up to him. 'I don't like good-byes.' My hand wrapped around his, extracting the bag handle he was still clutching. The luggage dropped to the floor. I leant my head against his chest. 'I killed a helpless woman. And I poisoned the father of my child.'

I meant to step away, but he held me tight. 'You are welcome here, Anna. Whenever you need a home.'

'I know,' I said, and kissed him softly. He buried his hands in my hair and pulled me close.

The way to Folkestone was short, accompanied by the sounds of timid drizzle and wind combing through trees. As the train took me back to London, I tried to shut off any feelings of sorrow or pity for Garret. He was a grown man. But to have abandoned Barry in St Giles was unforgivable. The boy was dear to me, almost like a son. And I had known that his mother would not be able to provide for him, and that she was not healthy enough even to stay alive until the boy grew up.

16

*T*he pipe clicked against the crystal ashtray. Black crumbs dropped from the one bowl to the other. Sherlock stuffed it with fresh tobacco and held a match against it. His face was lit by a golden flicker changing in intensity with each breath he sucked in. A flick of his hand, and the match went out and tumbled into the ashtray with a soft *pling.*

'What is so intriguing about this procedure?' he asked.

'I can see you focus. You empty your mind. The longer the process — pipe cleaning and stuffing take considerably longer than simply sticking a cigarette into your mouth — the more focused you are. Once you begin to smoke, it seems as though you let one thought after the other back in. Line them all up. Put them in order, so to speak.'

His nostrils flared. A thin sliver of smoke crawled up to the ceiling. 'Does it bother you?'

'What do you mean?'

'Watson has a habit of flinging the windows wide open when I'm smoking my pipe. And, of late, you have abandoned cigarettes. Perhaps the odour grew unbearable? A side effect of your pregnancy, I should think.'

I smiled at him. 'I like the stink of your pipe.' He huffed a large cloud. 'It is tangy with a sweet undertone. It reminds me of home, of a good thinking exercise, and of you.' It was an honest statement, yet I felt I had said too much again.

'Very well, then.' He settled back in his chair and focused at the ceiling as though a particularly brilliant thought might be found there. 'I paid a visit to Mr Hooks. He didn't speak much. He enquired whether I could get him out of Newgate. When I told him that was not in my power, he closed up like an oyster. As I was leaving, he said that all we were accomplishing was a postponement of what was bound to happen. He also said, "It is all there. Open your eyes, Mr Holmes."'

'He teased you. Perhaps he wanted you to reveal more of your plans?'

'I think so, too,' he said. 'I didn't reply, hoping my silence would provoke a reaction. But he didn't speak until it was almost too late. The turnkey had locked his cell and we'd begun to walk away. At that very last moment, Hooks ran up to the grated window and cried, "The Kaiser's favourite toy, Mr Holmes! Can you tell me what it is?"'

'What's that supposed to mean?'

'I don't know yet. I'll talk to Mycroft about it. The Kaiser's favourite toy. Reminds me of that children's story…' He trailed off, tapping the stem of his pipe against his teeth.

'Did you talk to Whitman?'

'No. He's a former government employee and my brother wishes to interview him. He might try to bribe him.'

I rubbed my eyes and stretched my tired limbs. My stomach stuck out — a watermelon atop a bony frame. Comical, almost. Quickly, I folded my body to hide it. Sherlock caught my reaction, but made no comment.

'Will Watson leave London now?'

Sherlock grunted softly. 'His wife is reluctant to leave. And I don't fancy that solution, either. Moran could simply follow.'

'Let's roam Whitechapel, then,' I said with a grin. 'Do you think Watson would like to join us?'

One eyebrow went up, together with a corner of his mouth. 'I'll dispatch a telegram.' He jumped up and left with energetic strides.

A short while later, he returned. 'We'll have to modify your shape, stuff your front, so to speak.' His upper body disappeared into a wardrobe. 'I retrieved a few things from my quarters earlier today.'

A handful of clutter was tossed onto the bed. Soon I was disguised as a pot-bellied, moustached, large-nosed version of a police inspector. Sherlock hid his face behind the large moustache he had worn at the solicitors' office.

We hailed a four-wheeler and made a detour to Watson's house. The doctor climbed in. Even in the dark, I could see his glowing cheeks, his shining eyes, his quivering moustache. 'I brought my revolver,' he said, as he settled into his seat. 'Hello, Dr Kronberg.'

I reached out and shook his hand. 'I see you are in a much improved state, Dr Watson. I'm glad.'

'We will not be in need your revolver today, Watson,' said Sherlock.

Watson's shoulders sagged slightly. He turned to me. 'I couldn't help noticing that you are still with child.'

'Yes.' All other words hung in my throat, none of them able to decide the order in which to slip out.

'If I can help...' he began, his hand twitching toward mine, then retreating before it made contact.

'It's too late. Thank you, Dr Watson.'

'Oh, well... Yes, I know. What I meant was...' He picked at his earlobe. 'My wife and I can't have children of our own. I am thinking we could perhaps adopt...' He trailed off. 'I would have to talk to her first, of course. I cannot promise. Not yet.'

I snatched his hand and pressed it hard. He noticed my struggle for composure and changed the topic. 'Where are we heading, Holmes?'

'Whitechapel. We'll visit a few brothels, pretending to be inspectors from Scotland Yard looking for a suspect.' He pulled Moran's photograph from his jacket.

Watson huffed with surprise. 'But Holmes! I have nothing that could prove my identity as an inspector.'

'I forged an identification card for my own entertainment a few months back. That should suffice. You two remain quiet. I'll speak.' He pulled his hat lower onto his face, effectively closing the topic.

We drove along Commercial Street, passing horse trams and omnibuses. At a narrow gap between two houses, we stopped.

'Careful, now,' said Sherlock as we squeezed through an alley onto Romford Street.

It was dark. No gas was wasted to light streets like this one. The air was thick with odours, indicating the lack of sewers, of regular visits by disinfectors, and of anything else that might prevent disease from spreading. Small animals scampered across the street, their ragged furs, distended bellies, and naked tails identifying them either as enormous rats or very undernourished cats.

We saw no women on the street, but customers were lining up on the doorstep of one establishment.

Refuse littered the pavement. Our progress was slow, and I could feel Watson growing uncomfortable. He bent his neck, perhaps to make sure he wasn't imagining it: every two minutes a customer was stepping in, and another stepping out, buttoning his fly.

'French,' I explained to him.

He looked puzzled and tried to wipe the curiosity off his face as though it were dirt.

'It's not that they are speaking it,' said Sherlock.

The penny dropped.

'Holmes!' hissed Watson, threw a glance at me, pulled up his shoulders, and began trotting a little faster to avoid any more comments on the matter.

'Twenty-one, I believe,' said Sherlock, as he came to a halt at a door with a dangling *two* on it. No trace of the missing digit. 'Remember: I speak, you remain silent.' He banged the silver knob of his walking stick upon the door.

A creak, and light seeped through a gap. A face appeared, and with it, the unexpected: a tall, healthy-looking woman, her figure a perfect hour-glass in an expensive silk dress. Her skin was smooth and pale, her hands slender.

She narrowed her eyes. 'Yes?'

Sherlock cleared his throat and flashed his card. 'I'm Chief Inspector Nieme. This is Inspector Dodder and Inspector Atkinson. You will want to invite us to a private room in the back of your house.'

'None of my girls is underage,' she said, not moving a bit.

'We know you are lying. But the illegal age of the girls you employ is not the reason for our visit. I'm unwilling to discuss this issue on the street and I'm certain none of your customers will appreciate hearing what I have to say.'

She stepped back, not taking her eyes off us. We walked into a small, clean parlour. A man the size of a wardrobe with abundant hair on wrists and neck received a nod from the madam, and stepped aside to let us pass.

'You will remember the female torso that was found under a railway arch not far from here,' he began. 'Pinchin Street, September 11, 1889, discovered by Constable Pennet.'

She nodded, flicking her eyes toward the door where the wardrobe-man was standing.

'We have evidence that has led to a customer of your house.' He extracted Moran's photograph and placed it on the table. 'Can you confirm that he is a regular customer, known to pay well to deflower underage girls?'

She remained composed, her face losing only the faintest trace of colour. Her voice was steady when she said, 'I can confirm that he is a regular customer of ours.'

'Thank you very much,' he said. 'The next time this man comes knocking at your door, I trust you'll bolt it and refer this at once to Division H on Leman Street.'

She nodded, eyes still stuck to Moran's face.

'Very well.' With that, he took the photograph, slid it under his waistcoat, and off we marched.

All five brothels we visited were exceptionally clean and well appointed — they were hiding their illegal, expensive, *special* services in one of the most dreadful areas of London.

'When I lived in St Giles,' I began, 'I wondered how many prostitutes there are in London. Around eighty-thousand, it appears, all aged twelve to thirty-five. This results in a ratio of roughly fifty to one hundred male Londoners per prostitute, if one assumed potential customers to be aged fifteen to forty-five, and if one leaves out every man too sick, too weak, or too poor. Considering the average fee and number of customers a prostitute serves per night, I arrived at a surprising conclusion.'

'You lived in St Giles?' Watson looked surprised.

I nodded, remembering that I'd never told him that much about me. 'My conclusion is that the average male Londoner capable of sexual intercourse visits prostitutes about once a week, regularly seeking comfort in the arms of a woman despised by society. A conundrum, don't you think?'

'Are you saying that—' Watson began, clearly offended.

'I'm certain she excludes current company, my dear Watson,' Sherlock interrupted, and beckoned us from the alley out to the main street.

'Please don't misunderstand me, Dr Watson. The point I was trying to make...' Watson's face still looked much darker than it normally would. 'I was about to criticise the hypocrisy of the situation.'

'I have never even thought of... of...' he huffed, eyes round, head shaking.

'That was not what I said,' I reminded him. 'What I said, or meant to say, was that it is quite normal for a man to bed a woman simply for the sake of bedding her, not listening to anything she has to say, and then to pay her and label her a low-life, a whore, and worse: dirt. Why is that?'

'Because these women are selling their bodies!' Watson threw his hands in the air.

'Do you believe they *want* to do that? Besides, most women of the middle- and upper classes do the same by marrying a man who can sustain their living standards.' I was perfectly aware that I was poking a stick in a bees' nest.

'Dr Kronb—!'

Sherlock slapped a hand over Watson's mouth. 'Control yourself. We are in disguise,' he murmured. 'Ah, there is the omnibus!' He waved at the driver and manoeuvred us to the main street. We hadn't seen any cabs for the past twenty minutes.

We climbed into the vehicle and were its only passengers, if one excluded an elderly couple sitting far in the back.

'I take it you are starving?' Sherlock asked before I had a chance to continue my discussion with Watson.

I frowned. 'Yes, I am.'

'Would you like to take a late supper with us, Watson?'

'Thank you, but my wife will be waiting. She'll be anxious. I'm puzzled, Holmes. When Moran learns that

Whitechapel isn't safe for him, he'll certainly avoid it. What is the use of this?'

'One of Mycroft's men will call at Moran's house tomorrow morning. He'll introduce himself as an Inspector from Scotland Yard and ask him where he has been on the days between the 9th and 11th of September two years ago. He'll let him know that the Yard received an anonymous package containing new evidence that suggests his involvement in at least one case of murder. He'll also order Moran to stay put for the next few weeks if he doesn't wish the police to believe he's guilty.'

'But why did we come here?' asked Watson.

'Because,' I said, 'there is money to be had. A gentleman rich enough to afford maidens on a regular basis is now the prime suspect in a murder case. The news will spread in hours. People believe the Pinchin Street torso was the Ripper's deed. Some daredevil will attempt to blackmail Moran very soon. Remember, Dr Watson, Moran's name — which he'll certainly not have used when frequenting brothels — was on the photograph.

'Moran knows we stole his photograph, among other things, and he knows we are behind this, but what he doesn't know is what evidence there is against him. It is very likely that the great Sherlock Holmes has found something dangerous, is it not? But Moran cannot wait to find out what it might be, because then it would be too late to run. He will not allow the manacles to close around his wrists. He will disappear. Soon. You and your wife should then be safe here in London.'

Watson, who had been bending forward more and more during my narrative, now leant back and blew air through his clenched lips.

We stepped off the omnibus at the Strand. 'Once he's gone, we will leave London as well,' said Sherlock to Watson.

'Do not forget that I remain officially dead until the day I walk into your practice, my friend. It is of utmost importance. Should Moran ever cross your path, contact Mycroft at once.'

Watson nodded. He stepped forward and took his friend's hand, then lost control and embraced him. The latter seemed a little stunned by the emotional outburst. He stood ramrod straight, wrapped up in his stocky companion. When Watson turned to squeeze my hand, I saw his eyes were wet.

After he had left, I said, 'I offended Watson. He offered his help and I offended him!'

'I'm familiar with this phenomenon.'

'It doesn't surprise me. He used to live with you. Does he ever get used to it?' I wondered.

'I can't tell. How curious! You don't seem to think I am ever offended. Although you offended nearly half of London.'

'I stated a fact.'

'Indeed. But after all these years, you must have learned that truth is usually not taken lightly,' he said, somewhat amused.

'I guess it's an uncontrollable reflex. So. You are offended?'

'No. I am simply excluded from your calculation.'

The smell of meat pies pulled me to the other side of the street, where I bought a large, steaming specimen from a pieman's trolley. 'How can anyone eat with this?' I asked as I shoved food past my moustache. 'It's disgusting how much becomes stuck in the fur. And why would I exclude *you* from my calculation?'

'Do you not?' He came to a halt. 'But you clearly excluded Watson, it seems.'

'I'm not sure I'd exclude an unmarried Watson, but the married Watson would never visit a prostitute. He respects his wife too much. You, on the other hand, have no wife.'

He threw back his head and barked a laugh. Then he offered me the crook of his arm. Without thinking, I slid my hand into it, but quickly removed it and took a step away from him. Two police Inspectors walking arm in arm would look rather peculiar.

'Why the sudden silence?' he asked a few minutes later.

'I realised that chasing criminals doesn't postpone birth.'

'And what would you like to do instead?'

I didn't like the tone. Nor the question, for that matter. 'Are Wiggins and his boys still keeping an eye on Moran?'

'Of course.'

We walked along the street, past the happy, the sad, the rich, and the poor. A mass of people trickled past me as water flows through fingers.

'What kind of life will you choose once Moran is arrested and you have three hundred thousand pounds at your disposal?'

'Is it time to decide already?' I muttered. I felt like saying *a life that has you in it*, but then I couldn't imagine him wanting to hear that.

He steered us through the back door of the hotel he had arranged that afternoon. We walked up to our neighbouring rooms. 'The bathroom on this floor has a tub,' he informed me and pointed down the corridor. 'I'll order tea for us.'

I locked the bathroom, shed my inspector disguise, and stepped into the tub — a small, cup-shaped thing. I folded myself into it, and listened to the gurgle of hot water from the spigot. Would I ever again wash with a worn-out flannel, hunched over a zinc bowl filled with tepid water from a street pump?

Steam rose from the water's surface, small wisps pushed about by my movements and breath, and by the child's occasional soft kick against its enclosure. The aroma of rose petals wafted through the room. I picked up a coarse brush and ran it over my arms. Streaks of red dots began to blossom where bristles scraped over skin. Burning followed suit, dulling the ache within.

～

I WAS WRAPPING myself in a dressing gown when I heard a knock. 'The tea, Madam. I brought it to your room.'

'Thank you,' I called, rubbed my hair dry, and left the bathroom. My body burned — a sharp vibrant feeling that almost gave the impression of me flying so fast that the wind was peeling off my skin. As a child, I'd often dreamed I could fly. But the dreams were frustrating — I was only able to fly a few yards before my feet would touch the ground again. I never reached any heights. I never soared.

Once in my room, I poured a cup of tea and drank it while slowly pacing in circles. I tried to sort through the many thoughts of Moran and what he might do next. I didn't even know whether he was still confined to his bed or had begun to move about. I decided to ask Sherlock.

'What is it?' he called when I knocked at the door separating his room from mine. I opened. He stood at the window, a pipe in the corner of his mouth, his eyebrows drawn together.

'Did your street arabs send any news about Moran?'

'The doctor is still attending to him,' he muttered absent-mindedly.

He barely looked at me; I nodded nonetheless. 'Thank you. Good night.'

I was about to pull the door into its frame when he called, 'One moment, please.'

I stopped.

Before I could enquire as to his reasons, he had stepped up to me and wrapped his fingers around my wrist. His other hand pushed my sleeve up a few inches. Red streaks glowed on pale skin.

'Why would you do this?' His tone was aggressive.

'That is not of your concern. I wish you wouldn't intrude into my private life whenever you see fit.'

'I was under the impression you'd invited me into your private life.'

I yanked my hand from his grip, and tried to analyse his expression. All I saw was annoyance. 'You know,' I whispered, 'you can simply say, "Anna, I wish this case were resolved already, so you would just disappear."'

I slammed the door in his face.

A soft thud followed. 'I apologise.' His voice was muffled.

'Stop offering your one hand just to use the other to push me away.'

Footfalls on the other side, softening, then approaching again.

'You are not to allow or forbid me anything.' I pointed an angry finger at the innocent door. 'You are not to steer me through life as though you know better than I. I don't tell you what's right or wrong for *you*. I respect your choices, even when I don't understand them. The fact that I once offered myself to you doesn't give you any rights over me.'

'Is the offer closed?'

The surprise in his voice hurt. I opened my mouth and shut it again. I stared at the door. Light seeped in through the crack at its bottom, divided by the two shadows of his feet. He wasn't moving. No sounds were coming from his side.

'Good night.' I blew out the candle and went to bed, hot with anger but ablaze with hope, which made me feel like a brainless fifteen-year-old girl. I could have slapped my face.

17

J buttoned the top of my dress, while observing the comings and goings down in the street. A brougham was waiting at the hotel's entrance, shrouded by light fog. I had slept longer than usual and was feeling oddly slow and heavy that morning.

Sherlock had left more than an hour ago to meet with his brother and talk about Whitman and the Kaiser's favourite toy — whatever that might be.

A knock interrupted my thoughts.

'Yes?'

'Your tea and breakfast, Madam.'

I walked to the door and unlocked it. The moment the door swung open, I saw my mistake. Parker grinned at me from behind Moran's back and produced a mocking, 'M'lady.' An almost perfect interpretation of the maid's timid voice.

Shock slowed all movements around me to a comical crawl. I couldn't step aside fast enough. The door hit me in the face. Stars began to blossom in my vision. Almost unnoticed, pain moved through me, past me, leaving only numbness behind.

I stumbled back and aimed a kick at Moran's shin. He answered with a swing of his fist. I ducked and saw his knuckles fly past my face; a sharp breeze brushed the side of my head.

Parker stepped forward. I was thinking fast. Not fast enough. I wished I'd been able to reach my revolver and shoot them both in the first second or two. The door shut. Swift steps, heavy booted, forward, forward. Too close.

Moran shoved a coarse palm in my face, kicked at my legs, and threw me to the floor. The impact robbed me of breath. A rag was stuffed into my mouth, An arm pressed against my throat. I blinked hard to wipe the light flashes from my vision, groaned as I tried to clear my windpipe and get air into my lungs. I kicked at the two without being able to clearly see where they were.

Moran's swollen and disfigured face drifted into view. I heard him mutter, but didn't understand what he said. I tried to kick and roll them off me. Parker was tying my legs together. I still had command over my arms. I pushed against Moran, against his weight on my chest and throat. I clawed at his eyes. He slapped my face. Once, twice, thrice. My ears sang. I felt my arms being pulled apart, one tied to each foot of the bed.

No! Only one was tied to the bed. The left one. I pulled up the right one and—

Moran's knee came down on my right elbow bend, his hand grabbed my chin. 'Bitch! Did you think I'd let you go? After what you did? The police want me! Do you think I'm so stupid that I don't see that you and Holmes are behind all this?'

He pushed his face closer to mine. The hornets had

attacked him savagely. He looked dreadful. I almost laughed at him. How could he be walking about so soon?

'God, how I want to put an end to you. But that stupid woman...' Spittle hit my face. 'She wants the child. God, how I detest that family!'

He rolled up his sleeves. Sweat dripped from his chin. His breath was a series of low, rattling bursts.

'Once that child is born, I'll take care of you.' Maniacal muttering. As though he didn't care whether I heard him or not. As though he had to tell himself that what he was about to do made sense in that isolated world of his.

What was he about to do? I moved my head to get a better view. His right arm was outstretched toward Parker. He grabbed the offered butcher knife. If I thought I'd already used all my strength, I was mistaken. The surge of terror mobilised an unknown wave of power. I managed to roll Parker off my legs and shove my knees against Moran's back. His body barely moved. He slapped me hard. Then a smile spread across his gleaming face. His incisors showed.

'You are lucky. If I kill you now — and believe me, I very much want to — she won't give me my money. So you'll have to wait for me, my *sweet*. Once you are ripe, I'll come for the harvest. For now, I have to satisfy myself with a small piece.'

All I could see was the knife, Moran's contorted face, how he bent over my right arm, his hand clamping down on my wrist, his knee on the bend of my elbow, welding my arm to the floor. I began to scream before the blade touched my skin. Terror beckoned pain before metal met flesh, before nerves could fire and blood could flow.

The noise I produced was muffed by the rag in my mouth. Snot and tears poured out of my nose and eyes. Soon the only other passage to my lungs was full of mucus. I felt the hacking, cutting, tugging. I tried to separate my brain from the searing pain. That birthplace of agony. My hand didn't belong. Couldn't belong. I barely managed to turn my head so my vomit wouldn't immediately end up in my windpipe.

'Careful with that,' snapped Moran, unplugging my mouth. I had almost inhaled the bile, the little my empty stomach was able to expel. Coughing, I fought for air.

He straightened up, wiped his bloody hands on my dress. 'Parker, search the room!'

The journals! Where had I put them? My brain stuttered and stumbled between two singing ears, behind bleary eyes. I couldn't think. I tried to scream for help. A palm slapped down on my mouth and nose. My lungs contracted in vain.

Moran bent closer. 'I'll take a vacation. I trust that you and Mr Holmes will try to find me. Let me assure you that your efforts will be unrewarded. I, however, will find *you*…'

The room fell into blackness, decorated with blinking dots and the screeching music of blood loss.

A click. I blinked. Slowly, my eyes regained vision. The door must have just fallen into its lock. Utter relief. But only for a moment. The journals. I still couldn't think where I had put them.

I moved the leftovers of my right hand to my face, running my sleeve across my mouth, chin, and cheeks to wipe the vomit off. With immediate danger gone, pain rushed in with overbearing sharpness.

The room was spinning, my vision blurry. I pulled at my left arm, inching closer to the bound wrist. The knot looked overwhelmingly complicated. I inserted my right thumb into the knot's various openings. So little control. Everything trembled, even the room, the bed, the knot. My hand, my whole right arm was aching so badly. I kept poking at the knot. Kept poking…until someone turned the lights off.

It dawned. How long had I been unconscious? My tongue was stuck to my palate. A metallic odour singed my nostrils.

My head was hammering, my hand about to rot off my wrist. I opened my eyes and inserted my thumb into the knot again, wiggling, pushing, until blood made the rope too slippery to move.

A knock. Then another. 'Ma'am?' It sounded far off. Echo-like. Then a scream. Who screamed? Who would have reason to make such ruckus?

A pair of scissors approached to gnaw the rope in two. My wrist slipped out and onto the floor before I could move it. Prickling ran up the freed arm. I flexed my fingers to wake up the numb limb, rolled on my elbow, and pushed myself up.

'Madam! Madam! I'll cut you if you move too much.'

I froze. She'd held her nerve. Most maids would have run away, screaming at the top of their lungs for male support.

The pressure around my ankles and knees disappeared. I began to move. 'Could you help me up, please?'

Her arm slid beneath mine. She was delicate, but determined.

'Sit on the bed, Madam,' she whispered, hesitant to give me orders.

'Could you please call for Dr Watson?' I said, staring at her and trying to recall the address. My eyes searched the room as though to find my composure. After a too-long time, I finally remembered. Before the maid left, she gave me a handkerchief to staunch the bleeding.

I gazed at the stump, trying to look at it from a detached, medical viewpoint. Not my hand, I told myself. Not my hand. Blood was oozing; a lazy pulsing of red. The white of the bone was visible; splinters stuck out. The severed tendon would have retracted by now, hiding somewhere, now useless. A ragged cut, blurred by my trembling and my leaky eyes. I wiped my face. A mess of snot and tears and blood. More pain. I had forgotten about the angry door and

Moran's punches. I lay my hand on the handkerchief and my aching head on the pillow. I needed to breathe for a moment.

Another knock and the maid entered, bringing a stranger with her.

'What happened here?' he demanded.

'Where is Dr Watson?' I asked. And where were Wiggins and his ragamuffins? I doubted Sherlock would employ a group of unreliable boys. Something must have happened to them.

'The doctor will be here shortly,' the maid assured me.

The man began pacing the room, stepping into the cut ropes and the spilled blood. 'Are you the manager?' I asked.

'Yes.' His eyes searched the room, apparently to catalogue the damage done, while calculating the resulting costs and deciding that it was I who would pay.

'You walk through the evidence, sir. One could almost believe you wish to destroy it.'

Shocked, he froze where he stood and, like an oversized spider, he lifted one foot, stretched his leg as far as it would go, and stepped to the side. This he continued until he arrived at the wall.

The door flew open and revealed a ruffled Watson. His eyes took in the mess, my state, the state of my hand, all in barely two seconds. 'I must ask you to leave. Should the police feel an urge to enter this room while I perform surgery on my patient, you can be assured I will lose my temper.'

I had never seen Watson angry. What a formidable friend he was. 'I'm worried about Wiggins,' I said once he and I were alone.

'Don't worry now. All is good. Explanations can wait.' He sat down next to me and gingerly took my injured hand into his, examining the wound. 'I'll have to do a few stitches. Are you still unwilling to take opium?'

'You'll have to give me morphia,' I said, pulling my knees up against my aching stomach. 'I'm in labour.'

That drug would help stall premature contractions.

Watson blinked, then nodded. 'You wish to keep it.'

I sighed. *Keeping* the child? I certainly didn't want to kill it. But wanting to keep it was an entirely different thing.

He pressed my healthy hand and bent down to extract a syringe, a tourniquet, and a small bottle from his bag. 'Make yourself comfortable.'

Soon a wonderful warmth entered my bloodstream, spreading from my arm to my shoulder, then into my chest and abdomen. Eyelids quivered. I wafted away. A bed of clouds. My right hand puckered a little. There, where my index finger used to be. That ghost of a limb tied me to reality for a flutter of time, until a soft *pling* cut me off altogether. I rose...

a heaviness lay upon me when consciousness dawned. A glass of water on the night stand reflected the evening sun. Watson sat next to the bed. His eyes were shut, his head lolling to one side.

I examined my hand. A thick bandage hid the stump and extended past my wrist. The ache was radiating to my shoulder. I could feel the silk thread pulling at my severed skin. My other hand slid under the blanket to press down on my lower abdomen. The uterus was soft. The contractions had subsided.

A snore issued from the armchair, then a cough. 'Hello, Dr Watson,' I said. 'It must be exhausting to have to stitch me back together again and again.'

'Ha! Indeed.' He laughed. 'You look much better already. Here, drink this.' He reached out and gave me the water.

I quenched my thirst and pushed myself up.

'Careful,' he said, lending me his arm. 'Blood loss and morphia have weakened you. Not to speak of the shock.'

'Was Sherlock here? And the police?' I pointed to the floor; the ropes and the bloody carpet had been taken away.

'Yes,' said Watson. 'Holmes came here shortly before the police. He is now hunting Moran. I have never seen him so furious.' He cleared his throat and added in a crestfallen voice, 'I had to remove the fractured proximal phalanx.'

'I wouldn't have been able to use it anyway.'

That last bit of index finger was gone now, too. As sharp as that end had been, it would have made healing of the wound impossible. He must have also needed the skin of the last phalanx to pull over the knuckle and make a suture.

'You are an excellent surgeon. Thank you, Dr Watson.'

He bobbed his head. I noticed a whiff of acid. Vomit was stuck to my hair. 'You look tired, Dr Watson. Are you all right?' I noticed his stubbly chin and cheeks, his tilted cravat. 'Is your wife all right?'

He cleared his throat. 'She is ill. But nothing serious.'

'Go home,' I said softly. 'I'm fine.'

'The police want to talk to you. They'll call on you tomorrow morning.' He rose and patted my healthy hand. 'I'll be back tomorrow after breakfast to change your bandages. Call for me should you need me before that,' he said. 'Oh! I almost forgot to tell you that Holmes wants you to know that the journals are at his brother's. I take it you know what he means by that?'

Relieved, I smiled and nodded. Sherlock must have taken them to discuss their contents with Mycroft. I hoped the two had found something of interest.

After he left, I rang the bell and asked the maid if she knew who had helped me earlier. She blushed and tipped her head. 'It was my sister, Madam. She isn't allowed up here.'

'Why?'

'She works in the scullery. Scrubbing pans and pots. She just wanted to see the nice rooms where I work. She just... She was new here.'

Could it be possible that the girl had lost her occupation so quickly?

'Oh. I see,' I said. 'Hmm... Could you tell the manager that the eccentric lady who lost a finger wishes to see the maid who saved her?'

Her hands clasped in front of her apron, fingers entwining.

'Alternatively, you could simply tell him that I wish to see him,' I added. She was visibly relieved. 'But before I can receive such a distinguished guest, I will wash and dress.' I sat up slowly, holding on to the bed frame for support should my feeble blood circulation betray me. And it did indeed.

'Would you like me to help you, Madam?' she asked, seeing me swoon.

'Thank you, but I think I'll be fine. I'll simply take my time.'

With a *Very well, Madam,* and a curtsy, she left.

I sat for a moment, then slowly stood and paused before I began moving. With my healthy hand sliding along the wall, I made for the bathroom. Nothing but fury propelled me forward.

No sign of Sherlock the following morning. The police had interviewed me and promised to arrest Moran and Parker. I had my doubts.

My hand puckered. Blood was seeping through the bandage and I needed to change it at once to avoid infection. Unwilling to wait for Watson any longer, I began unwrapping the gauze and soon noticed that it stuck to the stump. Tearing it off and opening the wound was out of the question. Watson had left bandages, but I found neither sterile saline solution nor disinfectant at my disposal. He probably believed I still had my doctor's bag with me. Or perhaps he wasn't thinking much at all, because his wife was more ill than he had admitted?

Were there any other sterile liquids I could use? I considered asking the maid to boil salt water or milk for me, but I assumed the scullery to be a rather greasy place and I didn't want any of the countless kitchen germs in my wound. That left only one thing: fresh urine.

I took a pair of scissors and clipped off the bandage, leaving only the patch that was sticking to the stump. Just as I was leaving my room to go to the lavatory, Watson walked up the corridor. 'My apologies for being late. I forgot to give you these,' he huffed, holding out two brown bottles.

Once back in my room, he poured sterile saline solution onto the last bit of gauze until it peeled off by itself. I was glad he had come — urinating on a fresh wound would have been rather painful.

Together, we examined the stump. Black silk thread pulled the skin tight over my knuckle. The flesh was swollen and had a tortured red gleam. I held it up to my nose and sniffed. It smelled of freshly cut meat, blood, silk, and yesterday's iodine. Underlying all those odours was a hint of stuffy sweetness — wound infection.

'It's beginning to smell,' I noted, and held out my healthy hand. Watson handed me the bottle. I poured a generous amount of iodine on a handkerchief, then dabbed the suture with it. He helped me wrap clean gauze around the stump and my hand.

I would watch this wound with eagle eyes. Should the infection spread, I could lose my whole hand. Getting used to the lack of a finger was one thing — writing, surgery, spreading pure cultures on solid media would need adaptation. But the loss my dominant hand was…unthinkable.

'Have you heard anything from Sherlock?' I asked when Watson snapped his bag shut.

'Unfortunately not. But I'm certain he is enjoying himself.' He bent closer and patted my healthy hand. I smiled down at his hairy knuckles. Watson was far from being as blind as Sherlock thought him to be.

'I'll leave these here.' He tapped on the bottles with solutions of iodine and saline, and four rolls of fresh bandages.

'Thank you,' I said.

'May I ask what you'll be doing now?'

I huffed a laugh. 'I'll pack my belongings and disappear. I have no idea how Moran found us or how—'

'Holmes told me that Moran caught one of Holmes's street arabs. That's how Moran must have got the information.'

I snatched Watson's hand. 'Wiggins?

'No. No, not Wiggins. Another one. I never knew his name. He…was shot in the back.' Watson shook his head, his moustache drooping.

'The poor boy! And I'm worried about Sherlock,' I said. 'I wish I had poisoned Moran, too.' But what *that* would have entailed! The thought was unbearable.

Watson looked a little confused. He didn't know I had poisoned James or how I had accomplished it.

'If you wish, I'll ask my wife as soon as she's better whether she'd like us to adopt your child.'

'You are an honest man, Dr Watson. Tell me, am I doing wrong? Planning to give my child away. Is that not…cruel?'

His gaze dropped to his hands that he now tucked in between his knees. 'I believe that a mother should do what is best for her child. If you cannot love your child, you must find someone who can.'

'Can the two of you love my child?' I whispered.

'What is not to love about a newborn?' He gifted me a

warm smile and rose to his feet. 'I have to go home and look after my wife. Holmes told me that the two of you might be leaving tomorrow, perhaps even tonight. Will you be writing to us, Dr Kronberg?'

I stood up. 'Yes, I will. Thank you, Dr Watson.'

He nodded and took his leave.

When I drifted about my room to pack my belongings and change into a walking dress, a thought hit me so hard it made me stumble. Just before Sherlock had arrested the Club — that group of medical doctors who used cholera and tetanus to experiment on paupers — I had possibly made a grave mistake.

Their leader, Dr Bowden, didn't trust me then, and I'd had to win at least some of his trust in order to gain enough information for the arrest of the entire group. So I'd demonstrated my ruthlessness by telling him an absurd lie: that the Kaiser was planning a war, and that we should use deadly bacteria as weapons.

Breathing hard, I sat down.

What if the Club's initial goal had been to develop vaccines? James's first wife and newborn child had died of tetanus. Would that not have been motivation enough for him to search for a cure for the disease? Had I changed the Club's intentions for the worse? Was I to blame for everything that came after my lie? James abducting me and my father to force me to develop bacterial weapons for warfare, James's order to murder my own father, Sherlock's near death, my own suffering, the unborn and unwanted child, Moran running free and possibly distributing dangerous knowledge on biological weapons, and finally James's death that I had actively brought upon him. What an avalanche of guilt that would be!

A knock at my door almost threw me off the armchair.

'A telegram for you, Madam.' A woman's voice. Its timidity indicated that it was indeed one of the maids.

'Just a moment,' I called, snatched the revolver from the night stand, cocked it, and hid it behind my back as I opened the door. With a curtsy, the maid placed a wire in my bandaged hand. I thanked her and re-locked the door.

Tante Christa erwartet dich mit Sehnsucht. Beeil dich. Hans.

THIS WAS SOONER than I had expected. I blinked. I had never heard Holmes speak German, and reading it now was most unusual. Aunt Christa is expecting me, and I should hurry. How interesting! No instructions on where to go. Perhaps that didn't matter.

Hastily, I threw the rest of my clothes into the bag, paid the bill, and left an envelope with twenty pounds for the scullery maid who had lost her post for helping me. I walked away from the hotel a mere fifteen minutes after the wire had reached me. At that point, I was sweating and shivering simultaneously.

I had to quickly disappear, but I also needed information. Without it, I was as good as blind. Sherlock had deposited his notes and Moran's journals at Mycroft's, so that was where I went.

I rang the bell and was frowned upon by the servant. 'This is a men's club,' he snivelled.

'I'm aware of that. I need to speak with Mr Mycroft Holmes. It's urgent. I'll wait here,' I said, pushing past him and settling in the parlour.

'Madam, I must insist—'

'I know you must,' I interrupted him, and for a moment I

considered using my revolver to convince the man. 'And I must insist, too. Mister Holmes is in grave danger. Go find him for me, if you please.'

He eyed me with suspicion, but his position didn't allow him to apply any personal judgment. He turned on his heel and swiftly climbed the stairs, taking then two at a time. His coat tails bobbed with each small jump.

Mycroft arrived only two minutes later. As Watson had the day before, he swept his gaze over my face and injured hand. He bade me follow him to a room in the back.

'I don't know where my brother is,' he said once he had shut the door behind him. 'But he asked me to return Moran's journals to you.'

I tipped my chin. 'Mr Holmes, I also need Sherlock's notes on our last case. Everything that might give a clue as to what James planned. I assume you made notes on your interview with Whitman?'

Mycroft folded his hands, his narrowed eyes piercing mine. 'You are aware this is highly sensitive information?'

'In that case, I shall go home at once and take up needlework.'

He held up a hand, warding off my acidic comment. 'Very well,' he said and made to leave. 'Am I correct to assume that you haven't had breakfast?'

'Absolutely.'

'You will be my guest.' He held out a hand.

'I thought women weren't allowed in this club.'

'It's my club. I make the rules.' He marched me one floor up. As none of the club's members felt free to speak, I heard only puffs and gasps as we passed various smoking rooms and libraries. 'Mayer, a hearty breakfast for my guest,' he called down the corridor before we entered his office.

Despite my short stay, I had already caused the violation

of two of the club's major rules. I tried to look not too delighted.

'Sit, please.' His hand waved me to a chaise longue. He slid behind his desk, opened a drawer and retrieved a familiar-looking stack. 'These were of help, Dr Kronberg. I was able to validate a number of Whitman's statements. My brother told me about your hornet bomb. What a pity you have no wish to be in my employ.' He waited for the reply I didn't give, then turned to a shelf and began sorting loose pieces of notes into a pile.

I lay down to let my blood circulation return to a state that didn't make the world tip back and forth. Soon, breakfast arrived.

Mycroft was still sorting papers long after I'd finished eating.

'I believe these are all the documents.' He dabbed a handkerchief to his brow. 'I'll bind them for you.' He punched holes through with a small knife, then pulled them together with a thick string, tying the individual sheets into one big volume.

'They are my brother's. Treat them accordingly.' With a thud, the makeshift book landed next to my plate. The tea in my cup rippled. Moran's journals followed, but with less force.

'Whitman provided useful information?' I asked.

Mycroft sat down, and nodded. 'Yes, he did so, but reluctantly. I will not bore you with the details, but my conclusion is this: Moriarty was solely concerned with Germany. I cannot fathom why that should have been so. It is true that since Bismarck's dismissal in March of last year, Salisbury has been unable to align British policy with that of Germany. But to see Germany as a threat?' He inspected his folded hands, his manicured fingernails.

'And yet...with the strength of the German industry

growing; with the rumours about the enlargement of her navy and military. With her scientists at the forefront of medicine, physics, and chemistry, and with her alarmingly unstable leader, it is logical that our government should grow concerned. But we have not, for we believe ourselves invincible. Hence, we do nothing.

'This is an utterly naive policy of splendid isolation!' He slapped a palm on his desk. The pen rattled in its holder. 'Nothing but arrogance. We don't even have a functional intelligence service! If we were to invade another European country — hypothetically speaking, of course — we wouldn't be able to manoeuvre through that country because we don even have *maps*. All because Britons are unwilling to invest any considerable budget, or even an inconsiderable one, or expend any effort in espionage. It's not gentlemanly. Ha! Moriarty was justified in gathering his own espionage organisation. However, it doesn't explain why he wanted to develop weapons for germ warfare, as there is simply no impending conflict.'

I swallowed my scrambled eggs. The knowledge that it was I who had pointed James toward Germany weighed heavy on my shoulders.

'May I ask where you plan to go?'

I cleared my throat. 'Brussels might be a good place to start. As far as I know, James attempted to change the Brussels Convention on the Laws and Customs of War.'

It was idiotic. I had no clue whether going to Brussels was a good idea, whether anything at all could be learned there. I didn't even know where one should start searching for information, other than in the stack that lay next to my plate.

He lowered his head, brow crinkled. 'Visit this man.' He wrote a name and an address on a piece of paper he tore from a notepad. 'I'll let him know you are coming. You can trust him to answer your questions truthfully, but don't trust him with your safety.' Seeing my puzzlement, he added, 'Don't tell him where you go or what you plan to do.'

'I...' I was about to say that I had never done anything like this. 'Mr Holmes, I assume sending wires or letters to you is out of the question. How should we communicate? And how can I get information to your brother?'

Unspeaking, he stared at me. It took a long moment before he cleared his throat. 'Sherlock and I are using book ciphers. Each letter is coded as a series of four digits, each identifying a page, a line, a word, and a letter. We need identical books, identical editions, otherwise the cipher does not work.'

'Would you like to use a different one with me than you use with your brother?'

'Of course I do.' He picked up the pencil again and wrote a second note. 'You'll find this one almost everywhere.'

I took the paper from his hand. 'The Bible?'

'Let us be specific, Dr Kronberg. Rheims' New Testament, Pocket Edition, published by Burns and Oates in 1888. Easy to remember.'

'Do you believe in God?' I asked. He snorted in reply. 'Not I. Thank you, Mr Holmes. For everything, including the delicious breakfast.'

I rose and offered my left hand in farewell. He pressed it and wished me luck. Whatever that might mean.

19

During peace time a scientist belongs to the world, but during war time he belongs to his country.

Dr F. Haber

~

I boarded the ship on a sunny Thursday afternoon. The appearance of a pregnant woman without husband or maid, but with two pieces of luggage, a bandaged hand, and a battered face might have been remarked on had she looked wealthy. I made sure to remain invisible with my simple dress, worn-out rucksack, and old bag until I was able to sneak into the first-class cabin I had booked for myself and my fictional husband.

I pulled off my hat and shoes, and extracted my new gun from the rucksack. It was a Webley Mark I, a standard issue service revolver with automatic extraction. I'd bought it for its higher accuracy and lighter weight, compared to the old revolver I already owned. The Webley's self-extraction function was of marginal importance to me. One shot was all I would need, and all I could hope to fire.

I placed the gun on the bed and unwrapped my bandage. The cool air felt good on the aching wound. I pressed around the suture; clear liquid seeped from it, but I felt no abnormally sharp pains.

I dabbed more iodine on the wound, then began to gingerly flex my fingers. The middle finger ached. Moran had cut it, too, but the injury wasn't serious. Watson had made three small stitches there. I watched with fascination. The pain in my wounds was expected, but the missing index finger tingled. My brain believed it was still attached. How odd.

I opened my revolver, removed the bullets from the cylinder, placed them on the bed, and snapped the gun closed. Holding my left arm out straight, I aimed at the doorknob and pulled the trigger repeatedly until my shoulder and fingers ached. The weakness and inaccuracy of my left hand and arm had to be exercised away, for using my right hand wouldn't be possible for weeks. I wasn't even sure whether I would even be able to pull the trigger with my middle finger.

I practiced for another ten minutes, then wrapped a towel around my hand and began hitting the doorframe, softening the force behind my punches. I neither wanted to attract attention by producing noise, nor did I wish to cause damage to my one good hand.

Force wasn't what I aimed for, anyway. I'd never incapacitate Moran with the little muscle power I had. I wanted speed and accuracy. And so I spent the ensuing hour and a half exercising the shooting and punching muscles of my left arm until they ached and trembled. All the while, I wondered how I could possibly stop a man as well trained as Moran. Come October, I'd need to have a good idea, and be prepared. But time and circumstances were working against me. I'd be either very large and about to pop, or weak from having just given birth. Moran's words kept ringing in my head: *I'll come to harvest.*

Sweaty and exhausted, I wrapped clean gauze around my injured hand and left the cabin to catch a bit of fresh air.

Passengers littered the deck. A few children threw bits of bread at the swarm of gulls that hovered alongside the boat. I sat on a chair, closed my eyes, and thought about anatomy. When it came to muscle power, I had no chance against Moran, or against most men, for that matter. I was small but quick, so I could escape if needed. But when the time came for me to run from Moran, I'd be at my weakest and slowest. Besides, he was a good marksman and could easily shoot me in the back, no matter how quick I might be. Once again I arrived at the conclusion that having been impregnated by James Moriarty was about the worst thing that ever could have happened to me.

I shook off that unhelpful sentiment and made a list of the weaknesses any man had, no matter his bulk or strength. Testicles were always an excellent target for an angry knee. But an attacker might expect an assault there. What else? Kidneys, surely. The throat, eyes, solar plexus.

I imagined Moran attacking me. He had done so three times and he had always come suddenly and unexpectedly. All three times, he used his whole body to stop me from escaping, squirming, and protesting. Chances were high that the next time he'd attack in a similar manner. I could run my knee into his groin. But what then? Use the confusion and pain to get hold of my revolver and shoot him? That would leave me with a three-step process to incapacitate or kill Moran — kick, grab gun, shoot. That plan had no room for flexibility.

I watched the people on deck, turning them all into potential targets. They walked about, chatted, joked, not knowing about the fictional danger my mind was brewing up. Knees, elbow bends, necks — joints always buckled, no matter how strong or weak a person was. Muscles were attached to bones by tendons. One could increase muscle mass through hard work and exercise, but tendons didn't get any thicker. With acceleration and force, I could break a limb at the joint. A frontal kick at the knee when Moran stood before me, a hard punch against his elbow when he held me at arm's length. But how could I be certain that my strength would be enough to snap his joints? I neither knew how to punch effectively, nor was I quick enough for such a feat. I could as easily attempt to stop a locomotive. One kick, one punch, one shot were the best I could hope for. When he came to *harvest…*

~

As NIGHT FELL and the ship's gentle roll began to weigh down my tired eyelids, I flipped through the pages Mycroft had given me. Along with Moran's notes, I would need days to read it all. Whether I'd ever be able to knit the bits of information together was an entirely different question.

From what my sluggish brain could understand of Mycroft's and Sherlock's notes, Whitman had provided information on the Kaiser's favourite toy: battleships. Wilhelm II had shown peculiar interest in the British Navy, and for the last two years or so he seemed to be planning to enlarge the German Navy. However, these were mere rumours.

The British government was more concerned with impending conflicts in South Africa that could result in a cut in profits from gold mining. Another weary eye was directed toward the new railway Russia was building, which might, in a few years, be used to ship weaponry and soldiers close to the Indian colonies, leaving the British Navy in an inferior position in this remote area.

If one were insanely paranoid, it might appear that the world cooked up powers to dismantle the British Empire. But wasn't Europe connecting her countries with one another and the rest of the world? Railways and steamships linked even the most far-away places with Europe and America. The telegraph enabled everyone to send a message from London to New York and receive a reply within hours. And telephones! Such a wonderful invention that allowed us to talk with one another even when many miles separated us.

The people of the modern world were confident that we were now intricately connected, too progressive, and all too civilised to settle conflicts with brutal force. Everyone believed that Europe would never again see a war in her territory.

20

*G*rey drizzle welcomed me to France. I didn't give the rain time to soak my coat. A cab took me to the station, and a train to Paris and on to Brussels.

I arrived late in the evening and rented a small room above the Café Metropole. My hand hurt, my feet ached, and I wished I could have gone to bed the moment I dropped my luggage on the floor. But I couldn't risk an infection.

I extracted the iodine bottle and a roll of fresh gauze from my bag, then made my way to the bathroom. I examined the stump and dabbed iodine on the wound. Should the thread continue to irritate the flesh, I'd have to pull it, and possibly make a fresh suture. I washed quickly, sneaked under my cover, and fell asleep with images of a lead-coloured sea pushing up against the fore, foam trailing along the hull, foam trailing over me, across my skin, a soft caress...

I ROSE at dawn to eat and quickly re-read the notes I had written the previous days. At nine o'clock, I hailed a cab. We passed the Jardin Botaniqe, turned right and right again, and came to a halt at the Rue Linné.

Apartment buildings crammed the street on both sides. Number twelve had a large blue front door with patches here and there bleached by time and weather. It stood open a crack, and I squeezed through. The courtyard was decorated with two rusty bicycles, several sacks of potatoes sprouting long white shoots, and a pile of wood under an oilskin. Where I had lived in London, these treasures would have been quickly taken hostage by many small and dirty hands.

I walked up a dark stairway until I found a sign with the name *Kinchin*. The bell knob had corroded and wouldn't turn. A doormat was lacking, and a line of dirt was brushed up against the door. It appeared as though no one lived there. Or no one ever visited.

I knocked.

A shuffling of tired feet on carpet, the clinking of a chain, the chirping of a key being turned.

A face showed in the door-frame, wrinkles trailing from the corners of his mouth down to his throat. The man eyed me from the top of my hat to the hem of my dress, then spoke in an extraordinarily soft voice. 'Mrs Kronberg.' He stepped aside, and held the door open for me.

'Mr Kinchin.' I held out my hand.

'I avoid touching people,' he informed me. He didn't inch away from me as I squeezed past, but he kept his distance while directing me to his sitting room.

The apartment was sparsely furnished. Knick-knacks were completely missing. Every item was arranged with exactness, perpendicular to the nearest wall or piece of furniture — the letters on his desk, the newspapers on his coffee table. Table, chairs, fireplace, hat-stand — invisible lines ran through his apartment, all crossing at ninety-degree angles.

He bade me sit, walked to a cupboard, and retrieved two cups. 'I made tea,' he announced, poured me a cup without asking if I wanted some, and pushed it to my side of the small table. I had no means to measure it, but I was certain that both cups were precisely two-thirds filled, their handles facing precisely ninety degrees to my left. He was right-handed. I was currently left-handed.

'Thank you, Mr Kinchin,' I said, noticing that he avoided direct eye contact. His mind appeared constantly busy, his gaze twitchy, his fingers tapping away on an invisible surface. Impatience oozed from every pore.

'I'll try to keep my visit short.' I pulled off my left glove and placed it on my lap.

'Mr Holmes informed me that you have questions regarding the Brussels Declaration on the Laws and Customs of War.'

I inclined my head, trying to observe the man without intimidating him. 'Yes. Are you aware of a new draft?'

His eyes twitched. 'No.'

'Would you be aware of a new draft should there be one?'

'I certainly would.' He leant back and looked at my throat.

I took my cup and pretended to be busy with a floating tea leaf.

'Why do you believe there is a new draft, Mrs Kronberg?'

'A mere suspicion. I am depending on information from an unreliable source.'

James had played games since we'd first met, or rather, since he had abducted me. His trip to Brussels could have been a ruse. I wasn't even certain why he would have taken pains to attempt to influence a new draft on the Customs of War. According to Sherlock's notes, James had appeared to be a man confident of his own success, but it wasn't clear what sort of accomplishment he'd attempted in Brussels. Sherlock hadn't been able to extract that information from anyone. Mouths were sealed, or simply couldn't provide an answer. His notes were littered with question marks. One of his entries gave me the greatest stomach-ache: *Potential effects in future warfare?*

'What, in your opinion, might a new draft include?'

'Exclude,' I said. 'It might exclude a passage that forbids the signatories to spread disease in enemy territory.'

My remark started an automaton-like reciting of information. 'Interesting! In 1874, delegates from fifteen European states came here to Brussels — a meeting initiated by Tsar Alexander II to agree on customs of war, to prevent torture and unnecessary suffering.'

The word *unnecessary* carried a trace of disdain.

'In one passage, the declaration prohibits the employment of poison and poisoned weapons, but doesn't mention the word *disease*. In fact, the term *disease* is nowhere to be found. However, records of the Brussels Conference show that this passage was meant to include chemical as well as biological weapons. Thoughtless and hasty, but what is to be expected? I haven't heard of any efforts to change and specify this passage. Besides, of what use is the convention? Not all of the fifteen governments accepted it, so it has never been fully ratified. Even had they all signed it, should one country attack another, do you believe anyone would press charges someone those using tear gas or disease in addition to machine guns and bayonets?'

'Then why make such a law at all?'

'The Brussels Declaration is not a law. It's an agreement, and worth the paper it's written on.'

I placed my cup aside and concluded, 'So the declaration is nothing but those in power clapping one another on the shoulders, affirming what good gentlemen they all are, representing fine governments that don't mean any harm at all. Until they do.'

'Precisely.' He pushed off his armchair and stood at the window.

The idea that James might have tried to influence a new draft now made even less sense. Even if this had been his intention, he had been in no position to initiate a meeting of two countries, let alone fifteen. Whitman stated he had no knowledge of James's activities in Brussels. I wondered if his spy friend knew more.

'I was waiting for this,' Kinchin said quietly.

'For what?'

'Since Koch isolated anthrax bacilli, I expected someone to use deadly germs for weaponry. But I never thought a woman would be involved.'

He slowly turned around, gifted me one second of eye contact, then announced he would make more tea.

I waited in my armchair, sorting through the many questions that swirled in my head.

'Why did you anticipate bacterial weapons, Mr Kinchin?' I asked when I heard him approach.

'It is the logical next step.' He sat the teapot on the table, sliding its handle to match the orientation of our cups. 'Two minutes.' A murmur directed at the tea leaves in the pot. 'Whatever scientists and engineers discover or develop, is assessed by the military, and if useful, employed. Not a single man can be shot with a gun without the prior invention of gunpowder. Without basic knowledge of anatomy, how can one aim a bullet straight at the heart? Without the telegraph and the locomotive, how would the American Civil War have ended? Where did you go to university, Mrs Kronberg?'

I felt the blood draining from my face.

He bent forward and removed the tea leaves, placed them on a saucer, then poured the dark golden liquid into my cup.

'Your interest in germs, warfare, and the Brussels Convention. Your face showing knowledge, not puzzlement, when I mentioned anthrax bacilli and Robert Koch. Your rather short hair, and lack of protest when I made my first assumption about the involvement of a woman. You didn't particularly hide it.'

'Leipzig,' I answered.

'Thank you. You see, I'm a collector of information that is generally hard to obtain.'

'Who would profit from a major conflict in Europe?'

A low chuckle pressed through his lips. 'You should ask who would *not* profit from a conflict in Europe.'

'Consider the question asked.'

'The most powerful country is, in this case, the one to profit the least.'

'England.'

'Naturally.'

'Which country would she fear the most?' I asked.

'Russia.'

'What about Germany?'

His eyebrows shot up — his strongest reaction to my questions thus far. He had an oddly impassive expression up until then, and I'd wondered whether something was wrong with his facial muscles. 'Certainly a country one needs to keep an eye on. Do you know anything about Britain's foreign policy? Or Germany's, for that matter?'

I shook my head. The little Mycroft had told me couldn't be regarded as knowledge.

'I thought so. Biscuits?' He gripped his knees, pushed himself up, and retrieved a tin box.

'Thank you,' I said and selected a biscuit. 'You avoid people, but you are not bothered by me sitting in your armchair.'

'I might be bothered very soon. It depends on what you have to offer.'

'I know very little.'

'Now you are insulting me.' His expression was impossible to read. The cadence of his voice was even, with only the slightest changes in speed and tune. It was hard to listen to him, for half the information — all that should have sounded between the lines — was missing.

'Politics never interested me much,' I replied.

'Let's begin with something less... critical. How did you manage to gain entrance to the Leipzig University?'

'I cut my hair and masqueraded as a man.'

'Obviously.' He leant back and waved his hand for me to continue. The hint of impatience felt alarming.

'I studied medicine. No one suspected me. I specialised in bacteriology and epidemiology, and spent some time in Koch's laboratory. Harvard Medical School employed me for four years. After that, I was employed by the Guy's Hospital in London.'

'The aim of Bismarck's foreign policy was to establish the German Empire as a *status quo* power,' he began. 'When Wilhelm II expelled him, we pricked our ears. Unverified information tells of a treaty between Russia and Germany. A dangerous constellation! However, that same source swears that the Kaiser let the treaty expire, despite the Tsar's efforts to renew it. Intentions are unclear. With the German Empire now united and strong, a leader with an obviously erratic temper represents danger.'

He poured himself more tea. A trickle of moisture crawled down the deep wrinkles at the corners of his mouth.

'It came to our attention that Wilhelm II made plans to increase his fleet and build a new class of battleships. With Helgoland now being the first German naval base in the North Sea, this could, in ten or twenty years, pose a threat. But I wouldn't count on it. Russia is the real threat to the British Empire.'

'Why?'

'Dr Kronberg was blessed with international fame when he isolated tetanus germs. Strangely, soon thereafter, he disappeared. Why?'

I had seen the *Times* on top of his neat newspaper stack, but the edges of the papers below it indicated his reading material was very diverse. A tiny bit of my life was in those papers, and I very much disliked that.

'I'm surprised how much information you extract from the papers,' I answered. 'You have a sharp and analytical mind; you remember details very well and put them together when a new and fitting piece is published. Considering all your other sources of information, such as connections with the government and the occasional spy, your mind must be crammed with data. I wonder whether this is the reason you stay away from the overwhelming outside world.'

He had contact with Mycroft and he had spoken of sources that certainly had nothing to do with newspaper reports. I guessed him to be a knot in a network of information traders.

'Why did you disappear and what happened afterwards?' he asked again.

'I've taken enough of your time, Mr Kinchin. Thank you for the tea.' I rose to my feet, took my glove and hat, and turned to leave.

'What a most unsatisfactory conversation.'

I stopped and turned to him. 'You must have noticed that I'm with child. I cannot allow you access to information that would threaten my life or that of my child. Good day to you, Mr Kinchin.'

'As I told you, chemical and bacterial weapons will be developed and employed when they are needed. It all depends on which country has the best scientists and the greatest motivation. Today, there is only one country that has both.'

'France, Germany, and Britain all have excellent bacteri-ologists,' I said.

A huff through compressed lips showed his contempt. 'Don't forget the chemists and physicists. And may I remind you that you are German? What side will you take should it ever come to open conflict? But the more pressing question is: why would a group of Britons want to develop weapons for germ warfare? Ah! Your face conceals the shock well. But your breath stopped for an instant. I made an educated guess. You have herewith answered my questions. Good day to you, Mrs Kronberg.'

I walked down the corridor, cursing my simple-minded-ness and the fact that Kinchin hadn't answered my most pressing question: why had James wished to develop bacte-rial weapons? My thoughts were interrupted by his shuffling footsteps.

'I have one more bargain to offer,' he said, 'you tell me about the weapons you have developed, and I will tell you about the Russian spy a certain Colonel Moran murdered in 1885.'

21

*W*hen the blue door creaked into its lock behind me, Brussels appeared different. Now, Europe was a chart covered with threads connecting and tangled, borders separating, powers shifting, governments haggling, cheating, prying, spying. Knowledge was, above all, the greatest power.

The old man up in his orderly room, tucked away in a disorderly house, had the knowledge to bring down governments. Mycroft had taken a great risk when he'd send me there. And he had played with me. Not one word of warning that Kinchin would already know that Moran was hunting me. I wondered whether Mycroft had also given away his brother. Most likely not. But I was expendable in Mycroft's eyes.

Nausea crawled up my throat. My body and that of the child were demanding food, making my stomach churn. I had learned much in the past two hours and I had given away much as well. Brussels wasn't safe for me anymore. Going back to London was out of the question, and travelling to a place where I could not understand the language made little sense. I needed more information, and it had to be in English or in German. I went back to my room above the Café, packed my things, and took the night train to Berlin.

My plan wasn't particularly intelligent, but it was all I could think to do at that moment. I would comb through libraries and newspaper archives and read as much as possible. The more I learned about my home country, the more I was becoming ashamed of my ignorance. I should have long known more about politics, should have read the papers more often. It simply hadn't interested me enough. Now, with Kinchin's information, my puzzle was growing larger and more complex, and it was beginning to reveal a picture.

On my first day in Berlin, I sent Mycroft a message with my whereabouts. On my fourth day, I wrote him a single line, *How is Sherlock?*

His absence worried me deeply.

~

I FLEXED the fingers of my right hand. The stump was healing well. A week ago, I had pulled the threads. The scar was still highly sensitive, and I was using the bandage to protect it from impacts, and not so much from infections. I had grown used to the lack of an index finger. Learning how to write with the pen pinched between my thumb and ring finger wasn't too great a feat. And once I was able to attain more flexibility with the middle finger, I would probably not notice the missing appendage.

For days now, my head had been spinning with information. Late at night, I lay in bed and could almost see the many threads of complex information and hypotheses flitting across the ceiling. A swarm of snakes, coiling and uncoiling, at times showing a pattern that made sense, at other times only chaos.

I watched the coiling and uncoiling, the swimming of thoughts, the forming and dissipating of theories until I fell asleep.

Soft rustling woke me. I forced my eyes to not snap open and my breath to flow regularly. I inched my hand under the pillow, sighing as though I were dreaming. The revolver was warm. My thumb found the hammer, my index finger the trigger. I had practiced with my left hand, but never used the weapon loaded, nor had I ever fired it. This would be my first time.

Prickling raced up my arm when I pulled back the hammer. The pillow muffled the clicks. My ears were pricked for a source of the low sound, but all was quiet. Where had the noise come from? Straight ahead and a little toward the wall, perhaps? I opened my eyes, swung out my arm, and pointed the gun toward the armchair.

A slender silhouette sat folded there, knees up against his chest, arms wrapped around shins. In the dark of the night, the glint of his eyes was barely visible.

'Hello,' I whispered, trying to calm my frantic heart.

'I had expected a certain degree of irritation,' he said, pointing toward the gun. 'Although not *that* much.'

I released the hammer, and placed the revolver on the night stand. When he walked up to me, I pulled my injured arm under the blanket.

He struck a match. Golden light spread as a wick caught fire. Frowning, he lifted a corner of my blanket and extracted my right hand from its hiding place. He pulled it closer, unwrapped the gauze, and examined the stump.

'He intended to take the middle finger as well?' he asked.

'When he hacked off the index finger, the middle finger was in the way.' Not wanting to upset him, I tried to speak as detached as I could. 'He cut it a few times, but damaged only skin and muscles.'

To prove my point, I wiggled my fingers, the middle finger following my orders reluctantly. My ghost finger wiggled, too, or so it felt.

His lips brushed over the scar. Warm breath followed. A soft caress of gauze wrapped around my hand before he fastened it. He took my other hand and ran a fingertip over the thin layer of callus on my knuckles. One eyebrow shot up.

'I know how little sense it makes to even attempt punching him,' I explained. 'But I'm unwilling to play helpless.'

I noticed how tired and worn he appeared. Dark shadows under his eyes, sallow cheeks, a two-day stubble. His jaws were working, and I placed my palm there. He pressed the offered hand against his forehead and sighed, 'Forgive me.'

'There is nothing to forgive.'

'Well, theoretically there isn't,' he muttered. A gruff noise. 'It's impossible to keep you safe at all times, illogical even; attempting it would cause more damage than good. Why does it bother me at all that I wasn't there to protect you? Yet *again!* Apparently, I don't even see it as a necessity to teach you how to use a revolver or how to land an effective punch. Look at you.' His head snapped up, his hand waved at me, up and down. A nervous and angry movement. 'You are a product of your sex. Your body invites attacks. Female, small, slender. With child, even! Everything screams weakness.'

'Why, thank you.'

He froze. 'I'm apologising. It would be appropriate to either accept or reject the apology. Don't try to make me believe there's nothing to ask forgiveness for. I'm not that stupid.'

With my palm resting on his cheek, I said, 'Apology accepted. But the truth is that it's I who must apologise. I should never have opened that door, never expected Moran to be too ill or too weak to seek revenge.'

A single nod. He took my hand and buried his face in my palm, then pulled back.

I trembled.

'I have to occupy your armchair. It was impossible to book a room at this time of night.' He rose to his feet.

'You can sleep in my bed. I'll work on my notes.'

He ignored my offer and rolled himself up on the too-small resting place. I rose and approached him.

'I'm not discussing the issue,' he muttered, eyes closed already and arms wrapped around his chest.

'Nor I.' I snatched the blanket from my bed and covered him and the armchair, then pulled on a dressing gown and busied myself with Moran's journals.

A moment later, he issued a soft grunt and a *Thank you*, then relocated to my bed. His feet began to twitch at once.

22

*T*he first light of the day trickled through the curtains. I rubbed my tired eyes and found myself in bed without the slightest idea how I had got there. My room was empty. I rose and dressed quickly, then tried to find Sherlock.

'Could you locate Moran?' I asked when I met him in the hall, eating breakfast in a far corner, mutton chops and thick glasses concealing his identity.

His face darkened. 'I wish I could have taken a horse-whip to that man.' His voice sounded like the scraping of a pipe cleaner when shoved through old and encrusted innards of a pipe. The tiny hairs on my neck rose.

He placed the butter knife aside with consideration. Perhaps because he was fighting the urge to stab someone. 'I followed him to the continent, lost him, then found a trail that lead me to Lyons. He wasn't there, and I couldn't find any information on his whereabouts. He's wanted in London. My brother informed the Sûreté — the French Security Police. No results as of yet. But at least I know where Moran and Parker can be found in three years' time.' A sideways glance at me.

The hall was empty save for us and the waiter, who drifted between reception, kitchen, and our table. We kept our voices low.

'He changed his plans,' I said. 'Last time I saw him, he told me he would come and meet me in October.' Moran wouldn't only take the child, he would also *take care of me*. It was a logical consequence; hence, not worth mentioning.

Sherlock straightened up, the muffin in his hand forgotten. 'Does he know when the child will be born?'

'All James could have provided was an educated guess. Moran might expect me to give birth in September or October.' I dropped my gaze to my plate. 'I'm not ready. I doubt I ever will be. Everyone,' I waved at my surroundings, 'seems to believe that my sex and the fact that I am with child should turn me into a happy round thing. But of course it doesn't! How can I ever forget what James and I did to each other, and that this child is the product of all that violence?'

Breakfast was placed in front of me. We waited until the servant was out of earshot.

'Isn't forgetting the least favourable solution?' A murmur, as soft and heavy as expensive silk.

'I came to know a very dark side of me.' I stabbed at my scrambled eggs. The knife screeched across the plate. 'One that commits murder, that manipulates and twists the minds and hearts of others. What makes me sick is that it's not my violent side that repels me the most, but the weakness my fear of it brings. I'm insecure as to what *else* I'm capable of. I'm the knife that used to cut apples into neat little quarters and now wonders when it will slice through a throat again. I would very much like to forget the taste of blood.'

'We all are capable of murder,' he said. 'It's essential to acknowledge that. We invented morals to disguise our violent nature. We allow men to beat their wives, we allow children to die in workhouses or to be locked away in asylums. All the while, we care only about how well dressed we are and what the neighbours might think. We are beasts of prey who work very hard on looking pretty.

'To be able to see these things for what they are is a curse and a blessing. I wouldn't want to lose my ability to observe just to lessen the hurt. And you wouldn't either.'

Light grey eyes settled on mine, sending a jolt through my belly.

I dropped my gaze. 'We'll set a trap. I'll pretend to be in early labour once we know Moran is close. But we need to let him know where we are without raising his suspicion.'

From the corner of my vision, I saw him tipping his head in acknowledgement.

'September would be best, I believe. It gives me a month's rest before the child is born. I need to buy clothes, and...' I exhaled a huff. I felt as though my time had long run out. 'Can you get help from the local police, or do we have to arrest Moran and Parker by ourselves?'

'We'll need the police as witnesses.'

I nodded. 'Of course.'

~

'HALF YOUR HANDWRITING IS UNREADABLE.' I let a sheet of paper flutter back to the floor. We worked in my room, notes littering the rug and tablecloth. Sherlock sat cross-legged amid the mess, saucer and teacup in his hand.

'I'd like to talk to Hooks and Whitman,' I added.

'Ah,' he said, clinking china on china. 'Unfortunately, two days after Whitman gave us his account and was released from Newgate prison, he was run over by a horse carriage. Very unfortunate. He died on the spot. It was supposed to look like an accident, but the pivots had been meddled with.'

'Moran and Parker did that?'

'Most likely. They had a strong motive and the opportunity. Whitman was killed late at night; the next morning, they attacked you and immediately left for the continent.'

'Mycroft didn't mention that.'

Sherlock raised an eyebrow. 'Did he not?'

I shook my head. 'I'm sorry about the boy.'

He didn't reply.

'What about Hooks?' I asked.

'Still in Newgate. He will be less inclined to talk, given the sudden death of his companion.'

'And von Herder? Or Dr Walsh?'

'Von Herder is a weapons maker. He had little to do with Moriarty's business, and will most likely have no information for us whatsoever. He merely designed tools, so to speak. Dr Walsh, however, might wish to talk.'

'This here,' I tapped my finger at the cryptic squiggles on one of Moran's letters. 'What does this... Diffusive... Rinssance mean?'

He took it from my outstretched hand, held the paper close to his nose, narrowed his eyes, and mumbled, 'Defensive Reinsurance Treaty.' He traced his finger along the lines, then tapped on a specific place. 'Between Russia and Germany perhaps?'

'Yes, of course!' I slapped my forehead and told him about Kinchin. 'If we can believe Kinchin's source — and I must add that the information wasn't corroborated — the Defensive Reinsurance Treaty was sealed between Germany and Russia and then was left to expire. The Kaiser seems to believe that occasionally smoking a cigar with the Tsar is sufficient for peacekeeping.' I wondered how Moran had come to know about the secret agreement.

'Hum…' said Sherlock, scratching his temple.

'I know. I find it hard to assess how much of what Kinchin said is a lie, and how much the truth as he perceives it. And how much of that was observed and reported correctly.' I had yet to tell him the most important message the man had given me.

'My brother seems to trust him, so we should as well.' He glanced up at me. 'To a certain degree, at least. Blind trust has never proved healthy. What else can you tell me about the good Mr Kinchin?'

And so I invited him into the small apartment of the old man. 'The house itself wasn't well tended to. Kinchin's door looked as though no one lived behind it. A layer of dirt was brushed up against the door; a doormat was lacking. He doesn't like guests, or people in general. He expected me; your brother had sent him a message. He is an elderly gentleman, sixty-five or possibly seventy years of age. His rooms are bare. Again, almost as though no one lived there permanently. But the place smelled of him. Old man odour, slightly sour and damp. His need to keep things in order borders on the extreme. Everything was oriented with edges parallel or perpendicular to one another. The surfaces used every day were shiny — the desk, the coffee table. Others had the finest trace of dust — the mantelpiece, for example. Both armchairs appeared well-used. He must have guests on a regular basis despite his solitary disposition. I cannot imagine him buying second-hand furniture. What he had looked expensive, but well used. I wasn't able to observe where he cooked.'

Sherlock opened his half-closed eyes.

'He made tea somewhere, but I didn't have a chance to look into rooms other than his sitting room and the corridor. I believe he has the money to employ a housekeeper and a maid, but he seems not to have either. Considering his occupation — or, should I say, *hobby* — it would only be natural for him to control information leaks as well as he possibly can. And an additional set of ears would surely pick up more than would be tolerable.'

'It makes no sense,' he interjected. 'He needs water to make tea and to wash — he has to have someone cleaning and ironing his clothes. You said the house isn't in the best shape, which indicates that it doesn't have water pipes and no connection to a sewer system. Or did you see any on the outside walls?' I shook my head. 'So where does it go? Where does he discard spoiled food? If dirt from the stairwell is brushed up against his door, he might as well be living in an entirely different place.'

I grinned. 'Circular scratch marks on the floorboards just outside his door.'

'Buckets.'

'Yes. Someone, perhaps the landlady, delivers his water and picks up his chamber-pot every day. In the hallway, I saw a set of seven sets of shirts and trousers, of which three were untouched, pressed, and starched. All of them identical. Delivered once a week, it appears.'

Sherlock slapped his knee. 'He doesn't waste time or useless thought. A most unusual man. I regret I haven't met him.'

'He said he is a collector of information that is hard to come by. I believe him. He trades and catalogues information to put it in order. Much like the meticulous order in his rooms. He uses existing information that might seem irrelevant when taken out of context. He puts it in context to create new knowledge.' My child kicked hard. I winced and rubbed the skin that stretched over the bulge, feeling how he or she moved about in the enclosure, probably complaining about the space becoming more and more constricted. *We both grow, little one.*

'Or discovers hidden knowledge,' he added.

'Yes. He told me he was expecting the development of bacterial weapons.'

'Hum… Did you tell him details about your work?'

'Of course not. He won't be able to cook anthrax poison with the information I gave him. But he certainly is intelligent enough to find all the information he needs to do so.' My words reminded me of something very heavy. 'Sherlock. It is quite possible that it was I who gave James the idea of using deadly germs for warfare.'

He placed the paper on the floor and gazed up at me. The little cogwheels behind his eyes visibly rattled. After a moment, he lowered his head. 'Let us get back to that later. I'm under the impression you haven't yet told me everything Mr Kinchin said.'

I tipped the contents of my teacup into my mouth, swallowed, and said, 'Indeed. The most important part I have yet to tell you. Come. Let's go for a walk. I can think better with fresh air in my nose.'

~

WE STROLLED along the *Unter den Linden* toward the Brandenburg Gate. The lime trees were in full bloom. Sunlight filtered through golden blossoms and hungry bees buzzed among them. The summer air vibrated. My mouth watered at the thought of fresh honey dripping from a warm slice of bread.

'Kinchin told me that in 1885, Moran killed a Russian spy in London. The spy went by the name of Pjotr, or Peter, as he was called in England. He used Smith as his family name. He spoke English and French fluently; his accent was almost unnoticeable. The man moved in upper social circles. Rich bankers and lower ranking government officials were among his friends. He played cards in clubs and drank copious amounts of vodka. On several occasions, he talked about the Russian railway system. One of his friends grew suspicious, because every time someone blurted out anything about Britain's position toward the Central-Asian Railway or her plans to counter the Russian threat of the British-Indian colonies, Peter would suddenly be sober. Whether Peter noticed the increased appreciation of his company or not, Kinchin couldn't say. But one day, an order was given to arrest Peter for treason. According to Kinchin, both the Special Branch and the military were involved. He believes this is how Colonel Moran came to know about Pjotr. Kinchin knew that Moran was Moriarty's man and he seemed to enjoy the fact that Moran is hunting me. Interesting...'

'What?'

'Never mind.' I flicked his question aside. I had referred to James as Moriarty. It hadn't escaped Sherlock's notice, either.

'Anyway,' I continued. 'From here the details become sketchy. Pjotr disappeared just before the Yard came to arrest him. The last time he was seen was in an opium den, arguing with a man who had been described as large, moustached, and highly authoritarian. Pjotr was shouting something about China, her abundant opium fields, and that all of that opium could only be claimed by the Russians. Very clumsy. Two days later, his body was found floating in the river. His throat was conveniently slashed wide open. According to the mortician, the man had bled out while he was drowning. How much, if anything, Moran learned from Pjotr before killing him isn't known.'

My roaring stomach interrupted me.

'Lunch?' he asked.

I laughed. 'Yes, I'm starving. As usual.'

We went to a nearby inn. While I ate, Sherlock pushed the

potatoes about on his plate, his face a mask of deep concentration.

'I don't see a connection. Russian railways don't reach China,' I noted.

'Hum,' he answered.

He didn't say much for the remainder of the day while we arranged and rearranged notes in my room. Fuelled by tea and driven by curiosity, we worked until the red sun peeked straight through the windows. Curtains billowed. The hot summer air cooled a fraction.

'This won't do!' he announced, took his hat, and was out the door in a heartbeat.

I stared at the closed door and back at Moran's journals. Petersburg. Eighty pounds sterling spent in the first week, thirty in the second week, one hundred twenty in the third. Horrendous amounts of money.

Moran had gone there only two weeks after Pjotr's body was found. What was the purpose of his trip? Sherlock's *This won't do* rang in my head.

I rose, wrapped a towel around my left fist, stepped up to the window, closed it, and drew the heavy curtains. Then I hit the reveal until sweat trickled down my spine.

'Don't pull up your shoulder,' he said. He shut the door and hung his hat on the hook. 'Take off your dress. It restricts you too much.'

I turned around, bowed, and said through heavy breathing, 'At you service, master.'

'Behave yourself!' A smile scampered across his face. Then he was all focus again. 'You'll need space to move when I teach you how to defend yourself.' Seeing my scepticism, he added, 'I've never lost a fight.'

The dress fell to the floor with a rustle. Heavy silk pooled around my ankles.

'Put this aside.' He pointed to the dress. 'And step away

from the window. We will open it. It's too warm for someone with the disadvantageous surface-to-volume ratio you have.'

I was glad for the breeze cooling my moist back, but I felt awkward standing in front of him only in my drawers, the loose maternity corset, and a fluttery camisole. And then I was supposed to...hit him?

'You can try to land a punch, but I recommend you hit my palms. We will perfect your technique instead of attempting to increase your muscle power.' He raised both hands to shoulder level.

I nodded and did as he asked.

'Now,' he said. 'If I place my feet as you do,' both his feet were now parallel to each other. 'I'm more prone to be tipped. Shove at my chest, if you please.'

I did, and he caught his balance by taking one step back.

'Now, put your feet like this and keep your knees slightly flexed.' One foot straight and closer to me, the other half a pace behind the first and at approximately forty-five degrees. 'You'll need a lot more force to tip me. Shove again.'

I did, and could barely move his upper body. I copied his stance.

'Punch my hand again.'

My fist hit his palm. How pathetic.

'Good,' he said. 'Now, use your *body* to punch, not just your arm.' He tipped at my shoulder and my hip. 'These must move. Look.' He showed a very slow swing that began in his ankles and extended to his fist. 'Simple physics.' His hands went up again, his expression expectant.

I punched, he nodded, and I kept hitting his palms, paying attention to how my body turned, experimenting with swinging in various angles and listening to the *slap* my fist produced with each impact

'Good,' he said again. 'The most important factor is that

you move quickly. Moran is heavy. He'll be slower than you.' His gaze dropped to my stomach. 'Or perhaps not.'

'I want to try something,' I said. 'How would you go about strangling me?'

One swift step forward and his hands were around my throat. 'Stay like that,' I said and ran my fingers over the weak points, testing my range for breaking his elbow joint, my right palm on his wrists, my left on his elbow. 'If I hit it like this, I could perhaps dislocate the joint, but I don't know if I'm strong enough.'

'Joints and soft tissues are the weakest points of the human body. There's almost no mechanical resistance. Your expert knowledge of anatomy will give you an advantage as long as you can develop a reflex to always hit these spots first.'

I nodded.

'Obviously we will not try to dislocate joints today,' he noted. 'Or on any other day, for that matter. But I believe we might be able to exercise your punches to such a degree...' He scratched his chin, his brow crinkled. 'We could pay the morgue a visit.' An amused mutter. His eyes shone with mischief.

The thought of him holding a stiff body up and me hitting and breaking its limbs was so absurd that I laughed out loud.

'Oy!' he called when I grabbed both his index fingers and bent them the wrong way, peeling his hands off my throat.

'Seems to work,' I noted, and kissed his abused knuckles before he could snatch them away. 'I'll write to the Institute of Pathology. What excuse would you prefer?'

'Hum.' He walked to the window and stuck his head out. 'I'll be Chief Inspector Nieme again. I'm on holiday, visiting a former colleague who wishes to consult me on an old case of his. A thought struck me, and I now require a corpse or two to simulate whether or not a woman could inflict the injuries that were observed on a murder victim six years earlier. And for that, I will need the assistance of my wife.'

'What if they send a wire to the Yard, enquiring about the existence of Nieme?'

'We will not give them enough time to receive an answer. We'll announce our visit a mere twenty minutes in advance. Besides, the good inspector is indeed employed at the Yard's Division H. But I doubt he has ever been to the continent.'

He ruffled his hair and walked back to me, raised his hands again, and nodded invitingly.

~

TWO DAYS LATER, we climbed the stone steps of the Institute of Pathology. A white-clad assistant beckoned us in, raised his eyebrows at me, bent to Sherlock, and murmured, 'Are you certain, Inspector?'

'Would I bother you if I weren't?'

Hearing Sherlock speak German needed some getting used to. 'It's not the first time,' I informed the assistant, but that didn't seem to appease the man at all. Only with an effort could he keep his eyes from flitting to my abdomen and prevent his upper lip from curling in distaste.

As we walked through the corridor, the sweet stench of death seeped into my clothes, hair, and nostrils. A large double-winged door screeched on its hinges, flapping back and forth, screeching again and again, until it finally came to a rest. Corpses were laid out, their stiff legs sticking into the narrow walkway between the rows of tables.

'Thank you, Mr Kleinmaier,' said Sherlock, and waved the man away. He left, visibly irritated by the impolite gesture. The winged door squealed and we turned to our work.

'Pick one,' I said. 'Did you notice the two cats near the

stone steps when we entered the premises?'

He hoisted up a medium-sized man and held him by the chest. Both of the corpse's arms were pinned to the torso.

'Lay him back down, please,' I said. 'One can always find two or more cats lingering on the Institute of Pathology's lawn. The medical students have their own theory about this. They believe the pathologists feed the animals pieces of liver to test for toxins.'

I bent over the body and broke the *rigor mortis* at both shoulders. The stiff flesh sang under the strain. I thought that perhaps I should feel ashamed. I had often dissected the dead and never felt the need to apologise when running the scalpel through cold skin, so where did the slight uneasiness suddenly come from?

'Sounds plausible,' said Sherlock.

I nodded at him and he picked up the corpse again. I stood facing the two and placed the corpse's right hand on my shoulder. The stiffness in wrist and elbow forced the arm straight.

'You know,' I whispered, 'the assistant here is representative of the unscientific, pseudo-educated majority of medical staff as I came to know them during my years as a physician. He believes that the child will be damaged when the mother looks at all these dead bodies. And *these* people who put superstition above knowledge then aim to solve cases of unexplained death.'

I hit with both my hands, my right against the wrist, my left against the elbow. The joint was dislocated with a sickening *plop*. I switched hands and hit the other arm; it didn't give as easily.

'I want to try this two more times.' I was glad my right hand wasn't hurting too much from the impacts.

He laid first the corpse aside and picked up a bulkier one. Perspiration was forming on his brow.

23

We spent our days on research and long, silent walks. Our progress was slow, occasional moments of understanding shining brightly in the semi-darkness of guesswork. What we had so far were only fragments of information. In August 1885, Pjotr was found dead in the Thames after arguing with a man who was suspected to have been Moran. Two weeks later, Moran travelled to St Petersburg and spent more money in three weeks than I had earned in a year.

In December 1887, James lost his wife and newborn son to tetanus. According to Moran's journals, only three months later, James paid him two hundred pounds and sent him through half of Europe. There were records of hotel costs in Paris, Brussels, Berlin, and again, St Petersburg. None of Moran's notes hinted at the purpose of his trip.

In the evenings, Sherlock exercised shooting and punching with me. It felt more like a polishing of my ego than a real improvement of my chances when faced with Moran.

'Exhale when you punch,' he reminded me. 'Focus on your hips, Anna.'

'Dammit, Sherlock! Try to swing your hips with a stomach like this. If you want me to use my whole body for a punch, I have to do it the way a very pregnant woman does it and not the way a man does it.'

A soft grunt and a nod. Then he waved his hand at me, beckoning. We were mostly dancing, trying to foresee the other's next step. He trained my eyes and reflexes, showed me how a heavy man like Moran would move, and what I had to expect. 'The sharp mind wins, not the heavy fist,' he kept telling me. I had yet to land a punch he couldn't block.

My shooting — although without ammunition — had improved. I could use both hands to aim and pull the trigger; Moran wouldn't expect this. But how much this short moment of surprise would help me in the end, I didn't know.

⁓

WE HAD RECEIVED a message from Mycroft earlier in the morning. Sherlock was deciphering it.

'Opium,' he muttered.

I placed my cup down, stretched my bulging body, and waited for him to continue. Should he continue, that is. He often spoke to himself in moments of deep concentration, when his eyebrows were drawn low and his lips formed a thin line.

He whirled around, his eyes gleaming, a long index finger tapping the note. 'Mycroft has filled a gap for us. Moriarty was invested in cotton and opium trades. We know his meticulousness. He would have known everything worth knowing and controlled everything worth controlling.

'Moran returned from St Petersburg with valuable information, which he reported directly to the War Office. He stated that Prince Nicholas of Russia planned a railway that would connect Russia with China — in effect, threatening Britain's opium resources. The Russians were already moving the Central-Asian Railway toward our Indian colonies. The War Office dismissed Moran's statement as unreliable.

'We know that Moran entered employment with Moriarty just before Pjotr was found in the Thames.' He pointed to Moran's journals on my lap. 'Then, in March 1890, the War Office dug up Moran's report because it had proved correct. The future Tsar inaugurated the Far East segment of the Trans-Siberian Railroad.'

He placed the note on the coffee table with a slap, rubbed his brow, and said, 'It's not surprising that Moriarty founded his private espionage club. My brother keeps complaining that no one in London seems interested in an overarching organisation to put the Foreign Office, the Admiralty, and the War Office under one wing. The purpose of the Central-Asian Railway is almost exclusively military. Hum… Moriarty's trading business wasn't listed as part of his assets. I wonder…' He began pacing the room, hands in his trouser pockets, shoulders drawn up.

'I see no connection to James's plans on using disease as a weapon. We need to talk to Walsh and Hooks,' I said. 'Now, one could speculate that he wished to spread disease to slow the building of railways and hence to protect Britain's resources. After all, the railway workers live under dreadful conditions; cholera and typhus outbreaks are all too common.' I rubbed my aching stomach and burning eyes. 'I don't know… We are missing crucial information, and all I can do is guess.'

'I never guess,' he said.

'Well, I do! And I test my guesses against the data I have

available. I try to prove my guesses and then disprove them. It's like playing with a variety of realities.'

'I'd call that theories and hypotheses.'

'Oh well, that's my working class background.' I smiled up at him. 'Poor sods guess; ladies and gentlemen hypothesise.' I bent at the hip until my lumbar region crackled.

'Lie down and rest. I can see how this tires you. Come.'

I took his offered hand and he pulled me up to my feet. 'I must be twice as large now,' I sighed. His eyes slid back to the notes.

I spread my heavy self out on the bed and watched his bent figure move over the scattered papers on the floor, his hands picking up a piece and placing it adjacent to another. The master of puzzles. I wondered what mysteries and excitements life would provide him once Moran and Parker were behind bars.

I watched him re-reading the newspaper clippings. He frowned at a rather recent one from the *Standard*. It stated that Britain and Germany were *friends and allies of long standing* and that any threats to the peace in Europe would be met *by the union of England's naval strengths with the military strength of Germany.*

'Sherlock?'

'Hrmm.' An irritated grunt. One that signalled *please do not disturb.* I looked up at the ceiling, waiting and thinking my own thoughts until he would be ready to leave our puzzle for a moment.

After an hour of no response, I rose, straightened my dress, packed the revolver into my purse, and made for the door. He didn't seem to notice.

I took a horse tram to the Museum of Natural History. My brain needed something else to think about. It was running in circles around the same useless theories, the same tiresome gaps of knowledge. I felt as though I had run the same muddy track over and over again, deepening the rut to such a degree that leaving it would cost great effort.

We were following bread-crumbs. We tried to peek behind a veil that James had created to conceal his plans and doings. Occasionally a message from Mycroft would arrive. More bread-crumbs yet. Hope, to move aside the blinds. Sometimes we believed a picture was forming, only to find it wiped off the slate by some new piece of information.

I sat down on a bench, a large beech tree providing shade, and then I let all I knew pass through my mind once more:

James had known about the Kaiser's plans to enlarge the German Navy — clearly a threat to Britain. The timing, however, didn't fit. The plans for enlarging naval and military forces were hatched after Bismarck was expelled, at least a year *after* we had found the first victim of James's medical experiments. The day of my abduction, however, fit quite neatly.

Mycroft had informed us that the Russians appeared to fear that England — her rival in the Far East and Central Asia — would join forces with a newly-powerful Germany. And, by extension, with Austria-Hungary, Russia's rival on the Balkan peninsula. England feared Germany's secret plans to increase military and naval strength, but confirming facts were so far lacking. In Foreign Offices across Europe, unsettling questions had arisen about the future of Germany's foreign policy, since Bismarck was gone and rumours of the French welcoming Russian overtures had begun to spread. Should France and Russia sign a treaty, Mycroft had written, the result would be a dangerous polarisation of the powers in Europe.

What looked like handshakes to common people was like arm wrestling to government officials. So whose perceptions were correct?

James couldn't possibly have foreseen these developments. Or could he? There had been tendencies. As a mathematician — and so, an excellent theoretician — he must have developed his own hypotheses. What precisely these were, and how they had played into the bacterial weapons he'd wanted me to develop, was a mystery to me.

I placed my hands on the cool grass, picked a few blades, rubbed them between my palms, and inhaled the fresh scent. Then I rose and went into the museum, leaving James and Europe behind, to spend a pleasant hour or two among pickled corpses of animals and humans.

24

*R*ows of glass cabinets and wood shelves gave off the familiar odour of old dust and beeswax polish. Years ago, I had spent many lunch breaks strolling among stuffed South American birds of every colour, skeletons of all sizes and shapes, and pale, malformed human stillborns floating in jars.

I rested a hand on my stomach, feeling the child within. Mycroft had ciphered Watson's messages, then sent them on to me. Mary, Watson's wife, had recovered from a severe cold. For a few days, Watson believed she might have tuberculosis. She was well now and dearly wished to adopt my child. We had agreed that once the danger had passed, I would return to London, and they would arrange for a wet nurse. Watson would assist during the birth. I wouldn't have to hold my child for even a moment. Why that thought would make my throat clench, I couldn't fathom. I wiped the sentiment away, focusing on the matter at hand.

The newly constructed museum was a three-winged building with high ceilings and a great variety of exhibitions of geological, petrographical, and zoological nature. Its newest exhibit interested me the most, so that was where I went: An account of how Dr Robert Koch developed what he had hoped would be a remedy for tuberculosis. The "cure" had been widely publicised the previous year. Had I not been in James's grip, I would have visited his laboratory. The past spring, Koch had admitted publicly that the remedy did nothing to stop the disease, but could instead be used as a test for it. The resulting scandal must have broken the man.

I leant over the glass cabinet with the newspaper clippings from November of the previous year, detailing Koch's presentation in August, reports of his colleagues' opinions, Professor Virchow's responses, and finally, the report of Koch admitting his grave mistake.

I found his premature announcement and resulting downfall strangely atypical for a man as meticulous as Koch. He would always test and test again, run various negative controls, then test yet again, and only when he was absolutely certain a hypothesis was correct would he publish it.

Perhaps the prospect of curing Europe's deadliest disease had caused this slip in discipline? But I couldn't quite believe it. Perhaps a colleague had dropped a word or two to a reporter, or one of Koch's usually careful and hesitant presentations had been rated too highly by his peers. A glimmer of hope must have wiped away all logic. I spotted photographs of consumptives pouring into Berlin, certain to find health. On their side, hundreds of physicians, convinced of fame.

I wondered where Koch was working now and whether the medical establishment would ever forgive that brilliant scientist.

An adjacent cabinet showed some of his work before he had been assigned a position as a government advisor in Berlin. He had served in the French War as a military surgeon, where he formed the first theories on the causative agent of typhoid fever. After the war, he'd gone back to his small practice and lived a quiet life. Then, around Christmas 1875, he'd isolated anthrax bacilli in his basement and killed all of his daughter's pet rabbits with repeated infection tests. Father and daughter then caught barn mice that suffered the same fate as their long-eared predecessors. In the process, Koch had proved that anthrax was caused by germs. His discovery was a sensation. As a result, he was offered government employment at the renowned Charité Hospital in Berlin.

Among all the snippets of information was a newspaper clipping from the year 1886. Just after his appointment as head of the Institute of Hygiene, Koch had made a short trip to St Petersburg to investigate an outbreak of cholera in a nearby town. According to the papers, he'd contained the disease and then he'd given a short presentation at the St Petersburg medical faculty before returning to Berlin.

My neck began to tingle. A hint of excitement spread from my shoulders. and down into my fingertips. The chances were extremely low that Moran and Koch had met, that ideas on bacterial weaponry had been exchanged. Frozen, I stared at the piece of paper, my mind moving around possibilities and impossibilities. I slapped the cabinet's wooden frame and left the museum.

The stairs to my room seemed unusually steep today. Halfway up, I was out of breath.

Sherlock was still sitting on the floor, surrounded by notes. 'You had a question,' he said.

'Not important.' I sat down huffing. My stomach hurt. My feet hurt. August was unbearably hot and I was unbearably large. How was it possible that I would continue to grow well into October? Sometimes I suspected two or three children in that enormous stomach of mine. But most women at eight months pregnant didn't look much smaller.

'Here.' He held out a cup of cold tea.

'Thank you. I need to talk to Dr Robert Koch.'

One of his eyebrows flickered upwards. I told him about my trip to the museum. 'I'd also like to use this visit to trick Moran.'

His eyes slid from my face down to my stomach. The corners of his mouth twitched. 'That might work. Dinner?'

'Let me catch my breath first.'

~

THREE DAYS LATER, I stood in front of Koch's house. I had sent a calling card the previous day. Now, my hand trembled over the knocker. He would throw me out, I was certain. Without wasting another thought, I grabbed the brass knocker and banged it against the wood. Three times.

A shuffled footfall, the clink of a chain, the rasp of a key being turned. The door opened a crack. A grunt, more shuffling yet, and a quiet curse.

'My apologies. These...letters!' the housekeeper groaned. Two large sacks were blocking the entrance. The woman peeked out over my shoulder, then back at me. 'Oh, I had expected Dr Kronberg.'

'Yes, that is correct,' I drawled in a poor attempt at staining my German with an American accent. 'Women can study and practice medicine in America. I'm Dr Kronberg.'

My title combined with my sex and my expectant glance sent her a step back her arm jerking the door open all the way until the handle hit the wall.

'Thank you.' I stepped in, my eyes sweeping over the abundance of letters. 'From consumptive patients?'

Another grunt. 'For a year now, Dr Koch receives two such loads every week. From everyone with consumption, or who has a consumptive relative.'

I doubted it. That would be more than fifty per cent of the European population. What I saw were perhaps two to three hundred letters. At the most.

She beckoned me through the hallway into the sitting room. 'Dr Koch will be with you shortly.' Then she disappeared.

I remained standing next to the door and closed my eyes. My mouth was dry. The large clock on the wall ticked and I tried to make my heart slow to its rhythm. Footfalls in the corridor. I took a deep breath and turned around.

He stood at my height — five and a half feet — and seemed to shrink a little as he recognised me. The knuckles of his hand turned white against the doorframe, one foot slid back an inch. I took off my hat so he could see the magnitude of the fraud.

'I am appalled,' he whispered, stepped in, and closed the door.

'I betrayed your trust. I apologise for this,' I said.

He snorted. 'With what do I deserve the honour of your visit, Mrs Kronberg?'

Odd, how quickly a university education and graduation can be wiped away. I pondered how I should answer. Shooting my thoughts and opinions at him would be of little help.

He continued in the high and thin voice so typical of him. 'My time is limited.'

'I'm still the same person. I worked hard to get a medical degree, just like you. I worked hard to get further in life, against all the expectations of society. Just like you, Dr Koch.'

He had been born into a family of mine workers. Both his parents were ambitious, his father an engineer and the foreman of a mine. They had barely been able to afford their son's tuition. Koch was a genius and a fighter. It had taken him years of hard work to shed the anonymity of small town medical practitioner and reach the fame as one of the most renowned scientists in Europe.

'The natural sciences are full of opportunities,' I continued, 'for men. I cannot accept such illogical limitations.'

He poured himself a brandy, then stood by the window. 'What is the reason for your visit?'

'In the spring of 1886, you visited a small town close to St Petersburg. You contained a cholera outbreak and presented your observations at the medical faculty in St Petersburg. Did you touch upon the topic of germ warfare during that talk?'

His eyes darkened, beard quivered. I imagined his Adam's apple frantically pushing the brandy down his oesophagus.

'I discussed the spread of disease in general.' He coughed.

'Have you ever been approached by the military?'

'Of course. I served in the war.'

'That's not what I meant. Did anyone ever ask you if pathogenic bacteria could be used in weaponry?'

His irritation was palpable. 'I work to heal disease, not to cause it.'

I waited.

After a minute or two, he lost his patience. 'No one ever asked such an absurd question.'

'Thank you, Dr Koch.'

The clock announced the ninth hour. He glanced at it, impatient.

'Your questions are highly… unusual,' he said.

'I'm aware of that. But it's of the utmost importance that I find answers. Did you mention, during your presentation or later in conversation with faculty members, historical accounts of the deliberate spreading of disease?'

His face hardened, his fingers tightened around the crystal glass. I had never seen him so upset. The usually quiet and rather shy man was boiling with anger. 'Dr Koch, I'm not asking you to forgive my bold behaviour. I did what I had to do. I'm not asking anyone to accept what I deemed to be right.'

He exhaled and slowly shook his head. 'I must apologise,' he said quietly. 'I have been a most unbefitting host. I didn't even offer you a seat.' He waved his hand at the armchair. 'Coffee?'

I nodded, and he called for the housekeeper.

Once the coffee was served he sat down, pinching the bridge of his nose.

'As I've already said, I discussed germ theory and epidemiology. And I gave several examples. John Snow's observations on London's last cholera epidemic was one of them. My presentation centred on water as a vector for cholera transmission. The epidemic was located in Kolpino, a small town at the river Izhora that flows into the river Neva only a few miles northeast and then enters St Petersburg.

'A faculty member was concerned about possible transmission of the disease to the city. I'd told him that the number of germs would be too dilute to cause infection, and that cholera bacteria prefer warm temperatures and gut contents to thrive. They would be weakened from such a long time in cold river water. But I also stated that if a number of cholera fatalities were to float down the Neva into St Petersburg, chances were that the disease would spread. A corpse can carry a great load of cholera germs. It would be much like a package dispatching deadly disease. I gave the example of Barbarossa disposing of dead soldiers in water wells in order to infect his Italian enemies. His attempt was soon discovered and not very successful. Floating bodies are conspicuous. People would be warned and measures taken.'

'Has a transcript of your presentation been published?'

'Of course.'

I studied the tips of my shoes and decided to not share my conclusions with him. 'I've always thought very highly of you, Dr Koch. And I still do.'

He nodded once — a stiff movement, the tip of his beard tapped against his chest.

'May I ask one more thing?' I didn't wait for a reply. 'Would you please report me?'

There was something in his expression that told me he had considered it at first. There was also amusement mingled with the surprise. I explained what I needed. He agreed, but showed discomfort when I wouldn't give him my reasons for the request other than it had to do with my safety and that of the child.

25

We needed someone to shine a light on this chaos of half-knowledge. Late in August, Mycroft did just that — the beacon arrived in the shape of a thick letter.

Sitting on my bed, I deciphered numbers to letters, words, sentences. The lamp on the night stand spilled its twitchy light over Mycroft's scrawl.

A soft knock and an, 'It's me,' announced Sherlock just before he picked the lock. He called it *exercise*. All the investigating without the satisfaction of solving the mystery and catching the culprit was depressing him.

'This arrived three hours ago. Read it,' I said, massaging my ankles and nodding to the eight pages I had just deciphered.

He took off his hat and unbuttoned his waistcoat, slapped cold water on his face, poured a brandy, and sat down.

Soft rustling of hands on paper, of paper on cotton blanket, breath pushed through nostrils, and the occasional *clonk* of brandy glass on night stand. I listened while stretching my abdomen. My ribs were being pushed out. Kicks to my stomach were sending acid up my throat.

'Hum...' he said, and rubbed his eyes. 'My brother appears to have found a good spy or two.' The snide remark was washed down with a sip of alcohol. 'And he's been able to extract information from the good Dr Walsh.'

He rummaged in the drawers of the night stand, took out his pipe and tobacco, stretched his legs, and began to smoke. Billowing curtains pushed at the clouds of smoke.

As it so often did, the clicking of pipe against teeth preceded his first comment. 'Admiral von Tirpitz plans to build a battleship fleet to rival Britain's in twenty years. He says the German Empire needs to expand in order to remain strong. The once-fragmented people will gladly believe him. The man who can convince others of his version of truth wields a dangerous weapon.'

'He speaks about Britain as an enemy,' I said. '*The* enemy, no less. Whether he really believes that or not doesn't matter. He certainly uses it to gain support for his battleship plans. If the Germans really wanted to keep that secret, they wouldn't have set up a naval base on Helgoland.' How odd, I was speaking of Germans as though I weren't one of them. But then, hadn't I always referred to *humans* as though I didn't belong?

'Indeed. But, then... politics are often clumsy. Driven by wants, rarely by needs. But this,' Sherlock pointed his pipe at the stack of papers, 'must have surprised even Mycroft.'

He threw me a sharp glance. 'The transcript of the interview with Dr Walsh worries you.'

I tipped my chin in reply. Walsh had stated that James saw Russia as the main threat to Britain. But he'd become more curious about Germany after I had lied about the Kaiser planning a war.

'Yes. It does worry me. But I'm also aware that my statement was only the last drop to flood the bucket. James was already involved in espionage and he already had the idea of using germs as weapons after Moran showed him the transcript of Koch's presentation in St Petersburg. Even if Koch hadn't talked about corpses transmitting cholera, someone else would have ignited the spark.

'Talk about germ theory and how disease is spread has occupied everyone's mind since the announcement of the tuberculosis remedy. Kinchin told me he had been waiting for this to happen.'

'I neither blame you nor your mentor, Anna.'

'I know. I am the one blaming myself.'

'One question remains,' he said. 'We've been able to reconstruct Moriarty's motivations and most of his actions. Russia growing into a threat to Britain's resources in India and China, thus threatening Moriarty's assets as well.

'And at the same time, the German Empire appears to be evolving into an aggressive power with a growing naval force and excellent — if not the best — scientists in the forefront of medicine, bacteriology, chemistry, and physics. An imaginative and analytical mind would very likely conclude that such a country had the potential to invent modern weapons that would kill with much greater effectiveness than anything seen before. Walsh stated that Moriarty's only wish was to defend the British Empire. A presumptuous lie! From what we have learned about that man, we must conclude that his motivation lay foremost with his personal interests and investments. And if Britain might profit from his actions as well, no harm was done. Ha!

'Now. The one question that has yet to be answered is what or whom precisely Moriarty intended to target with his bacterial weapons. He cannot have planned to spread disease in the whole of Russia and Germany. He had neither the resources nor the men to accomplish this. And it would have caused chaos. It was hardly to be controlled and might even have turned against him. He must have had a more precise aim. But *what* was it?'

I heaved myself off the bed and began pacing the room. Images of Moran stirring his tea and pouring more and more sugar into it, his insanely aggressive, but brilliant idea of packing deadly bacteria into sugar cubes. 'Moran and James favoured anthrax, and I found it impossible to change their opinion. The risk… They didn't care…'

Sherlock watched, unspeaking, calm grey eyes following me around the room.

'Oh!' I cried, holding my aching back. 'Bloody damn!'

'What is it?' He jumped up.

'An idea hit me.' I continued my rounds through the room, and Sherlock settled back in his armchair, pipe between clenched lips. 'We developed weapons for germ warfare,' I muttered. 'As you know, of course. The Kaiser's favourite toys are battleships. Russian railroads threaten British resources. The best place to spread disease is in isolated spaces. Battleships are isolated. Trains are isolated.

'Of course, I cannot be absolutely certain. I can only pick what seems most likely. James and Moran strongly favoured the idea of spreading anthrax. They didn't care that spores… Oh, you don't know — spores of anthrax bacilli are like eggs that retain the ability to hatch for tens, or even hundreds, of years,' I hastened to explain.

'Um…what was I saying? Oh! They did not care that anthrax spores can contaminate land for generations, that claiming anthrax-contaminated land is dangerous. Cattle will die, sheep will die, and people will die from eating anthrax-contaminated crop. The farther the spread of spores, the greater the danger.'

I rubbed my hot scalp. 'But none of that is a real problem when one plans to spread the disease in confined spaces where the targets are isolated for a sufficient amount of time. How long would it take a train to go from Moscow to, let's say, China's border?'

He scratched his chin. 'Four to six weeks, perhaps.'

'Perfect! Infect all the food and water that would be consumed on a train, and Russia is unable to deliver soldiers or draft animals anywhere beyond a one-week radius. Infecting all the men on a battleship is just as simple. James and Moran discussed the use of anthrax-contaminated bullets. They wanted those bullets badly! Even though their use on a battle*field* would make little sense. Sticking a bayonet through a soldier is just as efficient. But in a completely isolated space like a battleship — it does make sense. One contaminated bullet hits the target, or a small bomb, with anthrax spores as the payload — think of my hornet bomb! — and ninety per cent of the men contract the disease. Brilliant!'

His arm had wilted a little. The pipe hung limply from the corner of his mouth.

'What?'

He cleared his throat. 'Nothing.'

What had I said? I searched through all the words that had spilled from my mouth, but couldn't find anything particularly shocking.

He sucked on his pipe. The thing had gone cold. He lit it again. An impatient, almost aggressive gesture.

'It is easy to hypothesise the sequence of events,' he began. 'Moriarty earns part of his riches by trading opium and cotton from China and India. He hears about Moran's report on Russia's railway plans, he interviews him and offers him employment in order to gain more information.

'He sees the British Empire's limited interest in Russia's plans and her non-functional secret service, so he decides to form his own, while forging plans to protect his lucrative opium and cotton resources. He is aware that shooting railway workers will draw suspicion. But infecting and killing them all with a disease that a few of them were likely to catch anyway, and with no one expecting a bacterial weapon, and he has found the perfect solution — breed deadly bacteria and spread them among railway workers, soldiers, or civilian passengers.

'When he learns of the military purpose of the Central-Asian Railway, his plans change shape. He also hears of your lie about the Kaiser planning a war, so he sends his spies to Germany and doesn't like what he learns: the German Empire is increasing its naval and military forces. Even her bacteriologists are excellent. So he must wonder how long it might take others to arrive at *his* conclusions — how long until someone else thinks of bacterial weapons?

'That the Transvaal and the Orange Free State are regions with the potential for conflict is widely known, so he uses both, Germany and South Africa, as threats for impending conflict when he talks to you about germ warfare. He keeps his plans about Russia to himself, yet those are the very ones he is deeply concerned with. He learns more about anthrax from you and, together with Moran, decides that this disease is the perfect solution. It can be used to stop deliveries of soldiers and draft animals to India and China. Should there ever be a conflict, should Russia ever try to invade our colonies, he would be able stop them and keep his opium and cotton fields safe. And finally, he would be a hero. The man who saved our colonies.'

He rubbed his neck, then laughed out loud. 'Imagine Moriarty being knighted by the queen for his accomplishments!'

He placed his pipe on the ashtray. 'This is the first time I feel congratulations are in order for ending a man's life.'

I couldn't say anything. My eyes took in the papers on the

floor. *The power of knowledge*, rang through my mind.

'I'll verify the crucial points of our hypothesis with Moran, once we have arrested him. And I'll not communicate our conclusions to my brother. Not all of them. Not as long as it isn't absolutely necessary to share this information with the government.'

'I thought you trusted him.'

'Of course I do. I must think on the matter.'

I nodded, exhaling a sigh. 'I'll burn these.' I pointed at our notes — a cookbook on how to wage wars with deadly disease.

While we watched flames lap up paper, turning white into crumply black, I wondered whether solving a case always felt like dropping into a void.

'Two weeks until Koch reports me to the *Berliner Tageblatt*.' It almost felt like a vacation. 'I want to see my father's home once more.'

He looked at me, and I knew he understood. About one in two hundred mothers died during childbirth or soon thereafter. Infections took the greatest toll.

WE FOUND my father's house occupied by strangers. There were no chickens in the garden, no one cutting wood in the workshop. The old cherry tree was but a stump.

I was shocked. Apparently, I hadn't yet accepted that my father was gone. For a moment, I wished I had bought the property from the landlord, just to cling to a memory I wasn't ready to give up. When we turned away from my childhood home, I had no wish to ever return.

Katherina invited us to stay with her. She appeared older; her skin had given in to the gravity of grief. She had lost my father shortly before their planned wedding.

She had a small room for us. Her six children were long scattered throughout the neighbourhood, five of them married and surrounded by swarms of offspring. She couldn't understand my apprehension toward my own child, but she didn't say a word. *What would your father think?* was written all over her face.

Sherlock and I talked little during those days. It felt much like the moment of inhaling a deep breath just before an earth-shattering scream.

My thoughts were with Moran and James, with the future of Europe, and the sheer mass of information Kinchin hadn't shared with me. The night before our return to Berlin, I waited until Sherlock had fallen asleep. Then I dressed and made for the door.

'May I accompany you?'

'I doubt Moran knows where we are,' I answered, a little annoyed he felt the urge to protect me even there in my home village. 'But yes, if you wish.'

Unspeaking, he rose and dressed.

We walked to a clearing half a mile away. I sat down in the grass, placed my hand on my swollen abdomen, and shut my eyes. I could almost see my father's face now; it didn't look friendly. If he were still alive, he would despise me for even thinking of casting out a newborn.

I thought of all the young ladies — trained to behave nicely, be neat, have no wants other than to get married and be mothers — and of the young gentlemen — trained to see women as the lesser sex. It was hard to imagine a child of my own brought up that way, to grow into a woman or man like all the others.

The dawn of September brought an abundance of falling stars. We watched the night sky, and only the stalling of our breath spoke to the astonishment we felt as bright silver streaked across dark blue.

'I've never seen the Milky Way in London,' I said. 'There's too much soot in the air. The ancient Greeks believed it was Hercules' doing. He supposedly spilled his mother's milk.'

The forest around us was vivid with life. Scratching paws and claws, calling and screeching. Why these sounds scared people was a conundrum to me. As soon as the lights were out, imaginations of most went rampant, fuelling fears. Shouldn't one then conclude that people have little imagination during the daytime?

'Sunrise is a puzzling thing,' I continued. 'I'm astounded that people say "Look! The sun is rising!" But the sun never rises and never sets. Every observation depends on who we are, what we know, and where we stand. If I floated right next to the sun, if I had never heard of the human race, the absurd thought of the sun going up and down wouldn't even touch my mind. All I would see would be circular rocks revolving around a ball of fire. I wouldn't know anything about life on Earth.' ...*and how short it can be*, my mind whispered.

'I live in my own small bubble of education, with my own limited ability to see, smell, feel, and hear. No matter what I do, my viewpoint — my way of interpreting what I observe — is always tainted by what I have learned and who I am. Hence, I must doubt all that I see.'

I looked at him. 'It is a maddening thought. To be trapped in a cell, and to see that everyone else is trapped as well, and to know that I'm the only one who sees her private prison.'

He gazed at me. A moment of two minds connecting; a moment so intense that the air began to vibrate and the heart to weaken. Behind his eyes, I saw the weighing of consequences, the testing of hypotheses, the wondering whether it was fear or simply logic that held him back. At last, a decision was being made. He turned away.

26

*M*oran and Parker had arrived in Berlin. They'd found the trail of clues we'd laid to our hotel, and now they were waiting. Their plan was simple: wait for me to go from pregnant to non-pregnant, then *harvest*. Moran had picked a befitting term for his plans.

Perfectly on schedule, Koch had asked his housekeeper to report me to the papers. The article had made it to the second page and was published four days earlier: one of Koch's former students had appeared at Koch's lodgings and demanded an explanation for the failure of the tuberculosis remedy. However, said student was in fact not a man, but a woman who had disguised her sex for years, and — to put a crown on her audaciousness — she was most obviously in the family way. The housekeeper gave a colourful account of how agitated the doctor was after said student had left. She said that he wished her no harm and so had refrained from making her name public. The reporter then provided his own rather bloated opinion of the years of betrayal, the disrespectful treatment of Germany's most respected scientist (no matter his recent gaffe), and how wearing men's clothing was utterly unacceptable for a woman of any social standing.

As anticipated, Koch had a visitor who fit the description of one of the two men chasing me — that of Moran. He had been on his best behaviour, as should have been expected when conversing with one of Europe's best-known scientists. Koch had given Moran our address and then dispatched a wire to inform me of his latest visitor. He'd wished me luck and a safe future.

Should all go well, I'd write him a letter.

ON A MILD and rainy September morning, we began pulling in the lure. Sherlock had informed the local police using his forged identity of Chief Inspector Nieme. Two inspectors now lodged in the rooms adjacent to ours. He suspected the *Geheimdienst* — the German Secret Police — had been informed as well: two beggars neither of us had seen before suddenly appeared on the street below our windows.

My nerves had been pulled taut for days. My back muscles reacted, and so did my uterus. It was impossible for me to find a comfortable position and I had grown restless and abrasive. Once all this was over, I planned to spend a quiet month with rest, peace, and pondering Watson's offer again.

Sherlock and I got ready for step one: breakfast followed by a long walk with an *unexpected* outcome.

I kept my eyes on the pavement, occasionally leaning on his arm to pretend an urge to breathe heavily. He kept his face directed toward me, but his eyes searched the park. When his arm tensed, I knew he had spotted our pursuers. I pressed his hand to signal understanding. After another half hour, we strolled back to our hotel. In the last hundred yards,

I doubled over and produced a fake grunt. Sherlock's grip tightened around my shoulders.

'Excellent!' he said once we'd stepped into our rooms. I pulled myself together, rang the bell, and ordered tea. 'Second step,' he muttered, swung the heavy velvet curtains closed, and knocked thrice on each wall facing the adjacent rooms. Then he got his revolver, checked the chamber, and slipped a surplus of ammunition in his trouser pockets. I did the same, but my fingers were trembling. One bullet escaped my grip.

Two swift strides and he had covered the distance between us, picked up the bullet, and pressed my shoulders. 'All will be well.'

'I'm sorry,' I muttered, feeling a band tightening around my stomach. My thighs and lower back were aching. 'I'll lie down for a moment.' Clutching my revolver, I rolled up in a ball, hoping my uterus would calm down.

When the maid knocked to bring the tea, the sudden noise startled me. Sherlock threw me a quizzical glance, then went to open the door. I desperately wished he weren't so perceptive. If he would ignore my contractions, then I could possibly ignore them, too.

I kept telling myself that rest was the best aid against premature labor. If I could only find a little rest — if the space around me wasn't littered with guns, bullets, a missing index finger, an assassin and kidnapper, his footman, two police inspectors, and two men from the *Geheimdienst* — I could make this overeager uterus stop being so busy.

When I pressed my face into the pillow, a hand settled gently on my head. 'Is it time already?' he asked.

'No! It's another month. Dammit!' The cry of distress surprised even myself. 'I'll rest for a moment,' I huffed, trying to soften the panic, but noticing instantly that I was already on my side, curled around my cramping abdomen.

He retreated to the window, peeked through a crack in the curtain, then returned. 'Trust me now,' he urged and disappeared.

The door clicking into its frame and the ensuing solitude didn't feel safe at all. I rose, keeping a good grip on my revolver, walked to the door and bolted it, then pushed a chair under its handle.

I threw a one-eyed glance down to the street. Nothing moved. Footfalls in the hallway passed my room, but no one tried to force entry. I exhaled, struggling to rid myself of all the tension. The contractions were bearable. I still hoped they might subside.

Pushing all thoughts of Moran aside, I paced the room, careful to stay away from the curtains and trying to calm myself.

About half an hour later, someone knocked. I cocked my revolver.

'Madam?' The voice of a male stranger. 'Your husband informed me of your premature labour. I'm Dr Lehmann. May I come in?'

'One moment,' I huffed, thinking fast. It didn't sound like Parker, but the man had already proven that he could imitate even a female voice.

I looked down at my feet — no shoes, good. Tiptoeing, I reached the door, quietly removed the chair from the handle, and placed it aside. Then I softly slid the bolt aside, retreated to the bed and aimed the revolver. *Get it over with*, was all I could think.

'My apologies, Dr Lehmann, I'm unable to walk. The door should be unlocked. You may enter.'

The mouth of my gun was steady. One straight line from my pupil, along the revolver's barrel, to where the heart of a man of average height should be once he entered the room.

The door opened and a too-young looking blond man

made half a step forward, then froze, big-eyed shock directed at my gun. 'Why are you pointing that at me?'

If this weren't an inexperienced physician, I would eat a broom. 'My apologies. I thought you were someone else. Please come in and lock the door.' I lowered the revolver, but left it cocked; I leant against the bedpost and huffed through another contraction.

The man sorted his utensils on the night stand, muttering, 'And I didn't believe the porter's warning.'

I tried to ignore the large forceps, the dilator and speculum, the cranial perforator, and the blunt hook — tools to extract the child at any cost, no matter the bloodshed. 'What warning?'

'He said the police are involved. What have you done?'

The next contraction demanded my attention. Once it subsided, I barked, 'What have *I* done? Don't you think the police would be here in the room if they were looking for me?'

Embarrassment heated his face. 'I'll examine you now.' His hands were compacted to fists, his knees vibrated.

'Who called for you?'

'The hotel manager. He said your husband—'

'How many births have you attended so far, Dr Lehmann?'

He cleared his throat. 'Four.'

'And how many of these were demonstrations during medical school?'

'Four.'

'You will not examine me. Pack your things and make yourself comfortable on the other side of this door,' I pointed him out of my room. 'I'll let you know if I should need you.'

'Madam, the labor overwhelms your delicate constitution. You are out of your mind to reject the help of a trained medical—'

'Remember the revolver, Dr Lehmann.' I held up the gun.

He straightened up, declared me insane, shoved his utensils back in his bag, and left the room.

After having blocked the door again, I uncocked the gun and placed it on the night stand.

Despite Dr Lehmann leaving me in peace, my restlessness grew. Soon, the room seemed too small, the air too stuffy. I lay down, only to peel myself from the bed a few minutes later. I urgently needed to use the lavatory.

I cocked the gun and opened the door. The good doctor sat on the floor leaning on the wall opposite my room.

'Excuse me,' I muttered, then waited for the next contraction to come and to go so I'd be able to walk faster.

Down the corridor I went and into the bathroom. The wood panels on the wall swallowed my groans. The slick edge of the washbasin cooled my sweaty hands. I hurried to open the window. It faced out into a courtyard. With the breeze cooling my face, I felt better at once.

When the weight on my lumbar region grew too heavy, I leant on the reveal, shutting my eyes and listening to the chirping of sparrows, the chatter of children. As long as I heard them, I told myself, Moran couldn't be down in the courtyard. With each contraction, the band around my stomach seemed to pull in tighter and more painfully.

I paced, sat on the toilet bowl, paced again, then leant on the reveal, swallowing fresh air, laboured pacing, laboured resting, until the toilet bowl took all the contents of my stomach and then those of my bowels. Staring down at the mess, I finally accepted that my child was on its way. What impeccable timing!

With labor picking up speed and force, I wanted to be back in my room where I could lie down and be comfortable between contractions. The gun in my hand provided only small reassurance as I walked along the corridor, expecting

Moran and Parker to appear from nowhere. Lehmann was sitting cross-legged, his face showing annoyance, a sign that all was quiet.

I reached my room without surprises.

After having blocked the door once more, I undressed completely and slipped into my nightgown. The loose cotton felt wonderful on my taut body. I lay down on the bed and closed my eyes. Contractions were washing over me, through me, taking me away, up to frightening heights, only to leave me stranded and panting in anticipation of the next one.

The pain wasn't what I had expected. It didn't feel like hurt, like an injury. It felt more like very hard work while falling off a tall building. And I learned quickly that pain came fast when I didn't move about. I pictured the child descending more easily as my hips rolled from side to side from restless pacing.

I felt as though hours had passed when a noise pulled me out of my rhythm. 'Anna, it is I. Can you unblock the door?'

It took a while for me to cross the room.

'Are you alright?' Sherlock asked.

'Where's Moran?'

'Gone. Don't think of him now. I'm here. You are safe.'

'You seem more nervous than I.'

He laughed, and said that I might possibly be correct.

'I noticed you disposed of the physician.' He helped me back to the bed, where I knelt down and laid my head on the mattress, grunting. 'Do you want me to call for a midwife, or a more experienced doctor?'

I nodded. I had never attended a birth from this angle. He rang the bell and I was astounded at my own ignorance. How could I have forgotten about the maids providing almost anything one asks for? For once in my life, I lived in an isolation where consciousness had energy only for contraction and pause, to inch a small human out of my body.

'I cannot even dress my child,' I cried, once I had some air to spend on speaking. 'What a chaotic and naive person I am! I didn't purchase even one thing in preparation for this.'

A kiss on my forehead softened the worries. 'I'll ask the maids to get you whatever you need.'

His fingers combed through my hair and I felt myself relax. Then the next contraction hit. After it had passed, I said, 'I'll need plenty of towels. Ask Dr Lehmann for a pair of sharp scissors should the other doctor arrive too late, and... and iodine. Tea. I'm very thirsty. Clothes for the child. Blankets...'

Again, a long time seemed to have passed before the maid arrived, left, and finally returned with the requested items.

Sherlock placed the stack of towels on the bed, tapped a reminding finger on Lehmann's scissors on the night stand, and handed me a cup of tea while I resumed my pacing. By then, I was as slow as a snail.

He peeked through a gap in the curtains. 'A midwife and a physician will arrive shortly.'

I couldn't answer immediately. My back hurt so much. My tailbone was about to pop out, or so it felt. This contraction was taking too long.

'Good,' I grunted. 'Leave now.'

'I'll be right outside your room.' He patted the revolver in his pocket. 'Moran will not set foot in here. The police are guarding the hotel.'

'Thank you.'

'M'lady,' he said with a bow and a flourish, then left.

I laughed at his attempt to cheer me up until I felt something soft and pliable descend halfway into my vagina. An inaudible but tangible *pop* and the water bag broke, gushing its contents over my legs. An overwhelming contraction followed and a burning that shocked my core. My body was being split like an overripe melon. I bit into the headrest of the chair I was holding on to, muffling my scream, pressing and pushing because the urge to do so was uncontrollable.

So quick! I reined in my panic, urged myself to remain calm, to breathe, to relax my clenched limbs.

The next contraction came and I greeted it with a low and powerful growl. Wave after wave followed, tossing me about like a nutshell on an angry ocean. I let myself be carried away, pushing when my body commanded me to, resting when it allowed me to.

The child's descent was exhilarating. I put my hand between my legs and felt a smooth wet patch. I laughed again, bringing on another wave, pushing the child down farther.

Its head squeezed through that too-small opening of mine, setting my lower body on fire. Maddening elation came crashing down once the head was born. I sobbed when I heard a small noise like a kitten meowing. My fingers slid over its nose and chin, felt for the umbilical cord, and found it wound around its neck. I gingerly pulled the loop over the head, probed again, but the next contraction demanded my full attention.

I noticed the presence of strangers in my room. With my hand on the gun, I turned my head. A man and a woman, their eyes taking in the room. They moved toward me. Sherlock nodded from afar, then closed the door. Everything felt oddly dream-like.

I grunted and pushed once more, caught the child, and placed it on the towel between my knees. I was trembling hard. My body was about to buckle. I gazed down at the small and wrinkled baby. It twitched a little. The thought of a naked bird that had just fallen out of its egg touched my mind.

'A girl,' I sobbed. 'I don't even have a name for her.'

'Now, now.' A woman's soft voice.

When I picked up my daughter, she began to squirm. 'Help me up, please.'

Two sets of hands supported me and the newborn in my arms, then laid us down on the bed. The midwife pushed a towel between my legs and one under my buttocks, and the doctor covered the two of us with a blanket.

The clinking of medical utensils startled my daughter. She crinkled her nose. The midwife drew the heavy curtains aside while the doctor approached with a small tray, scissors, thread, and iodine.

'Wait with the cord cutting,' I said. I had noticed that newborns recovered quicker when the umbilical cord was cut after it had stopped pulsating.

I lifted her onto my stomach to keep her warm. 'She's so small.' I was concerned she would become ill because I hadn't carried her to term.

Eyes squeezed shut and mouth searching, the tiny girl moved her head a little. Gently, I pushed her up farther until she found the offered nipple and closed her lips around it. I gasped at the force. She pulled in a mouthful of breast and sucked with such strength as though she had practiced for months.

And I was shocked at her appearance, so unlike her father. Her hair was swirls of black, stuck to her head by mucous, water, and *vernix casoosa* the protective layer of white fat.

How curious! Although I had held many newborns in the past years, I was afraid I would break her. With soft touches, I massaged her ashen skin until it turned a healthy pink. She smelled so sweet.

My uterus contracted again. I inched my hand between

my legs and carefully tugged at the cord. The placenta had detached, and it slipped out onto the towel easily.

The physician rubbed disinfectant on his hands and wrists, then cut the cord and tied the end a few inches from the girl's navel.

The midwife handed me a cup of tea, helped me take a sip, then collected the placenta and bloody towels.

What a mess I had made.

The sweet warmth of my daughter pressed to my side demanded my attention. With her attached to my right breast, I reached out to Sherlock's glass of brandy, dipped my fingers in, distributed the alcohol on my hand, and let it dry. Then I probed for tears on my vulva. I couldn't find any.

I pressed a fresh towel between my legs and pushed down on my uterus. Warm liquid seeped into the cotton. I waited a minute, then examined the towel. The bleeding appeared normal.

The physician watched me from the corner of his eye. 'The young man outside your room believes you to be mad,' he said with a smile. 'He has a lot to learn.'

Exhausted, I leant back and watched the girl. She had fallen asleep. Both her hands were curled — one lying on my breast, the other on the mattress. Her fingernails were bluish and a bit flaky at the tip. Gently, I stuck my finger in her tiny fist and was amazed that a hand so small could exert such a grip.

What an adventure this must have been for her. I ran my thumb over the pressure marks on her forehead. The base of her nose was a little swollen. She must have collided with my tailbone on her way out. I remembered feeling as though the tailbone was about to be dislocated. I touched her fragile face, wondering how much it had hurt her to be squeezed through so constricted a space.

I let the doctor examine me and the girl, then he bade

farewell, and left with a satisfied nod. I forgot to ask his name.

The door closed with a shy squeal and someone else approached.

Sherlock came to a sudden halt in the centre of the room. 'The curtains!' he cried, dashed to the window closest to him and farthest from me. He yanked at the velvet. At that very moment, I heard a *clink* and a soft *plop*.

Time froze.

27

I curled around my child. A useless reflex. My body had no armour.

Sherlock's face turned toward me. His eyes were wide in terror, his face drained of all colour, his hand still clutching the curtain. Everything was so quiet, it hurt my ears.

He crossed the room. I saw him placing his feet on the carpet, saw the fabric of his trousers and shirt move and ripple, but I couldn't hear any of it. No footfalls, no rustling.

Then, all of a sudden, the world tore wide open.

Another *clink*, followed by a *plop*. And yet another. Shards hit the floor, shattering into a thousand pieces. The wind combed through empty sash bars. Curtains billowed.

Where did all the blood come from? My fingers flew over my daughter's face, neck, and torso. She protested with a cry, but she was unharmed. Red blossomed on my nightgown, spreading quickly.

I sensed Sherlock's shock, heard his frantic heartbeat, his blood being propelled through arteries and sucked back through his veins. The shout he tried to hold in. I heard my own blood leaking from my chest, the whispers of thick liquid crawling over skin, the crackling of moisture soaking through cotton. I heard the soft breathing of my daughter, restful and unknowing.

I sensed Moran's eye through the finder of his silent air rifle, sensed his sharp mind, prepared to disassemble the weapon in a flash and pack it in a bag, prepared to let a satisfied smile crack open his face. His brow was sweaty. His legs a little twitchy, eager to run down the flights of stairs to leave the anonymity of one of the many apartments in one of the many buildings across the street, to pick through the countless courtyards and narrow alleys Berlin had to offer.

I watched Sherlock hurl himself toward me, grab the heavy bed frame, and pull us out of the line of fire, closer to the now-darkened window. A furious growl rolled up his throat. His jaw muscles were bulging, the blood vessels on his temples stood out.

'So this is what he wanted. How disappointing,' I whispered. 'Dispatch a wire to the Watsons. But...later.' My eyes begged him to not leave me now.

A sharp nod. Then he bent over me, pulled at the strings of my nightgown, and pushed the fabric over my shoulder. 'A clean shot.'

That was probably the only good thing left to be said. One half of my ribcage was numb.

He pressed a towel onto each side of my chest to staunch the flow.

My mind had already catalogued which blood vessels had most likely been ruptured, which organs irreparably damaged. If the subclavian vein had been hit, and it looked very much like it, I had less than twenty minutes left.

He pressed me onto my back, took my right hand and held it to the towel. 'Hold this for a moment,' he said, then made for the door.

'Help!' he bellowed. 'We need a surgeon! Make haste!'

Running feet on floorboards, then a maid's voice. He barked an order at her to find the doctor who had just left and to call for the best surgeon, no matter the costs.

'I can hear you,' I whispered once he was back at my side. 'I hear your heartbeat, your breath cooling the perspiration on your upper lip, the blinking away of moisture in your eyes. I hear your pain and your worries, how your focus shifts between your fear of my death, your feeling of insufficiency, your rage about Moran, the helplessness that you cannot accept. I hear it all. Your...' A violent shiver ran through my body. 'Your complexity is beautiful. But it hurts me to see you so sad.'

'She looks like you.' He nodded toward my daughter.

'I know. How odd that I cannot recall why I feared her so.'

The world began to close in around me. Lights blinked on my retinae, blood loss screeched in my ears. 'I name her Klara Emilia. Promise me to keep her safe.'

The mere thought of my daughter and me being separated raised a flood of emotions I hadn't known existed in my silly heart. Why had no one ever talked about this? Why did all women talk about pain during childbirth when the pain from imagining the child being hurt, taken away, or having to grow up without a mother was unbearable?

'I'll keep you *both* safe.' A decisive growl that allowed no objection.

I felt his lips on my hair and wished I could turn my head to meet him. Warm breath caressed my cheek when he said that all will be well, that once I had recovered, he would take me and my daughter far away.

I listened to his soft voice and felt as though I had finally arrived home, but I wasn't certain whether it was only one of the illusions that helps everyone meet death without fear.

'Anna, stay awake!'

Have I been sleeping?

My gaze found my daughter. Her mouth was loosely attached to my breast, her tongue curled around my nipple. Careful not to wake her, I wiped my blood off her face, arms, and hands. My fingers trembled.

Pain began to spread, to vibrate and tear at bone and muscle. My heart was aching with loss, with opportunities not taken, lives not shared. What would become of her? What would become of him?

My mind drifted in and out of consciousness. 'Is it night already?' I asked, to demand an explanation for the sudden darkness.

'Not quite.' I heard him whisper. His voice didn't sound like his own. His hand warmed my cheek and supported my head, lifting my mouth softly to his.

He brushed a strand of hair from my face, then spoke about travelling across Europe to gain distance from Moran for a year or two. We would let Moran believe himself safe, let him think we had given up.

The low hum of his voice sent gooseflesh across my skin. Weren't we like two weights on a scale? I was so full of need, so heavy with it that I could make him slide toward me, collide with me if only I made myself a bit heavier yet.

A fleeting glimpse of a future that could have been, scampered past my vision. I saw his older self, smiling at his adopted family. Behind his eyes shone the restlessness of a caged animal, the urge to solve a riddle, to arrest a criminal, and to leave domestic life to stop the insanity from tugging at his underused mind. What a weight of possibilities and impossibilities.

My legs began to twitch uncontrollably. My field of vision was reduced to a pinprick, and in its centre — shockingly far away and much too small — lay my child. I hadn't even seen her eyes yet. Not knowing the looks of her eyes —

the look of her soul — disturbed me. I began to panic. My chest contracted.

Arms wrapped around me. A slender hand rested on my daughter's head. She began to stir and her eyelids fluttered, revealing the darkest blue — as smooth and deep and calm as the Pacific Ocean on a mild summer day.

I smiled at her.

My soul rose.

And finally, I soared.

28

*K*lara was wrapped in a thick wool blanket and safely tucked under my fur coat. My constantly hungry daughter had now almost reached the size of any other well-fed two-month-old girl.

Her head rested against my scar, radiating heat through layers of cloth and into hardened tissue, softening the pain within. Once we were farther out on the water, and clouds and fog concealed the November sun, I could expect the throbbing in my wound to reach the quality of a knife being stuck into it.

The distance to the harbour grew. I could barely see the boats bobbing up and down, the warehouses shrouded in smoke, the people lining the docks. Sherlock wasn't among them. We had agreed that a farewell could be said anywhere. Even in a doorway. I had stepped into the hansom without looking back. My few belongings, a stash of money, and a bag containing all the clothes my daughter would need during the next two or three weeks had been picked up and delivered to the ship just an hour before our departure.

The gale hit my face. Icy cold blew down my collar and

into my coat, making Klara cry out in protest, her nose searching for a warmer spot. Gently, I rocked her back to sleep. My sweet daughter. She would know nothing of her third big adventure. With her unusual birth and her mother nearly shot to death, the crossing of the Atlantic Ocean in winter must seem a small thing.

I didn't know what precisely I would find at the end of our journey. But it had become clear that staying with Sherlock wasn't good for either of us. He had loaded so much responsibility onto his shoulders that I had the impression he wouldn't be able to stand upright as long as I remained at his side. So I decided to remove a large part of that weight, and announced my plans to leave for America.

I hoped to find a medical school that would take me as a scientist or a lecturer — or rather as Dr Elizabeth Arlington, a name I was still trying to get used to. America was known to be progressive. And, I hoped, far enough from Moran and Parker. Sherlock would arrest them soon, and he would certainly enjoy the chase. I could forget warfare, biological weapons, and espionage, and focus on life and raising my daughter.

During my recovery, I learned what happened while I was in labour. Moran and Parker had exchanged their hats, coats, and trousers. While Moran sat on a roof, hiding behind a chimney and awaiting his chance for a clean shot, Parker had led the police on a wild goose chase across Berlin, occasionally showing himself at a distance. This would never have fooled Sherlock, but he had not dared leave me alone and unprotected.

He hadn't witnessed the charade.

He had instructed the police to search the buildings on the other side of the street, and the hotel. He instructed the hotel manager and staff were to keep watch and how to report effectively. He placed maids, servants, and policemen like chess pieces on a board.

Thinking of the birth she was to attend to and the doctor who would need light for his patients, it was the midwife who had foiled Sherlock's well-laid plans. She ignored his warnings, thinking we had all lost our bearings — and pushed the curtains aside. I wondered how often it was that ignorance ended lives prematurely.

Sherlock must have guessed my plans to leave long before I told him. While I lay in bed, healing, and nursing my child (and making all the doctors and nurses think I must indeed be mad, for who wouldn't take a wet nurse under such circumstances?) he'd tried to convince me to come with him.

Once I'd almost said yes, when he spoke of the South of France, where warm winters would lower the risk of my daughter falling ill. He knew of a laboratory in Montpellier where he wished to experiment with novel coal tar deriva tives — aniline dyes, which are used to stain cells. He planned to adapt them for a diagnostic test to identify various forms of post-mortem tissue damage, and he believed I could also modify them to stain bacteria.

He offered the two things I wanted the most — safety for my daughter and science for myself. But I was tired of the mortal danger he revelled in. Moran and Parker, who had eluded us for so long, would try to find us.

So I stood in that doorway to say goodbye. I held his hand, unable to tell him that I loved him, unable to say I hoped one day, perhaps when we were both a little wiser, to meet again.

I gazed at my hand that had held his only a few hours earlier, knowing I would never feel his touch again. And yet I had let him go so easily. The calluses, the missing index finger, its odd shape. I liked it the way it was. It was a hand that had no wish to hold anyone down.

I blinked the burning from my eyes and pulled Klara's cap lower over her face. Within a week of her birth, her nose and ears had begun to look like her father's. How odd that seeing her face and being reminded of James didn't bother me the least. It was her lovely face, and hers alone. Thinking about her and her father, I was surprised to see how unreasonable my fears had been. She reminded me of the good things in James. Even if there had been so very few. When I looked at her, I never thought of the violence and manipulation that dominated the relationship we'd had. I thought only of those brief moments of mutual respect.

I gazed out at the leaden sea merging into a leaden sky — a continuum of dark bluish-grey that would surround me for the two weeks to come. Soon, storms would toss the vessel about, and most passengers would be sick. Only infants wouldn't be bothered by the constant rocking and rolling. To them, it was reminiscent of the womb and the movement of a mother's hips.

I inhaled the salty air, let the cold sting my nostrils and the back of my throat. Then I turned away and made for my cabin, wiping my slate clean, preparing myself for a new beginning.

— END —

Keep reading for a preview of *Silent Witnesses*

SILENT WITNESSES

PREVIEW ANNA KRONBERG BOOK 5

Only two people in this world know my name.
I am one.
The other is believed to be dead.

PROLOGUE

Boston, 1893

*I*f there is a memory that best describes those balmy weeks of late May and early June, it is that of a small, silent child sitting under a mulberry bush.

Nothing seemed to escape her notice, those sharp grey eyes she inherited from her father. She would watch Zachary's every move — how his black hands grew paler as a dusting of loamy soil covered his skin, how his sun-bleached shirt darkened along his spine as he plucked and dug and mowed. How his large brown eyes twinkled in the shadow of his straw hat.

Whenever I think back to those days, I see myself standing at the bay window, gazing out into the garden, watching my daughter and her fascination with the world, and wondering what it was that made her so quiet.

She was two and a half years old and had not spoken a word.

It was the time of late spring cleaning. Margery excessively aired out the house, washed the lace curtains, knocked the dust out of mattresses and rugs, and polished tables, cupboards, and floors until our home smelled of beeswax and linseed oil, with a faint bite of turpentine.

Those were our days of peace and quiet, a time that was much too short and far away.

With each day closer to Klara's third birthday, my fear of Moran grew. The man had hacked off my index finger with sadistic pleasure, shot me in the shoulder and very nearly killed me.

He was a constant itch at the back of my neck. There was not a night I didn't lie awake going through all the precautions I had taken over these last years. And I always came to the same conclusions: Anna Kronberg had disappeared. Moran would not find us. My daughter and I were safe.

How blind I was.

~

CHAPTER ONE

All the silent witnesses ... the place, the body, the prints ... can speak if one knows how to properly interrogate them.
    Alexandre Lacassagne

COREY HILL CLIPPED the sun in half. Houses lining the embankment were painted orange, and a fiery red was bouncing off their windows. The Charles River swept past me. A crew of rowers stroked the calm water, their boat as sleek and white as a tern.

I shut my eyes, inhaled the scents of muck and burning coal, and could almost picture the Thames. And the city I'd once called home. The men I'd loved and left.

The air was growing chill. It was time to go.

I slung my bag over my back, and mounted my bicycle. The brisk ride through the Common, across the channel, and down Dorchester Avenue pumped heat through my body as darkness began to descend on Boston.

I turned into Savin Hill Avenue and trundled to a halt some distance from a freight train. For a heartbeat, I thought it abandoned — an old toy forgotten in the middle of the road. But there was movement, lights and noise. Lanterns danced like fireflies around the engine's snout. Cries pierced the rising fog, and farther east, a ship's horn blew.

Cold sweat broke out along my spine, gooseflesh followed. My heart kicked my ribs as my mind hollered, *Not Klara! Not Klara!* Despite the unlikeliness of a small child climbing a picket fence and walking two hundred yards through the neighbourhood unnoticed.

But even the strongest logic could not put a damper on fear I had cultivated for years.

I dropped my bicycle by the side of the road, and ran up to a clump of people waving their arms and throwing harsh words at one another. I squeezed past two burly men, asking what had happened. Irritated murmurs and an elbow to my side were the only replies. Eventually they parted, and my gaze fell on a man who sat folded in on himself. Head between his knees, he heaved and wept. His hat lay in the grass.

I crouched down and touched his shoulder. 'What happened?'

'I...I...'

I waited, but that was all he managed.

'He saw her too late. Couldn't stop the train. She was... I mean...we *think* it's a woman.'

I looked up at the man who had spoken. The bruised sky reflected off his spectacles — two flecks of dark violet in a soot-covered face. 'He's the driver?'

The man nodded.

'He ran over a person?'

Another nod.

'And you are?'

'Name's Smith.'

'Dr Arlington. I'm a physician. When did this happen?'

'Um... A few minutes ago?' He cleared his throat, and pulled at a small chain that dangled from his trouser pocket. 'Eleven minutes.' There was a click as he snapped his watch shut.

'Have the police and the coroner been informed?

'I...' He blinked. 'I'm only the stoker, Miss.'

'Summon them. And point me to the victim, please.'

'Which...part do you want to see first?'

Throats where cleared, eyes dropped. The stoker's gaze stumbled up along the railway.

'I need a lantern,' I said, snatched it from one of the bystanders, and walked away before he could protest.

I had only ever seen one railway accident — a collision of a passenger train and a costermonger's cart. The man had died on the spot. His screaming horse had had to be shot. That train hadn't been going fast. But this...this was a disaster.

I forbade myself to think too deeply about the shreds of white fabric snowflaking the grass, the dark liquid spattering steel and snowflakes and earth. The gloom leaching all colour from the blood.

The muttering of onlookers faded, the snatches of enquiries of who, when, and why.

My gaze snagged on something golden, a wisp of silk wrapped around a wheel. I bent down and held the lantern close to it. A lock of fair hair. Blood.

Klara's hair was dark and short. I pressed a fist to my heart, gulped a lungful of air, and made my way toward the engine.

Bits of scalp with long hair spattered track ballast and anchors ahead of me. I almost stumbled over a bump covered with a dark, checkered blanket.

More than a decade of medical training and still my stomach dropped at the sight. I directed light to the blanket, picked at a corner, and pulled.

It was barely recognisable as a head.

The lower jaw was missing, as was half the scalp, the skin of chin and cheeks, and one ear. Moths fluttered in the beam of my lantern. One caught its powdery wings on the victim's lashes. The forehead was badly abraded, eyebrows shaved off. Blood crawled from the neck wound.

I knelt and inspected her eyes. She'd died with her eyes open. They were clouded, her pupils constricted, the whites bloodshot. I touched my finger against one eyeball. It felt cold.

Carefully, I turned the head face down. The vertebrae had been ripped off, and the large foramen was visible. I slipped two fingers through the opening and into the cavity. The brain was lukewarm.

Frowning, I wiped my hands on the grass, and shrugged off my bag.

I WAS FOUND several minutes later. Or rather my legs poking out from beneath the engine were found.

'May I ask what you are doing here, Miss?'

An overly authoritative voice. He must be police. I inched back out, and heard the fabric of my jacket crackling against rock. A seam gave.

I wiped my palms on a handful of grass, brushed off my knickerbockers, and stood.

'PC Lyons, Boston Police Department.' The man had yet to extract his hands from his pockets, lift his hat in greeting, or abandon the cigarette than hung from the corner of his mouth.

'Dr Arlington. I was about to examine the torso.'

A lazy lift of his eyebrows. His gaze slid down to the mangled shoulder joint peeking out between two wheels.

I shone the lantern onto the mess. 'She was dragged quite a distance before the train came to a halt. Her head lies about ten yards farther down. One foot was severed as well, and is on the other side of the tracks. I need to move her to reach her rectum. Perhaps you could assist me?'

He stopped chewing his smoke. 'Excuse me?'

'I measured the temperature in her brain, and found it to be sixteen degrees too low. I need to take her rectal temperature for comparison.'

'You...what?'

'As I said, I'm a physician.'

He took the lantern from me, and knelt down to peek under the train. 'Why were you taking the temperature of the...dear god!' The light wobbled as he pressed his face into his elbow bend.

Before he could drop the lantern, I took it from him. 'Has the coroner been notified?'

'Umpf,' he squeezed into his sleeve.

'The core temperature was twenty-eight degrees Celsius. Or eighty-two degrees Fahrenheit. Whichever you prefer. Body temperature lowers by approximately one and a half degrees Celsius per hour after death. The accident occurred less than fifteen minutes before I took the temperature of the brain. The neck wound indicates that the head was severed by the train — meaning the head hadn't had time to cool down faster than the rest of the body. But I need to make sure that the temperatures do match before I draw my conclusions.'

PC Lyons had regained some of his control. He stood, slid a hand into his pocket and pulled out a fresh cigarette. With trembling fingers, he struck a match and lit his smoke. The flare gave his eyes a devilish glint. 'Meaning to say?'

I refrained from asking whether the police didn't educate its officers on the most basic post-mortem procedures, or whether he'd slept through it.

'It means that the victim must have died around noon,' I explained. 'She must have been placed on the tracks when darkness fell. The train schedule should narrow it down for you. Is a post-mortem surgeon on the way?'

'The coroner has been informed,' PC Lyons said, and sucked at the cigarette as if his life depended on it.

I couldn't interpret the flat tone of his voice. Perhaps he was trying to appear hardened, but I found it useless to ponder the matter. 'Would you help me move the body so that I can take the rectal temperature?'

The ember pinprick near his mouth flared and quivered.

'Well,' I said. 'Two people won't fit under there anyway.'

I crouched down. 'Should anyone wish to move the train, I'd be much obliged if you would stop them.'

The track ballast crunched and shifted under Lyons' boots. 'Should have told them yourself *before* you placed yourself in harm's way,' he muttered.

Again I squeezed between train and sleepers, the track ballast cutting sharply into my elbows, hips, and knees. I placed the lantern next to the body, calmed my breath, and let my eyes roam.

She wore the pitiful leftovers of a chemise and stockings. Skin was torn from her belly, breasts, and hips. Bones protruded through flesh. A kneecap hung limply from her leg. Blood was everywhere, and yet the total amount must have been merely a pint. Much of it had clotted before the force of the impact ripped her open.

'Well, then,' I muttered and got to work.

Upon my huffing and grunting, PC Lyons grew worried and peeked under the engine. Seeing that I was tugging on a bloody thigh, his pale face disappeared at once. 'What are you doing?' he hissed.

'I'm moving her, so that I can take her temperature. She's on her back and I can't reach her rectum without the risk of breaking the thermometer, so I will measure inside her vagina instead.' That was probably a bit of information too delicate to share with the good constable.

'Her eyes were cloudy,' I continued. 'And her blood had already clotted. More evidence that her death occurred several hours earlier.'

Lyons said nothing.

'Aha!' I said more to myself that to Lyons. 'The temperature in the vag…of the two body parts is identical.'

I wiped off my thermometer, stuck it back into its cardboard cylinder, and into my bag.

Then I touched the victim's lower abdomen, pushed bits of intact skin around, and pressed into her flesh. 'It appears she was pregnant. I mean…with child. Possibly fifth or sixth month. From the state of her skin I'm guessing her to be between twenty-five and thirty-five. Rigor mortis present in the extremities was released by the impact of the train.'

I examined her limbs down to her clenched fists. 'Her hands are cold, as can be expected in this season…' Unfurling the stiff fingers of her right hand took some effort. 'No blood or skin under her fingernails as far as I can see.'

Rocks crunched as Lyons shifted his weight from one foot to the other. 'It would be best to wait for the coroner.'

'I'm qualified to perform post-mortems, Constable Lyons. It is imperative to examine the body as soon as possible. If you would write down the address of the coroner, I will send him my report tomorrow morning.' I bent back the fingers of her left hand. Something white — or yellow? — was stuck to her palm.

I picked at it and held it close to the light. 'I've found a flower petal in her left hand. Hmm. From a rose, I believe. Yes, definitely, a yellow rose. A bit early for roses, isn't it? But it might have been grown in a hothouse.'

I directed the light toward Lyons' boots. 'It would be best to block off the area, and ask that the train not to be moved until all evidence can be collected in daylight.'

Silent Witnesses will be released in February 2018.

～

Get Annelie's Bookish & Writerly News:

www.anneliewendeberg.com

ACKNOWLEDGMENTS

I'm deeply indebted to my husband and to my children, who by now, have had to suffer three years of wife/mom writing — I love you, you are my home, my life, and my passion.

I bow to my developmental editor, Sabrina Flynn, for slapping me repeatedly for those plot-twists gone wrong, for unnecessary mushiness softening the necessary gruesomeness, and to my Holmesian-Pottermaniac, Rita Singer, for pointing out the fairy piss and unicorn farts. You both helped Holmesifying my weird Holmes.

Many thanks go to my lovely copy editor, Nancy DeMarco, and to Susan Uttendorfsky for the final proofread.

My dear beta readers, Bryan Kroeger, Kirsten Lenius, Ruth Griffin, Elena Hofmann-Smith, and Karen Schoch-McDaniel — thank you for your feedback and for volunteering as test subjects for my story.

Note: No beta readers were harmed during the production of this book.

I'd like to thank the great people at the Asexuality Visibility

Network (www.asexuality.org) for sharing their views of and experiences with asexuality – one potential facet of Sherlock Holmes – with me. And a big thank you goes to David Jay, for letting me bug him with so many (awkwardly private) questions about the many shades of asexuality.

To all my readers — thank you! Thank you for reading what leaks from my weird brain onto paper. Without you, I wouldn't have half as much fun doing what I'm doing all these long nights. A writer without readers is only a very unhappy scribbler.

APPENDIX 1

DR KOCH & DR DOYLE

*I*n November 1890, Dr Robert Koch announced a demonstration of his highly anticipated remedy against tuberculosis — a disease that killed more people in Europe at that time than any other.

One unknown country doctor's greatest wish was to attend Koch's demonstration. This doctor travelled more than a thousand miles to see the man he admired. Ticketless, he knew he wouldn't gain admission to Koch's presentation, so he tried to sneak past the man guarding the entrance — to no avail. However, the following day he was allowed to read the notes of a physician who did attend the demonstration. He also visited three clinics that tested the remedy, and finally went to see Koch's laboratory.

Not regarding what the whole world desperately wanted to believe, this country doctor put observations and facts together. The following day, he reported his conclusions in *The Daily Telegraph* — in essence, his article stated that Koch was wrong. The remedy had no effect in treating the disease, but might have great value as a diagnostic test.

It took Koch three more months to admit the exact same thing publicly.

The (yet) unknown country doctor's name was Arthur Conan Doyle.

Twenty years later, Doyle was the first fiction writer to use bacterial pure cultures as murder weapons, long before the Germans pioneered this technique in World War I.

> *No, Watson, I would not touch that box. You can just see if you look at it sideways where the sharp spring like a viper's tooth emerges as you open it. I dare say it was by some such device that poor Savage, who stood between this monster and a reversion, was done to death.*
>
> *The Adventure of the Dying Detective*, Dr A.C. Doyle

STRANGELY, a lot of Sherlock Holmes fans believe that Doyle was but a Watson.

APPENDIX 2

It is a strange thing to look upon these utterly insignificant creatures (microorganisms), *and to realize that in one year they would claim more victims from the human race than all the tigers who have ever trod a jungle.*
    Dr A.C. Doyle

1343 The Mongols catapult thousands of their own dead soldiers — infected with the bubonic plague — over the city walls of Caffa. The incident potentially triggered the spreading of the Black Death through Europe. ***Approximately 25 to 35 million died.***

1763 Captain Ecyuer, Commander of Fort Pitt, orders small-pox-infected blankets to be given to the Native Americans. Subsequently, Sir Jeffrey Amherst, British commander of forces in the American colonies, conceptualises a similar plan. *Number of fatalities: unknown.*

1915 Anton Dilger brews anthrax and glanders pure cultures in his basement in Washington DC, not far from the White House. He and his men infect draft animals the US delivered to allied forces. The German Biowarfare Program of World War I was the first national offensive program and the first with a scientific foundation. It also represents the first systematic use use of agents of disease in warfare. *Number of fatalities: unknown*

1920 The Soviet Union launches its Bioweapon Program. Although a signatory to the 1925 Geneva Convention and the 1972 Biological Weapons Convention, the USSR employs over 50,000 people at 52 clandestine bioweapon sites. In the 1980s and 1990s, bioweapon agents were genetically altered to resist heat, cold, and antibiotics. The annualised production capacity for weaponised smallpox, rabies, and typhus, for example, was 90 to 100 tons. Human experimentation on typhus, glanders, and melioidosis in the 1920s, alleged use of tularaemia against German troops in the 1940s, as well as accidents, resulted in *more than 100,000 deaths.* The 'Biological Shield of Russia' is the new bioweapon program under President Putin.

1932 Shiro Ishii heads the new Japanese Bioweapon Program. In his large research complex Unit 731, he tests deadly disease and surgical procedures on more than 3,000 prisoners and is responsible for some of the most notorious war crimes in history. In scientific publications, his victims were referred to as 'apes.' The field trials were terminated in 1943; several of the key scientists, including Ishii himself, were granted immunity by the US Biological Weapons Developmental Program.

Investigator Edwin V. Hill reported to the Chief of the U.S. Army Chemical Corps in 1947: *Evidence gathered in this investigation has greatly supplemented and amplified previous aspects of this field. It represents data which have been obtained by Japanese scientists at the expenditure of many millions of dollars and years of work. Information has accrued with respect to human susceptibility to these diseases as indicated by specific infectious doses of bacteria. Such information could not be obtained in our own laboratories because of scruples attached to human experimentation. These data were secured with a total outlay of $250,000 to date, a mere pittance by comparison with the actual cost of the studies.* (Hill 1947). ***580,000 Chinese civilians died.***

1943 The US Biological Weapons Program is launched. No evidence exists that the US ever used biological agents against an enemy in the field.

2001 Letters containing anthrax spores are mailed to several news media offices and two senators in the US. The two prime suspects were US American bioweapon experts. ***5 died***

Made in the USA
San Bernardino, CA
14 February 2018